WHEN BUNNIES GO BAD
The Sixth Pru Marlowe Pet Noir

"... Simon's wacky humor—darkish but surely not black—provides more than enough entertainment."
—Booklist

"Pru's method for communicating with Beauville's nonhuman residents is cleverly conceived, and Simon neatly incorporates these exchanges into her tale...animal lovers will be delighted."
—Publishers Weekly

"This was my first Pru Marlowe novel and I can safely say it won't be my last. ...Clea Simon does an excellent job of mixing humor, romance, and mystery into one coherent and exciting tale."
—San Francisco Review of Books

"Simon brings intrigue, wit and a profound love for animals to Pru's latest adventure. And readers who enjoy a whodunit with unusual characters, animal connections and—dare we say it?—velveteen prose should hop to it."
—Richmond Times-Dispatch

"Simon's mysteries are lighthearted with a fair amount of humor in the mix. Her animal characters are as three-dimensional as the human characters. She makes Pru's ability believable and realistic in how she interacts with the animals. She draws you in with the first paragraph and keeps you engaged to the final word."
—The News Gazette

"So, what's the big secret? Not telling. But readers will absolutely love this fun, witty mystery that hits on all points!"
—Suspense Magazine

KITTENS CAN KILL
The Fifth Pru Marlowe Pet Noir

"... this quirky series has a devoted following among the *Animal Planet* crowd, and the unique premise has its own appeal."
—*Booklist*

"... cozy fans will enjoy spending time with Pru and her two- and four-legged friends."
—*Publishers Weekly*

PANTHERS PLAY FOR KEEPS
The Fourth Pru Marlowe Pet Noir

"...[Pru] remains an appealing hero, and fans of animal mysteries will find plenty to keep them entertained here."
—*Booklist*

PARROTS PROVE DEADLY
The Third Pru Marlowe Pet Noir

"Pru Marlowe can hear what animals are thinking? The wonderfully talented Clea Simon makes it a delight to believe it. Clever, original and completely captivating!"
—Hank Phillippi Ryan

CATS CAN'T SHOOT
The Second Pru Marlowe Pet Noir

"Simon excels in creating unique and believable animal characters as well as diverse and memorable humans, and this sequel is just as good as *Dogs Don't Lie*. A perfect read-alike for fans of Rita Mae Brown and Shirley Rousseau Murphy."

—*Booklist* Starred Review

"Fast-paced... readers will relish this fun caper."

—*Mystery Gazette*

DOGS DON'T LIE
The First Pru Marlowe Pet Noir

"Simon writes a high-quality cozy mystery, well paced and plotted, with plenty of twists, and set in a New England small town full of intriguing characters. Pru's struggles to deal with her abilities make this stand out among other animal mysteries, and the sad story of Floyd, the heart-broken Persian, will touch the heart of cat lovers everywhere. Recommend this series to fans of Blaize Clement and Rita Mae Brown (especially those who have grown weary of the Mrs. Murphy novels). Watch this series closely. It could well sprint to the top of the animal-cozy genre."

—Jessica Myer, *Booklist* Starred Review

"Simon, author of the Theda Krakow (*Probable Claws*) and Dulcie Schwartz series (*Grey Matters*), launches a delightful new pet series that will appeal to fans of Shirley Rousseau Murphy and Rita Mae Brown."

—*Library Journal*

Fear on Four Paws

Books by Clea Simon

The Pru Marlowe Pet Noir Mysteries
Dogs Don't Lie
Cats Can't Shoot
Parrots Prove Deadly
Panthers Play for Keeps
Kittens Can Kill
When Bunnies Go Bad
Fear on Four Paws

The Theda Krakow Series
Mew is for Murder
Cattery Row
Cries and Whiskers
Probable Claws

The Dulcie Schwartz Series
Shades of Grey
Grey Matters
Grey Zone
Grey Expectations

Nonfiction
Mad House:
Growing Up in the Shadows of Mentally Ill Siblings

Fatherless Women:
How We Change After We Lose Our Dads

The Feline Mystique:
On the Mysterious Connection Between Women and Cats

Fear on
Four Paws

A Pru Marlowe Pet Noir

Clea Simon

Poisoned Pen Press

Poisoned Pen Press logo

Copyright © 2018 by Clea Simon

First Edition 2018

10 9 8 7 6 5 4 3 2 1

Library of Congress Control Number: 2018930055

ISBN: 9781464210099   Trade Paperback
ISBN: 9781464210105   Ebook

Poisoned Pen Press
4014 N. Goldwater Blvd., #201
Scottsdale, AZ 85251
www.poisonedpenpress.com
info@poisonedpenpress.com

Printed in the United States of America

For Jon

Acknowledgments

Much gratitude to eagle-eyed readers Brett Milano, Karen Schlosberg, my agent Colleen Mohyde, and, of course, Jon Garelick, as well as John McDonough and Erin Mitchell for their assistance and advice, and to Lisa Jones, Frank Garelick, and Sophie Garelick for their loving support. Mistakes and errors are mine and occur despite all the best efforts of these generous people! Thanks as well to Sarah Byrne and Peter McDonald, whose winning bid at the 2017 Bouchercon auction will go to support Frontier College, a cross-Canada literacy organization. It is because of their generosity that Bunbury Bandersnatch appears in these pages. Auctioneer Donna Andrews made a similar donation so that Jane Burfield's much-loved Carson and Squeeks could be remembered in these pages as well. Purrs out to you all!

Chapter One

The bear was fast asleep, but he wasn't the one snoring.

The black bear, a young male, lay on his side wrapped in rope netting, a small hillock of thick midnight fur. From where I stood, a good twenty feet away, he could have been fake—an oversized stuffed animal still in its wrapping from some upscale toy store, like the one I used to pass in the city. Only the slight rise and fall of that rounded side warned me against reaching out and running my hands through the lustrous coat that stood in contrast to the tawny weave of the ropes that bound him. That and the state warden who was approaching gingerly, tranquilizer gun in hand.

"Can you shut him up?" the warden, Greg Mishka, called out to me.

Greg was examining the net that held the bear, following a trailing line to a tree several feet behind the beast. He was moving slowly and very carefully with good reason: a bear that size could tear the rope around him like so much lace.

"On it." I turned toward the other slumbering mammal, this one much less attractive in its natural state. Sleeping off a drunk, that is, and sloppy with it, a thin film of drool coating the side of his face that leaned against a rotting tree stump.

"Come on, Albert." I used my foot, none too gently. Unlike the bear, this animal didn't command my respect. "Time to go home."

"Wuh?" With an ursine snuffle, the bearded mess blinked and woke, after a fashion. The eyes that stared up at me over his unkempt beard barely focused. Still soused, I suspected, though the smell of stale beer could easily be a holdover from the night—or the week—before. "Pru?"

"Yeah, you're dreaming." I kicked the prone man one more time, lest he get the wrong idea about what kind of dream this was. "Get up. Time to go home."

"Pru?" Greg, this time. I turned to see the dark-haired warden had maneuvered around the animal, quite quietly for a man his size. "I could use a hand. From both of you."

Leaving Albert to shake off his own form of hibernation, I walked back to the bear. His body was still caught in the netting, but a huge muzzle now covered the bear's snout and mouth, and shackles—almost like human handcuffs—held his front and rear paws together.

"You should have waited." I glanced at the warden, at the gun that now rested against the tree and the oversize syringe he was putting in his bag. Greg was built like a linebacker and I knew the bear was out cold. Still, protocol exists for a reason.

He nodded his acknowledgment as he pulled a heavy green tarp from his truck bed. "I figured I could get the BAM into him, the way he was." The butorphanol, azaperone, and medetomidine cocktail was standard fare for wildlife removal. "I hate to do this to the poor thing." He spread the tarp beside the sleeping bear. "But I have no idea what they gave him, and I don't want to find out by him waking up in the truck."

"Where do you want me?" Most men, I wouldn't give such an opening. But Greg and I were colleagues, sort of, and I knew his mind was on this task at hand. It has to be, with wildlife management. As cuddly as this creature looked, he could kill in seconds—and would, if he felt threatened. Still, when I heard a snicker behind me, I knew Albert had roused.

"Hindquarters, please." Another snicker. Albert might be our town's animal control officer, but he never really got over junior high school.

"You." Greg had taken Albert's measure quickly enough. "I need you to help. Lift his midsection."

"Me?" Albert's voice squeaked, as if a mouse were hiding in his unkempt beard.

"Come on," I growled. Albert feared me—feared most women, actually—more than any wild animal. "Time to make amends."

Albert might weigh almost as much as Greg, but I'd bet I'm stronger. Between the three of us, we got the poor creature onto the tarp and then, using the lift, into the cage in Greg's truck.

"Where are you taking him?" The effort had woken Albert to the point of curiosity, not his natural state. He stood staring as Greg checked the latches, absently picking twigs from his beard and shirt.

"The vet will check him out, and then we can release him." Greg turned from Albert to me, his face serious. "We don't need to hold him while we investigate."

"Investigate?" That squeak again, but Greg didn't answer. I didn't either, at first, and simply watched the warden drive off. Then I brushed the leaf debris from my own shirt and started back toward my own, much less bulky, ride.

"You're lucky, Al." If he couldn't hear the anger in my voice, that wasn't my fault. "Luckier than that bear. You got a warning."

"Pru, I—" I turned and he fell silent. The dead-eye stare I'd perfected back in the city was as effective as that tranq mix, at least on creatures like Albert. He didn't need me to tell him that drugging and trapping bears was illegal, and if he knew anything about me by now he'd know that I sympathized more with the poor creature in the back of Greg's truck than I ever would with him, even if he weren't involved in poaching.

Back in my car, I realized my hands were trembling. Rage, not fear, affects me that way, and I was grateful that Greg had responded to my call. I'd found the bear when I'd come looking for Albert. I handle most of his responsibilities here in my home-town of Beauville, but sometimes his signature is needed—and I have no patience for waiting. When he hadn't answered his cell, I'd driven out here, hoping to find him in the clearing, a half-mile off the county road. I had no desire to venture into the ramshackle structure Albert and his friends called their camp, and which gave the term "man cave" new meaning.

What I found instead had prompted me to call for help right away. I had feared he was dead at first—the bear, not the man—and when I'd then stumbled on Albert, snoring on his stump, I was very close to making sure he followed. Crisis averted, or at least contained, I took a deep breath, hoping to release that adrenaline. Only when I saw Albert waddling up to my window did I start to think I might have another outlet for my anger.

"Pru!" He waved as he came close, his flannel shirt pulling loose from his stained denim. "Pru, wait!"

Another breath and I rolled down the window. "What is it, Albert?"

"Can I get a ride?" He was panting from his short sprint, and had the grace to look abashed as he shifted from foot to foot. "I can't find my keys."

I closed my eyes for a moment. Albert had endangered a more glorious creature than he would ever be. And to top it off, he smelled. My GTO hadn't had that new car smell in decades, but it was my pride and joy—restored to better than its 1974 heyday through hard work and hard-earned money. Still, unless I was going to help him search, I had to do something. I doubt he'd have any sense of where he might have lost his keys—and I couldn't discount the theory that one of his buddies had taken them, though more likely as a prank than as any kind of state-ment about his condition or ability to drive.

Besides, I had a feeling he wasn't alone.

"You got Frank with you?"

If the portly man standing by my car found my query odd,

he didn't show it. Too dim to dissemble, he merely blinked and nodded.

"Okay," I sighed. "Go get him."

I watched as he rambled over to his truck and half-expected to hear a shout as he found his "lost" keys still in the ignition. I would have no such luck, however. But at least, as he made his way back toward me, I knew I'd have some decent conversation on the ride back to town.

"Hi, Frank." I nodded as Albert lumbered back toward the car. The triangular head that poked out of his flannel shirt blinked in acknowledgment. Frank may be a ferret—his sable coloring and distinctive facial "mask" making him resemble a streamlined version of a raccoon—but he's one of the more personable denizens of Beauville. Certainly more than his person, Albert.

Seeing him peer around, safe inside his flannel nest, I was glad I'd agreed to give the pair a ride. Frank was curious about the woods. He smelled the bear, I could tell, and his busy nose was picking up scents I couldn't even begin to catalog. Still, such curiosity was best left unsatisfied. Albert might survive out here for a few days, if he'd had to. There had to be some provisions in that shed besides more beer. But Frank is small for a carnivore, and these deep woods were not his territory. Besides, Albert brought himself out—and into whatever trouble was brewing. Frank was an innocent bystander and, from the way he craned his head around now, I suspected that he'd spent most of the day huddled in some corner of the truck cab, waiting for the drive home.

Given my druthers, I'd have taken the ferret and left the man behind. I could learn a lot from the sleek creature, I knew, but it was pointless. I'd only end up coming out here again in the morning.

"Hop in." I popped the lock and tried not to look as the larger of my passengers angled his large rear toward me as he maneuvered into the bucket seat. "So none of your buddies is meeting you out here?"

It was a leading question, and not too subtle. But in addition to my curiosity about his keys, I knew Albert wasn't capable of figuring out how to capture a bear by himself—nor dispose of one, once he had it, for either its pelt or for some canned hunt.

"Nuh uh," he said, shaking his head in what seemed even then too vehement a rejection. The movement must have spooked his pet, who ducked back inside his shirt.

"Okay, then." I rolled toward the road, easing the classic chassis over the pocked dirt. Once I got to the state road, though, I floored it, venting my fury in speed. My GTO was made for this, especially with the modifications I'd been working on recently. Besides, I enjoyed how Albert was thrown back in his seat as we crested the hill, silenced by my speed. I knew Greg or I would get our answers eventually. Someone was helping Albert, and someone would be asking about that bear.

We wouldn't find the body for another day.

Chapter Two

Since Frank had retreated—asleep, I figured, after what must have been a tense day—I focused my queries on Albert.

"Tell me about the bear." I didn't look at my passenger as the trees flew by. Didn't need to. I could feel him clench up in the seat beside me, and since I was on a straightaway back toward town, the curves of the state road evening out as we drove through the valley, I knew it was in response to my query.

"The bear?" He paused, and for a moment I thought he was going to deny any involvement. Never mind that he was found snoring yards away from the prone animal. "It's my job," he stuttered after the pause became too obvious. "It was a—whatchamacallit?—a nuisance."

"A nuisance animal? Hardly." I may not work for the town in any official capacity, but between Albert's indolence and my, shall we call it, sensitivity, I end up handling a lot of Beauville's animal issues. Some of that is purely mercenary. Although I inherited my mother's house free and clear, I still have to pay taxes on the huge old wreck, which had been built back in the days when Beauville's mills had translated to prosperity and families were larger. And bourbon alone isn't enough to keep me warm under those ten-foot ceilings when the winter snows cover the Berkshires.

Some of what drives me, as Albert well knew, is preference. Animals like that bear—or the misunderstood pets who make up most of my practice—have more of my sympathy than does the average Beauville native. With reason: none of them can lie any better than Albert can, but unlike my portly colleague, the cats and puppies and canaries of our beaten-down little town don't even try to deceive me.

"I read the same notices you do," I lied. I did keep up on the alerts from the state police, reports on errant wildlife with the temerity to encroach on human habitation. I also knew Albert rarely noticed them, nor the more mundane notices—the ones to do with license renewals and the like. Well, not unless he needed one of the fliers to sop up spilled coffee. "There's been nothing about a problem bear."

"Just came in," he said, with a burp. I turned my gaze from the road to eye him with suspicion. I really didn't want him sicking up in my car. He hadn't turned green, though, so I figured it was safe to continue.

"Who were you hanging out with—today, that is, at the camp?"

"No one." He sounded sullen as a teen. I risked another glance—a hard-eyed stare this time. "Only Paul. He must have taken my keys."

I let that one go. Paul Lanouette didn't seem like a prankster. Leaner than Albert and nominally more intelligent, he was also more ambitious. I thought back to the man I'd known since high school and had avoided even then. Tall and rakishly handsome, at least before the drinking began to show, Paul was an operator, always looking for an edge. Something he could turn to his advantage, a trait I hadn't seen him outgrow, whether he was plying it on one of Beauville's less-perceptive women or in the series of odd jobs—contracting, painting, what-have-you—that he was always hustling, with that crooked grin and the light-brown hair he let go unfashionably long. The bear wasn't particularly pretty, but Paul might have been behind the illegal trapping, if he'd seen some score in it. Anger, as much as a desire to get my fragrant colleague out of my ride, made my foot grow heavy.

"What were you going to do with it?" If Albert noticed that I'd ignored his denial, he didn't let on. At the best of times, Albert wasn't the sharpest tool in the woodshed, and as I neared town, I pushed into a final burst of speed that had him wide-eyed and gasping.

"Nothing." Another hiccup. "Pru? Could you…?" I squealed to a halt and let my passenger tumble out, gagging, to the pavement. We'd reached Albert's putative workplace, and I'd gotten all I could out of him. Putting my baby blue GTO into park, I debated going into the modern brick building myself, while Albert was still on all fours in the small lot. I might not have an actual position there, but I had my own set of keys for those mornings when Albert was "delayed." There were reasons I didn't want to set foot in that building, however.

"You going to clean that up?" The main reason stepped out of the foyer—Detective Jim Creighton, senior man at our little town's cop shop, whose precinct shared an entrance with the animal control office. With that sun-bleached buzz cut and the jawline of a comic book hero, he might look like a boy scout, but he and I had a history.

"He's not my pet." We both paused to watch as Albert finished up, staggering to his feet and wiping his mouth with the back of his hand. "And that's no furball."

"Albert, get a bucket." Creighton sounded tired, but the note of command was hard to ignore. "Clean that up."

"Yeah." Albert glanced from the officer to me. If he expected me to speak up for him, he was mistaken. "Sorry."

"You went out about that bear?"

I nodded. I respect protocol, at least where animal safety is concerned. Before I'd called Greg, I'd left a message for Creighton. If any charges were going to be levied, they would probably go through him. Not that I felt good about that. The handsome cop was working too many hours these days—Beauville was changing, but his budget wasn't—and I knew his resources were stretched thin. Still, if Paul Lanouette had fled the scene, leaving Albert and the animal there as some idea of a prank, I'd push for endangerment—of the bear, not Albert.

"It was a young male," I filled Creighton in. "Drugged but otherwise apparently unharmed. Greg's bringing him to wildlife rehab to make sure."

Creighton nodded, but from the tilt of his sandy head, it was clear he had another question queued up. I turned away, hoping to ignore it—and Albert—but he didn't hold back long. "And he didn't tell you anything?"

Now it was my turn to pause. Creighton didn't mean the chubby town official, who was in the process of throwing as much water on himself as on the soiled pavement. He was smart enough to know that I knew that too.

"We're talking about a bear, Jim." My non-answer drew a silence that spoke volumes. Creighton knew more about me than was comfortable. About my sensitivity, in particular: a gift that I was still working to understand myself.

If I had to explain it, I'd say I could hear what animals are thinking. They don't talk to me, per se—well, most of them, anyway—and they don't necessarily think along the lines that you or I would, or, at least, they don't share the so-called social graces. But for the past two years almost, thanks to a bout of fever and, perhaps, some neural damage done during the wild nights of my former life, I've been able to pick up on signals from the creatures around us that most humans can't. It's the nuts and bolts of food and safety, family and survival, mostly. Instinctive reactions, that I hear as words voiced inside my head.

Sometimes, I get their take on us—unvarnished and usually not very flattering—and sometimes what they notice helps me see the world in a new way. That wasn't the case with the young bear, though. For starters, he was out cold, in a dreamless deep slumber. Besides, as I'd implied to Creighton, even at the best of times, I have trouble getting anything from truly wild animals—you don't need any special gift to understand that they are often confused, if not afraid, around us.

In terms of communication with this other male, I was grateful to be able to answer somewhat honestly. Jim Creighton may not be an animal whisperer, but he has an uncanny ability to read me.

"Anyway, I'm glad I caught you." I breathed a little easier, as Creighton seemed ready to leave that dangerous topic and move on. There was no way I could explain what I did, and questions could only lead to trouble. "A lady called about her lost cat."

I nodded, waiting for details. That Creighton would field such a call wasn't that strange. Beauville is a small town, and when Albert isn't answering his phone the message directs callers to reach out to the police for any animal emergencies. One of the reasons the tall, lean man in front of me looked so tired.

"Maybe you can help her out." He handed me a Post-it note with an address scrawled on it. "Or maybe you'll want to hand this one off to Wallis."

I glanced up sharply at that, but my sometime-beau was grinning. He seemed to know that I did, in fact, often confer with Wallis, the tabby who shared my big old house.

"You don't know Wallis very well if you think she'd want me looking for another cat." I turned it into a joke, glad to be able to lighten his mood as well as his workload. "But I'll leave Albert here with you. He's lost his car keys, apparently. I'm pretty sure Lou at the garage has a copy, if they don't 'turn up.'" I made air quotes around those last two words. Creighton shared my opinion of the slovenly mess of an official, who now stood staring at the particularly un-distinguished puddle he'd made. "He was hanging with Paul Lanouette, though, so maybe Paul will ride to the rescue."

"I'll take care of it." He turned toward our erstwhile colleague. "You go find that kitty."

Chapter Three

Out of consideration for Creighton, I didn't peel out of the parking lot. He wouldn't ticket me, but I knew he'd had complaints. I did floor it once I was out of sight, however. Creighton might have made a joke of it, but a lost cat is a serious thing. Most domestic animals trade off something for the right to loll about the house, and felines are no exception. Yes, your kitty might daydream about hunting those robins nesting on the porch, but the reality is she or he is just as likely to be scoped out—and scooped up—by any of a half—dozen predators native to our area. Coyotes, fishers…even some of the larger raptors can make fast work of a pampered puss, and since we've brought 'em indoors, it's our responsibility to keep them safe.

Besides, the neighborhood I was heading toward—Pine Hills, a rather obvious name—had its own issues. Although it was adjacent to one of the older parts of Beauville —situated on the other side of a rock formation that had served as a barrier to the original settlers—it might as well be a different town. All new construction, in an area that had still been woods when I was growing up, the development was separated by more than just the cobble, as the big stone outcropping was called, or the patch of forest around it, which the developers had left intact—and which I now drove around. McMansions, the sprawling homes of Pine Hills would be called anywhere else, with garages as big as the ranches less than a mile away and manicured lawns instead of the meadows that were coming into bloom. Not that all the houses here were that much bigger than my mother's rambling three-story, I saw as I slowed onto the new blacktop. But my tumbledown Victorian had some history—dating from when Beauville had an industry that wasn't seasonal. Pine Hills, however, had no real connection to the area—not the sad little river that had once powered the mill or even the conifers and birches that gave the area its name. Anyone who lived there had likely moved in the last year, or—more likely, I realized as I let centrifugal force take me round a turn—was renting for the summer. And that meant any pet was new to the territory, too.

Creighton's joshing aside, Wallis would have a heyday with this. Yes, in the dishy cop's terms, I "let" Wallis out. Once I was able to communicate with my feline cohabitant, I no longer felt comfortable dictating the terms of her life. But she and I had both lived in the city before coming here. Plus, we had spoken often of the risks and rewards of her roaming free. In truth, I believe my tabby was smart enough to stay indoors mostly, contenting herself with sunning on the porch. With cats, so much is about appearances.

Helen Birman's showed just how distressed she was. I'd pulled up to the silvered clapboard—at least her house had been built in a traditional New England style—half expecting to have to explain. Some owners call to their pets to come in, and if they don't, feel they've done all they could. The elderly woman in the blue cardigan who greeted me anxiously wasn't one of those. Red-eyed and clutching a handkerchief as if it were a security blanket, she looked so distressed that I feared that "poor Marmalade" had already come to harm. But no, she explained, as she pulled me inside a sitting room that brought up nightmares of Laura Ashley, the orange tabby—a lifelong house pet, as I'd expected—had simply disappeared. It wasn't until Ms. Birman realized that a window screen had come loose that she'd figured out what had happened.

"I called and called." Her voice caught from the tears. "I've walked all over. My companion, Tillie Gershon, is making up signs for me."

She held out the prototype: the photo showed a chubby cat with a rather smug expression on her face, as well upholstered as the small sofa where we sat. "Reward," read the text, above a phone number that—yes—had the area code of the city.

"Do you think people will call?" She must have picked up on my raised brows. Given her age, I suspected the appellation meant the industrious Tillie was a paid assistant, and I wondered at an aide who would leave such a dear old thing alone. "I hate to think that because I'm not local…"

"It's fine." I conjured up a smile for her. I've met mice that were less timid, and the woman perched on the sofa beside me was in real psychic pain. I didn't want to add to it by suggesting that many in town wouldn't want to spend the money on a toll call—or that they might resent the newcomers. I had a hard enough time straddling that line, and I'd only been away a few years. "You do know that most house cats that find themselves outside simply hide until they're found?"

"But I called for her." Stress won out over logic as she kneaded the handkerchief. "I did, and she always comes when I call!"

"She's probably scared and disoriented. There's a lot more outdoors here than she's used to." Fear can make the most sensible among us panic, and a large part of my job was to translate. In this case, not only from pet to person, but also from urbanite to Beauville, as few others in this town could. Feeling for her, I made a snap decision. "I'll tell you what. Why don't you wait here by the phone, and I'll go look? If I can't find her right away, I can put down some traps. They're completely safe, humane traps," I rushed to reassure her as she started. "We'll put some of her favorite food in, and maybe we'll get her when she gets hungry."

More likely, we'd end up with a couple of confused raccoons. This wasn't the city or even suburbia, but the plan was still worth a shot.

"I called her name." She wasn't hearing me. Either that, or my original impression of her as an intelligent, competent adult was very off.

I patted her hand like I would smooth the coat of any frightened animal, and she grabbed onto it as if it were her missing pet, her cool, smooth fingers closing anxiously around mine. Her distress was real. I was more concerned about Marmalade, however, and so I extracted my digits and backed out of the paisley den.

"Marmalade," I called aloud. I could almost feel Ms. Birman's pale eyes on me as I made my way around the side of the little house. "Marmalade!"

I was heading for the window where the orange cat had last been seen but I took a roundabout route, wanting to distract the distraught woman. I was also hoping to pick up some stray signs of the cat's passing, if not the kitty herself. "Marmalade?"

No luck. And once I reached the window, I stood, back against the wall, trying to open my mind. As I've explained, animals don't usually speak directly to me—none but Wallis, anyway—but I can often pick up what they're feeling. Fear, hunger—these were what I was searching for, the other usual motivators, like lust and the drive to protect a family, having been largely ruled out by Marmalade's status as a spayed, older female. Not that we ever really give those over, but on balance, a warm, safe home and steady meals likely took precedence for the missing feline.

It would help, I knew, if I had the orange cat's real name. "Marmalade?" I tried to picture the old lady's lined and worried face, hoping that loyalty, if not affection, would evoke a response. I could understand some resentment: cats are dignified creatures, and being named for fruit preserves would make that hard to maintain. But seeing as how a plump older house cat was basically a marshmallow snack waiting to happen out here, I thought maybe the feline would make an exception. The transition from city to country is hard for people, but at some level the cat would've figured this much out. "Kitty?"

Bingo—I got a hit. A sense of confusion, topped with curiosity about a stranger—me, apparently—in the area. Marmalade didn't get to meet many people these days, I gathered. Still, I found it intriguing that the cat could pick up my signals as well as I could hers.

"You around here? What happened?"

A flash of panic, as I made the connection. I was lost, consumed by the terror. Fear on four paws, I felt my chest tighten. My breathing quickened to a pant as I desperately sought a way to retreat, to back further into my little sanctuary. My safe space, here, in the dark…

Of course. I rounded the corner to the back of the house and saw the brush at the edge of the property rustle. Could have been a squirrel or even the wind, but I could sense the wild out here—and apparently Marmalade could too. I turned back toward the house, where a silver-gray lean-to nestled up against one wall. Sure enough, when I peeked behind the trash enclosure, I saw two green eyes staring up at me. How a twenty-pound feline managed to squeeze into the space between the covered attachment and the wall was beyond me, but as I squatted to face her, I did my best to convey my intent. I pictured the sofa with its overstuffed cushions. The nice old lady, her veined hands wringing the handkerchief. The cozy blue cardigan. When that didn't give me anything, I visualized the cat treats that Wallis indulged in.

"*Reina.*" The word popped into my head.

"Reina?" I said the name out loud, softly, and extended my hand. She reached out gingerly to sniff. "Are you ready to go home?"

"*Home? What is home?*" She might be a house cat, but she wasn't dumb. I looked down into her green eyes.

"You know 'home.'" I pictured the house I had just left—and waited. "Don't you?"

"*That's not…*" She blinked, and I lost her. "*Predators.*" Even a house cat has a sense of what's out there, which was my cue.

"Let's go then." She emerged and let me slip one hand under her, hefting her to my chest. "Your person is going to be so relieved."

"*Predators.*" The word echoed in her mind as she strained to see over my shoulder—back into the woods. And it occurred to me, that while she was relieved to be going back inside—what intelligent domestic animal wouldn't be?—she wasn't totally comfortable. The cat in my arms was still nervous about the predators out there. Either that or she feared that the dangers of the wild were going to follow her into that cozy house.

Chapter Four

I left the happy reunion feeling rather satisfied with myself. The old lady didn't have to know that my special sensitivity had helped me find Reina—or Marmalade, as she insisted on calling her. As did Tillie, who appeared to be roughly the same vintage as her partner, although a head taller, and who'd rushed in after us, slightly breathless, with a ream of now-unnecessary posters. I figured this was what they call a teachable moment, and I used it to educate the longtime couple about feline habits. And when I suggested that their precious pet was too regal for a name like Marmalade, the purr I got from the orange tabby made me feel like I'd earned her approbation too.

But as I did a quick shop and then began the drive home to my own feline housemate, an odd fragment of doubt began niggling at me. "Predators," the cat had said. That made sense. Despite her years of indoor pampering, Reina's instincts had informed her of what was out there. What I didn't understand was why she seemed to think that being indoors wouldn't be an adequate defense, almost as if she had left the house for a purpose. As if she needed to protect her people. Granted, feline vanity could explain that—no self-respecting queen wants a stranger to see her as weak. But, like I've said, I don't really hear what animals say to me, so much as what they feel. No, Reina really believed that whatever was out there was threatening her home or the old couple who loved her so.

Well, maybe the cat had a point. Those old ladies probably wouldn't last long out in the woods either, and Beauville could be mean, especially to newcomers who so clearly had more money. Or maybe it was simply that all that orange and white fur hid the intellect of a day-old kitten. At any rate, I'd done my duty, and so I then did my best to put the thought aside as I pulled up the pitted gravel drive of the old house I called home.

"And you thought I'd be insulted by the comparison?"

As soon as I walked in the side door, Wallis jumped to the floor. She'd been watching for me out the kitchen window, of course, alerted to my approach by the familiar vibrations that precede even scent. Now she twined around my ankles in a manner that looked very much like a typical house cat. Except, of course, that she was using the contact to better plumb my thoughts and memories, which explains why she was mentally grilling me even as she leaned in.

"You really think we're all alike?" A paw reached up. To an observer, Wallis would appear a supplicant—an affectionate kitty begging for treats or attention after a day alone. I knew better. I could feel the needle-sharp claws piercing my jeans.

"I'm sorry." I knew better than to deny it. Wallis has always found it easier to read my thoughts than I hers. I just wasn't aware of this until after my awakening. "It was that what she was thinking bothered me. I took her too seriously, is all."

The bit of flattery had a core of truth: Wallis was an exceptionally acute observer. That was probably one reason it worked—that, and the half a rotisserie chicken I fetched from my bag. Wallis was still a cat, after all.

"Bird." Maybe I was picking up her ravenous appetite or maybe it had just been a long day for me, too. But when I ripped the cooked carcass in two—knives and forks seemed overly fussy at that point—we both fell on our meals like the beasts we were, and all conversation fell silent.

Only after, when Wallis was busy cleaning her white mittens

and I the few dishes that had accumulated since the previous night, did she bring the topic up again.

"*Why do you concern yourself?*" The thought surfaced in my mind with the taste of fur.

"Wallis." I could growl too. The tabby knew how her grooming while we conversed discomfited me.

"*You splash all over when you bathe.*" Her nonchalance couldn't hide the tiniest edge of apology. "*An individual could get….wet. But why?*"

"It's my job," I responded. Her silence showed me that she knew I wasn't being totally honest. "Okay," I added. "I was curious. I mean, it seemed odd to me. Doesn't it to you?"

A twitch of her black-tipped ears—a quick back and forth, the feline equivalent of a shrug. "*We worry about you,*" she said. "*Especially the clueless ones. We're not…heartless.*"

"No, I know." I dried my coffee mug and hung it beneath the cabinet, next to my mother's old favorite. I'm not sentimental, far from it, but I did experience a pang. When I'd first moved back—ostensibly to take care of my mother in her final illness—I'd revolted against her orderly ways. But with the hospice nurses handling most of her daily care, I'd found myself falling into old, observed habits. When someone is lying there, waiting to die, an act as simple as washing a cup can be comforting.

"*And you wonder why I groom?*"

"What do you have to be anxious about?"

She didn't answer, which could have been because she was now twisted around, meticulously licking the base of her tail, where her herringbone fur joined into dark rings.

"And it's not like I get involved in everyone's life." I paused. My mother suffered horribly from the town busybodies, the cliquish mavens who blamed her for my father's alley-cat ways, and I didn't think they'd be much kinder to a pair of same-sex newcomers, seeing any divergence from the norm as an affront that had to be punished. Those nasty neighbors—along with my mother's rigid clampdown of a response—were behind my fleeing this town all those years ago. That and the knowledge that I was more like my old man than my mother, or so I'd thought.

"I'm not," I said aloud. An image of Albert came to mind, slovenly and inept.

"*Prey animal.*" Wallis was even less sentimental than I am, but in this she was right. Left to his own devices, Albert would be eaten alive. It was only because he'd grown up here, drinking and fishing with so many of our town's more respectable citizens, that he had the title of animal control officer. There's no actual list of qualifications for the position, and his predecessor had been a glorified dog catcher, more or less. Of course, in the decade or so since Albert had inherited the position, the standards for what constituted animal control had grown and changed—and that was where I came in.

"I couldn't leave him out there." I put the last of the dishes away and reached for a tumbler. "I mean, he gives me work. And odds are, he'd have survived—it's already pretty warm out—and I don't need him pissed off at me." I didn't mention Frank. Wallis had strong feelings about the ferret.

"*Prey,*" was all she said, and I know enough to let her have the last word.

Besides, I had other things on my mind—and men other than Albert. Creighton, specifically. Despite our testy exchange earlier, we'd become something of a steady thing over the last year. Maybe it was the tension between his boy scout ways and my own bad-girl tendencies, but I was anticipating an evening's recreation with my favorite officer of the law.

But after a long hot bath and a second tumbler of Maker's Mark, I was beginning to think I'd been stood up.

"*Springtime.*" Wallis leaped to the sofa, where I was sprawled pretending to read. "*Time for roaming.*"

"Creighton's not—" I stopped myself. I'd been the one to resist my beau's push toward monogamy. Not that I had anyone else lined up, not anymore. But Wallis wasn't talking about the sandy-haired cop. "Who else in this dump of a town would you have me take home, Wallis? One of the crew at Happy's?" I occasionally still drank at our local dive.

"*Huh.*" She dismissed the idea with a little bark-like cough that made me wonder if a hairball was in the offing. "*There are other alpha males around.*" She circled, settling the cushion to her liking. "*Or we could go back to the city.*"

"That we could," I said. I'd given up arguing with her. And after I drained the last of the bourbon, I gave up on my date, too, and dragged myself upstairs to bed.

Chapter Five

The call, when it woke me, was not going to be an apology. I knew that even as I saw the familiar number glowing on my cell in the first morning light. I may not have Wallis' instincts, but I had enough sense to know that if Creighton was calling this early, it was official.

"Morning, sunshine." That didn't mean I couldn't rib him a little. I'm an early riser—a holdover from my breakdown, when I didn't sleep for nearly a week straight—but the sun was only just breaking through the new foliage. "How're they hanging?"

"Pru, I need you to come by the office." As I'd suspected, his voice was all business.

"I need you too," I teased, even as my curiosity grew. "But you know I've got my morning rounds."

"After, then." He was not in the mood. "Right after, Pru. This is serious."

He hung up, and so it was with piqued curiosity that I dressed and prepared to start my day. I made myself a pot of coffee, which I drank black and hot. If I could have, I'd have girded my loins. Most of what I do isn't onerous. I like working with animals. Prefer them to people, in most cases. And when I can help them out—whether that be alerting the state warden to a bear in distress or locating that frightened cat—I feel pretty good about it.

But some jobs are barely worth it. I was thinking, of course, about my first gig of the morning—walking a little ball of fluff named Growler. That was his private name, of course. Like Reina—aka, Marmalade—the petite bichon frisé had been given a much less dignified name by his human. She called him Bitsy, for which he'd never forgive her. She was pretty rude to me, too, of course, but I didn't have to live with her.

"Good morning, Mrs. Horlick." Even having taken time to caffeinate, I was early, and the harridan at the door was not pleased. She'd be in the same stained housecoat all morning, I suspected, though, at some point she'd touch up the lipstick that caked in the corners of her mouth like so much dried blood. Still, she eyed me with eyes closed to slits. The look was supposed to express disapproval, I reckoned, or maybe disdain. I figured it was just as likely the smoke from her unfiltered Marlboro that made her squint so. At any rate, I had as much control over one as the other, and about as much personally invested. And so I conjured up my most fulsome morning cheer and, plastering a big smile on my own face, sallied forth. "Is Bitsy ready to go out?"

My blatant disregard of her scorn wasn't just a petty bit of revenge. It was also Animal Training 101: Don't respond to bad behavior. Any response may be seen as a reward, even a response you might deem a punishment. Better to ignore the unwanted behavior, as most animals will come around in order to get the attention they crave.

"Bitsy." She flicked the ash off her burning butt and then picked a fleck of tobacco from her lip. "Amazed you've got time for any dog at all, the way you run that man ragged."

The smile on my face stiffened, but I held my tongue. My little romance was fated to be common knowledge in a town this size. That didn't mean I had to like it.

"Getting him to do God-knows-what." Behind her rough caw, I could hear the scrabbling of claws and a muted plea. "*Out! Out, please. Out!*"

"I think I hear Bitsy." I craned to see past her—difficult, as she had planted her worn carpet slippers in the doorway. "I hope he doesn't have an accident."

"*Please!*" The short sharp bark was more protest than plea—the little dog had more self-control than his mistress. But it worked, as without another word, old Horlick turned back into her house. As she padded toward the basement door, I made my silent apology, hoping Growler would see my ploy for what it was.

"No funny business." As the white pup scurried toward freedom, his person's eyes remained on me. "I hear what you get up to."

I managed to keep my smile in place as I reached up for the lead that hung inside the door. Funny business? Some secrets I didn't want to get out.

"See you soon," was all I said as she closed the door in my face.

"*Come on, walker lady.*" The fluffball's voice sounded gruff in my head as he waited for me to attach the leash, but his snowy puff of tail was wagging furiously.

"At your service," I responded, my voice soft. We'd reached a comfortable understanding, Growler and I, over the time that I'd been walking him, but the leash was part of the pantomime we both had to play, at least while we were still in view of the Horlick house. "Where will it be?"

"*River!*" In his succinct bark—and the more articulate telepathic command behind it—I heard the longing of a great spirit stuck in a miserable situation. Tracy Horlick might feed the tiny beast and house him, but she had no idea how proud a spirit existed inside the cute toy. Even her hiring me was, I suspected, more about her own need to dominate—and to have a direct line to the source of some of Beauville's juiciest gossip—than about caring for Growler. She might still be trying to figure out my connection to animals, but she knew I'd fled town years ago, and that my return—and my subsequent romance with Creighton—was the source of speculation. Still, the bichon in her custody had made some kind of peace with his situation. He'd also learned to make the most of our daily excursions into the outside world.

"*Oh, Donald!*" The toy's snuffling translated to words in my head as his wet leather nose sniffed a curbside tree with interest. "*You've got to stay out of the garbage.*"

I smothered a smile as he left his own mark on the poor maple and moved on, "reading" each pit stop as avidly as Tracy Horlick did the gossip pages.

"*No!*" The yelp stopped me short. Had my charge been bitten by something? But those black button eyes said it all. "*Not the same. Not!*"

"Of course." I responded immediately. "I'm sorry." I was. For all that I might find Growler's cataloguing of the neighborhood dogs' escapades amusing, these daily rounds were more than entertainment. Although Tracy Horlick released him into her fenced-in yard for nightly relief, his outings with me were how Growler stayed in touch with his community—his real peers and colleagues. Despite my sensitivity, I could never hope to replace other dogs in his life.

"*Carson, you dog…*" I got a sharp image, almost as if it were my own memory, of a shepherd-pointer-lab mix, big as a small horse and full of fun. The big rescue had had been by this morning, I gathered, and I could almost taste the tennis ball in his mouth. Just then, another shape came into the picture, her glossy brindled coat flecked with red and brown and warm from the sun and play. "*Squeeks, huh?*" I started. Growler usually had less interest in females. I didn't know if it was the Boxweiler's association with Carson, or her own inquisitive nature that had made her stand out.

The image faded as Growler moved on, a little quieter and, I thought, a tad lonelier. Those two dogs had been having fun in real time, while he was left with the traces of play. No wonder my assumption—that he was a gossip like his human—had insulted him. I knew he'd find my pity worse, and so I kept my thoughts carefully shielded as we continued around the block. It was a technique I was slowly learning—Wallis said a week-old kitten could do better—but I figured at least it showed respect. By the time we reached the edge of the old development, Growler's internal "voice" was back to its unselfconscious volume and that stub of a tail was vibrating madly again. When he stared up at me, eyes bright, I knew my efforts had been worthwhile.

"River?" I didn't have to offer twice. With a quick glance around to make sure we weren't seen by any of my human colleagues, I bent and unsnapped the lead. Growler took off like a pint-sized rocket, bounding over the leaf loam and damp moss like a white superball. Carson and Squeeks—Roxie, I gathered, was her real name—loved to frolic in the water, and their recent visit added a piquancy to Growler's lone romp. I followed as closely as I could—I knew how important this free time was to him, but still, he was a small dog and, as the bear yesterday had reminded me, neither of us were the most ferocious creatures out there.

"Took you long enough." Tracy Horlick squinted down at her pet on our return, almost an hour later. After our romp by the river, I'd had to spend some time brushing Growler's coat, but I was pretty confident she wouldn't see anything to complain about.

"It's spring." I offered in return. "Bitsy's a healthy dog, and he needed a good run."

"Huh." She used her cigarette as a prop, drawing on it as she turned her gimlet eye up to me. "You're not getting any extra, you know."

"All part of the service." By my shin, I felt the thrumming of that little tail. Thanks enough, in my book.

"Might have thought you were running off with him." She

narrowed her eyes once more, though that could have been because of the smoke. "Maybe that's how you're hoping to stay out of trouble."

I didn't know if she had her own psychic powers or if she was simply looking to cause trouble. But I handed her back the lead at that and, with a silent farewell to the bichon, made my way back to my car. I hadn't forgotten my appointment with Jim Creighton. For forty-five minutes, though, I'd relished my freedom as much as Growler had.

Chapter Six

If I were a dog, I'd have smelled something off. If I were a cat, I might have been more attuned to the posture of the clerk and the two deputies in Beauville's sole police station when I walked in. Maybe it was the old memories. In my teens, I'd been dragged in here more than once. Not for anything too serious—joy riding in someone's "borrowed" car or smoking a joint behind the high school. That was all they'd caught me at, anyway. And since I'd been a minor, the cops back then had been willing to release me to my mother, who would come in with a face like thunder to take me home.

That's the best reason I can think of for why I didn't question the downcast eyes and averted faces of Chuck and Harry, Creighton's two deputies, or the flat affect with which Kayla sent me back to his office. We'd gotten past the smirks and jokes by then. I knew Chuck Carroll from high school, and even Harry Staines—older than us both by a year or five—had stopped grinning like a hyena when I came by for Jim.

As soon as Kayla buzzed me in, however, I felt the hair on the back of my neck start to rise. Maybe it was the nod, in place of a greeting, or that my own friendly "hey" was, by default, addressed to her neat French braids. But while I walked down the corridor to Creighton's office, I found myself once again thinking of my youthful scrapes—and the icy terms in which my mother would evoke my absent dad on the ride home.

I should have known another factor was at play. Growler would have, for sure. Pitiful human that I am, I had to wait until Creighton glanced up from the paper he held before him to see that something was indeed very wrong. I couldn't read whatever it was—he knows me well enough so that he turned the page over as I took the room's one spare chair. That was par for the course with Jim. No, it was from the flat, dead expression in his cool blue eyes that I could surmise that whatever it was, he thought I might be involved.

"Good morning to you too, Jim." I worked to keep my voice level. Like any sensible animal, I wasn't going to let the stone-faced man before me see that I was rattled.

"Sit." I did. He knew how to use the command voice as well as I did. "Tell me again about yesterday."

I opened my mouth, but the smart-aleck comeback stopped in my throat. The man sitting on the other side of the metal desk was not my lover at this moment. Not the wry, funny man I'd grown quite fond of bedding. This was a cop, plain and simple. I knew what he was asking about, to some extent, and so I answered as truthfully as I could.

"I was in the office—Albert's office—when I got a call about a fishing license. I forget who called. Some real—" I caught myself—"tool," I completed the thought. "Walz or Walls or something like that. One of those summer people who think we exist for their pleasure."

Creighton's brow furrowed in impatience.

"Anyway, I wrote it down and I can find it for you. I started giving him the spiel about applying online, but he stopped me to say that he'd already filed out the forms and sent everything into Albert. He wanted to know where his license was, and he wanted it now. So, yeah, I started rifling through the mess on Albert's desk, because, well, I am covering for him. I didn't find the application, but I did uncover a bunch of other stuff, including our state registration forms and the authorization for my latest invoices. It was a nice day, and so I figured he'd be out at that camp where he and Paul and Ronnie hang out. I mean, it's on state land but it's kind of an open secret."

I paused, and Creighton nodded. "Anyway, when I got out there, I found Albert—and that bear. I called Greg, and you know the rest." I stopped to take in the man across from me. "I never did get back to Walls, or whatever his name is.

"Why?" I figured I deserved some kind of explanation. I didn't think it was about the bear.

"You arrived when?" I didn't think he would answer with another query.

"Around three, I think." I stopped to calibrate. "Yeah, that's about right. Greg was there within the hour."

"And during that hour?" His voice had a chill I didn't recognize.

"I sat in my car and read." My curiosity was really piqued now, but so was my sense of danger. I eyed the report to see if I could make out anything, even facedown. Creighton's hand moved over it protectively. "If Albert says anything different, he's lying. He was dead asleep. And, yes, before you say it, I could have woken him while I waited. I didn't want his company, though. I wasn't going to try to free that bear alone—I'm not a fool—but if he'd started to come to, I'd have roused Albert and gotten him into my car. I pulled up close to him, just in case."

He nodded, and I gathered that my story fit with the facts as he'd seen them. I didn't add that I was more concerned for the ferret who was Albert's constant companion than the portly animal control officer.

"You didn't go into the shed—their 'camp'?"

I recoiled at the thought. "No! I don't even want to guess..." I stopped. "Wait, I do. A still? Drugs?" Albert might be a town officer, but I wouldn't put it past him. And some of his friends...

Creighton only stared.

"No, Jim," I repeated, letting my own query slide. I searched my memory for what he could be getting at. "It was locked, I think. I must have seen the padlock on the door, because when Albert told me he lost his keys, I would've told him to go look in there, otherwise. And, no, before you ask, I didn't see Albert's keys either. You think I would've driven him back to town if I didn't have to?"

"I don't know, Pru. That's what I'm trying to figure out here." A note of sadness had crept into his voice, and I leaned forward. I'm not the affectionate sort. Some would say I'm rather like a cat in that way. But there was something in his falling tone, something around his eyes, that almost made me want to reach out to him, even as the hackles along the back of my neck rose in alarm.

"Jim?" I swallowed, my mouth suddenly dry. "What happened, Jim? What did you find?"

"Pru, you know I can't…" He looked down at the paper beneath his hand, and I knew then it was bad. "It's police business."

"If it involves you, then it involves me." I kept my voice low. The man had been pushing for more of a connection, but as I spoke, I also knew it was the truth. "And it sounds like I'm in there, too."

A sigh released the last of the stiffness in his posture, leaving my boy scout sweetheart visibly deflated.

"We found a body, Pru." He met my gaze then, his eyes filled with pain. "Someone died out there, locked inside the shed."

Chapter Seven

The rest was pretty easy to piece together. The trapping of the bear was illegal. Albert was playing dumb—not that much of a stretch, for him—and still claimed not to have found his keys. But a search of the shed was an obvious first step in the hunt for whatever drugs or apparatus had been used to subdue the beautiful wild beast. And when Creighton cut the lock he'd found more than he'd bargained for. That was why he hadn't come by last night—this last was confirmed by a tip of his buzz cut as I figured it out aloud.

"How'd he die?" Creighton's eyebrows shot up at my words. If he thought I'd be squeamish, he should know me better by now. "I mean, if you wanted me to know who it was, you'd have told me, right?"

"Pru, really…"

"A gunshot would've woken Albert." I paused, considering the amount of drink that had probably been consumed. "Probably. Stabbing? A fight?"

"Pru—" A little louder.

"Do you think I'm too girly to take it?" I'd seen the violence one human could inflict on another. "Do you think I'm one of those city people who see Beauville as some kind of paradise?" Despite his partial thaw, this was too far.

"I think you're a civilian. No," he corrected himself, "I think you're a possible person of interest in a suspicious death. So, no, I'm not going to share information with you."

I couldn't help it. A smile tweaked the corner of my mouth. He must have seen the twitch of my lips, because he frowned. "Not more than I have, anyway. Pru, this isn't a local matter anymore. I've got to get the staties involved, but I wanted to be the one to ask you those questions. I really hope that will be all that's necessary."

The rest of what he'd said—"suspicious death," and, more to the point for me, "person of interest"—began to kick in. I opted for a clinical approach, so cool, Wallis would be proud. If I was being looked at, it definitely wasn't a gun death. I don't own a gun. I do, however, own a knife—a small, sharp blade that accompanies me everywhere. "A stabbing?"

His stare was as cold as my reasoning, but his silence answered me. He hadn't asked for my knife. "I get it." I did. He was protecting me, as much as he could. He was gallant in that way. I stood, and lingered for a moment. "You know, if you need to unwind..."

"Pru, please." He stood too—to make sure I was leaving. "We'll be in touch."

We'll be in touch. I pondered those words as I walked back down the corridor. That was a new one, and I didn't think it was simply the involvement of the state police that had my golden boy holding me at arm's length. Yes, a man had died, and Creighton was trying to shield me. But those weren't words of comfort, by any stretch.

Maybe they meant nothing, but my instincts with men had been honed by considerable experience. Wallis would have a field day with it, I knew, as soon as I got home. She'd pounce on my mood like an errant rodent, not only scoffing but stressing that with a simple dismissal my boy scout beau he'd actually freed us. We could move back the city now, she'd say, wrapping herself around my ankles as if to replace his caresses with her own. She might have a point. I could get a good price for the old house now, while the summer people were here and shopping. So why didn't I? Maybe I was getting old. Or maybe I just didn't like the idea of giving up my territory to new money. Having my house taken over by the kind of folks who automatically assumed any native was a country bumpkin lacking in the smarts to make it anyplace else.

Speaking of such, I shouldn't have been surprised to see Albert waiting by Kayla's desk. It was early for Albert and I doubted he'd stopped drinking once I'd dropped him off yesterday. Without a ride, he'd likely bunked down in the office, with poor Frank in tow. He certainly stank as if he hadn't showered, and I didn't think the ferret was to blame. Chuck had made himself scarce—or, okay, maybe he was out on a call—but poor Kayla was stuck, and I saw her wince as the slovenly man leaned forward and breathed on her.

Albert was in no shape to be out, but Creighton must have put the fear in him. Because after Kayla sent him back to the benches, he simply stood there, shifting from foot to foot, as wide-eyed with terror as an oversized hamster in a cat shelter.

"Hey, Albert." I nodded and made to pass.

"Pru, wait." He reached out to me, but one glare and his hand dropped back by his side. "Can you—"

I was already shaking my head. As much as I'd tried to brush off the reality, a man had died, and Albert had been at the scene. I wasn't going to speak up for him to Creighton. Jim would be as fair to Albert as he deserved, and I had no pull if the state police were getting involved. Nor was I going to give the bearded hulk before me a heads-up about what the cops wanted to know. I might not like being blindsided by Creighton's line of inquiry, but I respected his technique. A man had died, and he was going to get to the bottom of it.

"It's Frank." Albert cut off my wordless rejection. "I'm worried."

"Is he all right?" I kicked myself. Creighton had his responsibilities, but I had mine too. Albert and his pet had been out in the woods for an extended period, and I knew the little mustelid had been frightened. With everything else going on, I hadn't pursued the matter further.

"What? Yeah, yeah. He's fine." Relieved that my instincts weren't entirely shot, I turned to leave. "But Pru, if I—you know—if they lock me away, will you look after him?"

I paused to size him up. Considering his bulk, that took a moment. "Albert, what did you do?"

"Nothing much," he said, with a shrug that bounced the belly beneath his beard. "Only, you know, sometimes things happen."

"Things happen?" I knew Albert liked to drink. He'd never been violent, though—at least not with me. Then again, he was afraid of me. Of most women, I believe, but of me, for sure. And then I remembered—he'd blamed Paul for making off with his keys.

"Albert, what were you and Paul doing out there anyway?" A horrible idea began taking shape in my mind. I knew what Lanouette was capable of—and framing a drinking buddy was the least of it. "Besides drinking and trapping some innocent animal?"

"Nothing." He scuffed his sneaker on the ground like a little boy. "It's just, you know, Paul doesn't have a job. And I do."

"Uh huh," I said aloud, as my dread grew.

"He thinks, you know, that he's smarter than me." Another scuff, even as he peeked up to see if I was listening. "Like he can boss me around."

"Albert, did you—?" I stopped myself. I didn't want to hear another lie, and I had something I needed to say. "Look, Albert, I know you're a Beauville official. I know you're smart." That one hurt, but I needed him to listen. "But you don't have to prove that to anyone. You don't have to prove anything to anyone. So if Detective Creighton or any other officer asks you anything, you tell him—you tell any of them—that you want a lawyer."

"A lawyer?" If he wasn't scared before, he was now. He stared up at me, wide-eyed with terror. But before I could say any more, Kayla interrupted.

"Albert? Detective Creighton is waiting for you."

"I'll look after Frank," I promised, as the clerk led the speechless brute away.

I wasn't being paid to take care of Albert. That didn't stop me from worrying about him as I crossed the foyer to the office he had just vacated. I didn't think he'd killed anyone. Then again, anything was possible—and if the staties were involved, I couldn't be sure that Albert would get a fair shake. To me, he might be a big, dumb lout. To them, he might be a bird in the hand. A fat, hairy bird that didn't have the sense to protect itself.

I couldn't help but worry over this as I crossed over to the lout's office and opened the door. The rustle of paper alerted me to the desk's other regular occupant, who had apparently just dived for cover.

"It's me, Frank." I went to refill my travel mug, then thought better of it. I had no idea what Albert brewed in that pot, but it wasn't coffee by any of my definitions. "You okay?"

"*Cat, dog…Albert?*" A triangular head popped up from the open desk drawer, the whiskered snout busy cataloguing all the scents I had brought in with me.

"Yeah, I saw him." I nodded toward the door. "Next door."

"*Next door.*" The ferret climbed onto the desk blotter. I might have been projecting, but he appeared dejected. "*Box,*" he said.

I caught my breath, stopping myself before I could respond. I'd had a vision, along with that communication, of four close walls and a low ceiling—an animal's idea of hell. "Box" meant "cage," I figured. Yes, Albert was at the station next door. He'd gone in voluntarily, just as I had, to answer questions, but I could not in good faith promise that one interview would be the extent of it.

I didn't want to lie. Frank is an intelligent animal, smaller beasts have to be, and this little predator had survived on his wits more than once. Not only that, but he and I had a connection. In large part, I suspected, that was because he knew the respect I had for him. In some measure, it was also because we both had to deal with Albert. Frank had to because the human was his support and provider, by some accident of fate, despite the disparity in intellect and character that by rights should have had that relationship reversed. And me, well, you could say the same factors came into play for me too. Albert's laziness and ineptitude made it easier for me to earn a living, without any close scrutiny either. A more astute observer might have noticed the attention I paid to animals, rather than their humans. Albert was not that. Was there something deeper, as well, at least between the sleek animal now looking up at me and his unkempt person? I didn't know.

What I did know was that Frank was telling me something about himself, rather than reading my mood. The fact that he came out to greet me, that he now sat up, his long body stretched at attention, let me know that he was trying to communicate.

"You don't have to be nervous," I replied. That one word— "*box*"—echoed in my head. "If—something happens, I'll make sure you have a home." I'd take him in, if it came to that. What Wallis would say, would be another matter.

That was poor comfort, and the animal knew it. Ferrets are high-energy creatures, usually scurrying and sniffing like mad. But Frank appeared despondent—snuffling at Albert's desktop like he already missed the man.

"*He doesn't know,*" he said, at least in his fashion. What I was getting was a deep sense of uncertainty and, for lack of a better word, displacement. "*He can't know…*" Disappointment. Well, I'd be disappointed too if I were paired permanently with Albert. "*He doesn't know,*" I heard again, almost as if the poor animal felt responsible for his person's imprisonment, if not his ineptitude. No self-respecting ferret would let himself be grabbed up. Then again, no ferret would have gotten involved in such a…well, hare-brained scheme.

"You're not responsible." I longed to reach out to the ferret. Not only was his fur eminently inviting to stroke, but physical contact can amplify my connection. Frank was one of the more intelligent and discerning males in Beauville. It hurt to see him in any psychic pain.

But if I've learned anything with this sensitivity, it's that I need to be aware of boundaries. Sometimes—often, even—the animals in our lives welcome our touch. At other times, we must respect them and let them be. And so when Frank didn't respond to my words—or the thought behind them—I could only watch as he climbed off the desk onto the seat cushion that probably still smelled strongly of his person's presence. I watched him circle once, like a cat, and then curl up into the deep sleep that ferrets are known for.

Poor guy. I waited as the thoughts of Albert drifted off into vague dreams about hunting some shiny object. A fish, perhaps, as seen through water, and the anxiety, if that's the word, fading into something more solicitous and protective.

Frank was a neutered male, I knew. Albert was not the most law-abiding member of the Beauville establishment, and, despite his title, I didn't think he'd necessarily observe the state laws about ferrets. But he'd adopted Frank when a vacationing family had surrendered him to our county shelter, an adult animal no longer being as cute as a cub, at least not to a young teen who had discovered other interests, I gathered, from the few memories Frank had shared. And his original owner—probably at his parents' insistence—had had the surgery done, though probably more to make the little animal's musky scent more palatable than out of any strict adherence to the laws in the state of Massachusetts. From this, I had always assumed that Frank had no offspring of his own. Now, picking up that sense of responsibility—and, was it guilt?—I wondered. Maybe it was me, but I couldn't see caring that deeply about the man I had just seen in the police station next door.

Then again, I mused, it could be fatigue. Wallis could get snippy when she was due for a nap, and she had often pointed out the same about me. We're all animals, after all, and our vulnerabilities are heightened when we're tired, hungry, or scared. And so, making a mental note to follow up with the slim sleeper once he woke, I began to rummage through Albert's papers. My talk with Creighton had reminded me about the caller. I might not have an answer for him, but at least I could let him know. And if I ended up resubmitting his fishing license application, well, then, that was something I could bill Albert for, once he was back at his post.

If… I caught myself. No, Albert might be a mess of a man, but he wasn't violent. Though I'd been around long enough to know that when people drink and emotions run high, people can get hurt. Was there a molten core of wounded pride underneath Albert's bulk? Could he have lashed out after one too many insults? A man of his bulk, unconscious or not caring…

No, I told myself. Odds were, the body wasn't even one of Albert's friends. Lots of people come through this little town of ours, and a shack a half mile from the road might appeal to folks for a variety of reasons, none of them honest or kind. I didn't know who Creighton had found out there. I certainly had no reason to assume it was anything but an unfortunate accident.

Besides, I had my own priorities to see to—and other clients who needed my attention. I pulled the spare chair up to the desk as I realized the magnitude of my quest. Albert didn't file anything. I wasn't totally sure he read anything—or could, for that matter. While Frank snoozed, I worked my way through notices about changes in hunting and fishing regulations, all clearly marked with "PUBLIC POSTING." Two letters about overdue water bills for Albert's apartment, which were surprising in that I didn't think the man bathed or drank the stuff. And then, under a grease-stained sports page from the local rag, I found it: my note about Jack Walz, a summer resident who wanted a fishing license.

With a sigh of relief—I really didn't want to excavate any deeper—I sat back and reached for the phone. Only to have it ring as I lifted it.

"Beauville Animal Control." If it was Walz, I could honestly tell him that I had been about to call him back.

"Hello, Officer?" The high voice was breathless. An older person, I thought, and scared.

"May I help you?" I stood and reached for a pencil I'd seen earlier. If someone was being threatened or an animal was in danger, I'd pass the info onto Creighton's office and head right out.

"I hope so." A man, I thought, but frail sounding and upset. "It's my Sage, you see. She's gone missing."

Chapter Eight

Summer people. I know their distress is as real as that of any creature flushed from its den, but as I repeated Sage's Pine Hills address to memorize it, I couldn't avoid the thought that they bring it on themselves. Bad enough that they uproot themselves with the change in the weather, but they inflict massive changes on their pets, too. Granted, some animals are more territorial than others. Most dogs will be happy enough anywhere, as long as you're there with them, while cats, as Wallis frequently reminds me, just want to be in their proper home, with or without you.

Still, this is what I do—reconcile the ways of man to dog—and it wasn't the poor pet's fault that his person had placed him in an unfamiliar setting. So, with a sigh that might have woken Frank were he not so completely out, I abandoned the pile of paperwork half sorted, only pausing to fish out a liquor store flier from the previous winter—along with a pen suspiciously like one I'd lost weeks before. Scrawling "out of office—back soon" on the flier's back, I pocketed the pen and searched for something tacky to stick it to the office door. In my hunt, I found that message from Walz again and pocketed that too. No matter what I felt about Beauville's wealthy transients, I had given this guy my word.

The rest I left for Albert. As I locked up—I'd found a scrap of duct tape for the notice—I looked over at the cop shop on the other side of the foyer. The waiting area appeared empty, but that didn't mean anything. Albert could easily have gotten out while I was working through the mess on his desk. In fact, if he'd seen me in there, he'd feel more free to amble on down to our little town's old main drag and console himself after his ordeal with a liquid lunch.

I found the idea of the bearded man bellied up to the bar at Happy's oddly cheering and was almost whistling as I drove away from the shared lot. I even managed to wait until I was down the block before I let my baby-blue baby roar.

●●●●●

Sage, and her person, weren't that far away. Nothing in Beauville is, and from here, in the commercial center of town, I could take the county road, which looped around the gentle slope Beauville was built on and the big stone outcropping that divided it. This made for a scenic drive, and after the disruptions of the morning, it felt good to put my foot down, to let my GTO's muscular engine do its work.

Not that I was alone. This late into spring, the birds were beyond caring. Nests had been made and eggs had mostly hatched. Now everyone was either trying for a second chance or readying for their fledglings to take off. Memories of my own mother came back as I heard the squawking of a particularly outraged robin. She'd have been even more appalled if she knew how her little girl had been bullying her brother, stealing the food literally out of his mouth the moment mom's back was turned. Well, I wasn't going to tell, and as I drove out of earshot, I found myself wondering if the little male was going to survive. The little female as well, for that matter. Life isn't easy for any of us, and even we tough ones can get tripped up.

Well, they weren't my concern, I told myself as I pulled off the county road and circled back around the cobble. My sensitivity had made me more aware of the struggles around me, much to Wallis' scorn.

"*Really?*" I could hear the rolled "r" of her guttural purr in my head. "*Worried about the robins now? And what about that rotisserie chicken?*"

Shaking the memory free, I checked the address one more time. I'd had no answer for her the first time she'd confronted me on what she called my "human hypocrisy," back when I first realized I could hear her thoughts. I hadn't come up with an answer since.

New Birch Street—a few blocks from where I'd met up with Helen Birman only the day before. Recalling the old lady and her errant pet, I slowed to a more reasonable speed as I maneuvered through the freshly paved streets. Sage's person—a Mr. Ernest Luge—was further back than Helen and Tessie had been, and as I drove, the houses got bigger and uglier. The developer who had lacked imagination when it came to street names had also been missing common sense. Beauville, a former mill town, is situated in a valley. The older houses, like mine, climb the gentle slope on the west of the river. The first new houses, like Helen and Tessie's clapboard, perched on the same slope and continued the old New England-style, on the other side of granite outcropping that had once defined this town.

This warren of McMansions, though, had been tucked into a cleft of the rise. Easier to build on, I figured, but that also meant it was cut off from the regular breeze that flows up the valley along the river. I was sweating by the time I found the right address.

"Mr. Luge?" I'd wiped my brow on my sleeve as I'd walked up to the house, hoping to make myself more Pine Hills-presentable, but I'd still been somewhat surprised when the tiny white-haired man had answered with a smile. "I'm Pru—Pru Marlowe, with Beauville animal control."

It felt odd to announce myself that way, but I was here in a semi-official capacity. I'd let him know later about the freelance services I offered.

"Yes, of course." Nodding agreeably, my host stepped back,

gesturing me into a frosty living room. When he'd opened the door, I'd noted his age in his lined face and the way his slim body hunched forward. What I hadn't seen was the cane, nor the way one leg dragged as he maneuvered. "Please, come in."

I did, just enough so he could close the door. This much air conditioning shouldn't be wasted.

"I should get some information and then head out." Especially if Luge couldn't do the searching himself, I wanted to get moving. A lost pet is serious business—and this wasn't going to be as easy as the situation with Reina. As I started to explain: dogs aren't like cats. Beyond the obvious, they don't behave the same when they're lost. I needed to know this Sage's age and breed to plot out where she might have gone. It was still bright day, but I wouldn't give a domestic dog much of a chance out here at night with the coyotes. Like that robin, they had young to feed, and even as we closed in on high summer, their awareness of winter was always near.

"You didn't get my message?" The smile was confusing, and I shook my head. Like so many of the animals I dealt with, I viewed bared teeth—even unnaturally white ones—with caution.

"I'm sorry. I called the office." He waved me over again, moving quickly despite his disability, and this time I followed. Not so much because of his gesture but because I'd picked up a faint signal—"*nice man! Treats!*"—from an animal somewhere deeper in the house. "Sage has been found. She's home safe and sound. I was just giving her some dinner when you rang."

"Ah, of course." I wasn't surprised she was getting treats, considering how frantic her person had been. The rest fell into place. "My cell isn't hooked into the animal control office phone," I said aloud. "I'm freelance—I'm a local animal behaviorist and, well, pet-care specialist." It sounded better than dog walker and for all I knew, he needed some help training Sage. "I help out when Albert, when our animal control officer, is … otherwise engaged."

"Well, I'm sorry you had to make the drive for nothing." He looked up at me, pale gray eyes bright. "Would you like a cold beverage?"

"Sure." While I didn't want to put the little man out, I did want to meet the pooch in question. Maybe she could give me some hints as to her person's pet-care needs. Also, there was something off about the happy little grunts and barks that came from the kitchen. Something missing. "Is that Sage I hear?"

"You have good ears." Moving at a jaunty, if awkward, pace, he led the way into the kind of kitchen I'd only seen in magazines. "Hey, baby!" His voice took on the singsong quality people use with their pets. "We've got a visitor!"

"Hey, Sage." I peered over my host's shoulder to see the large dark eyes of a Chihuahua stare up at me. Apparently utterly unfazed by my appearance in her kitchen—or by her recent adventure—she licked her chops and sat. Awaiting those treats, I imagined.

"How are you doing?" I spoke out loud, crouching on the floor by the little dog. The words were primarily for the benefit of the man who was busy by an oversized stainless-steel fridge. For the dog, I held out my hand, palm up. It was the closest I could come to a dog's submissive posture without alarming my host, and by letting the Chihuahua sniff my hand, I was offering her a more detailed introduction than anything words could do. "*And how would you prefer to be addressed?*" I posed the query silently to further demonstrate my willingness to let her take the lead.

"*What? Sage. Sage will do.*" Her damp nose was busy, roving over my hand. "*Hmm…cat, dog—dogs. What's that?*" She paused, and I wondered if she could pick up the bear from the day before. "*Weasel?*" No, Frank. Of course, in my hurry. I had neglected to wash my hands. "*Well, well, well.*" her nose trembled over my fingers and into the base of my palm. I waited for the moment of contact, for the chance of a greater connection, but it was not to be. "*No treats.*" She pulled away.

"Sorry, girl. I don't have any treats." That, I dared risk out loud.

"You haven't finished your dinner!" The man standing beside me sounded affronted. "Sage!"

"She appears unharmed." I rose and turned toward him, a query forming in the back of my mind. An animal who won't tell me her true name may be holding other things back as well. "She's probably had a fright, which could explain the loss of appetite. But I'd be happy to take her in for a checkup." Despite his facility with the cane, I wasn't going to inconvenience him further. Besides, a drive to county would give me the chance to get some answers.

"No, no." He shook his head and handed me a glass. Iced tea. I took it and watched as he squatted and the dog leaped into his free arm. He held her close as he stood, her delicate paws reaching up his chest. "She wasn't out that long. I'm sure it was just the excitement." Leaning his cane against the counter, he stroked her velvet head and held her close. Even if the man didn't address his canine companion with her preferred name, theirs was a love scene, and I was intruding—an impression that was amplified when the dog turned to stare at me. I was about to make my excuses and duck out—leaving these two to their reunion—when it hit me what was missing. Even as the little toy focused her dark eyes on me, I got no sense of agitation. None of the distress—part fear, part excitement—that I would expect from a domestic animal that has experienced the wild, even briefly.

"Are you sure?" Doc Sharpe, our local vet, would squeeze her in as a favor to me. "She's such a good girl." I extended my fingers once more, this time silently forming the questions as she lowered her head: "*What's going on? How are you?*"

"She is!" Her person shifted, moving her wet nose away at the last moment as he bent to kiss the top of her chocolate head. "Who's a good girl? Who is?"

"*Oh, please!*" Sage—or whatever her true name was—whined,

but it was the affectionate sound of a long-suffering pet. As if on cue, Luge reached for her foreleg. The paw he held out to me, ever so gently, was trembling in the way that Chihuahuas do. Not with fear or stress, I sensed immediately, as I touched the leather pads, but with happy anticipation.

"I'd say she is," I commented, although the question hadn't been for me. It was a natural response to the query in those deep dark eyes that now pleaded with me, asking in the manner of spoiled pets everywhere, "*Treats?*"

Chapter Nine

I couldn't say I was satisfied as I drove back to what I still thought of as "real" Beauville. But Luge and the dog he called Sage seemed happy enough—and after the old man took my card, I figured I shouldn't risk any possible future appointments by overstaying my welcome. It wasn't until I was cruising through our meager downtown that I realized I'd never even heard what happened, or how the lost pup had ended up found.

"Probably hiding under a cushion," I muttered to no one but the birds as I pulled up to the curb in front of our one Chinese restaurant. Fish are as dumb as you'd think, but they were still grateful for the weekly cleaning I gave their big tank. Besides, the little sucker fish who was supposed to do his own version of that was a notorious gossip. He filled me in on who'd come by and with whom—the restaurant's bar was a popular rendez-vous—as I replaced the filter and tested the pH. That was about as exciting as the rest of my day would get. When you start your day with an interrogation—even by a good-looking cop—it's all downhill from there.

• • ● ● •

"*The company you keep.*" Wallis jumped off the windowsill and sauntered in my direction as I let myself into the house. "*I don't know why I bother.*"

"Good evening to you, too." I placed the grocery bag on the table and headed for the fridge. Wallis might expect to be served first, but I yearned for a beer.

"*If you simply went for what you wanted…*" She twined around my ankles in an almost pet-like fashion. "*You wouldn't need to drink.*"

"'Want,' Wallis." I twisted the cap off and took a pull. Cold and refreshing. "Not 'need.'"

"*Whatever.*" Another figure-eight and an anticipatory purr began to rise. She knew me well enough to know that once the beer was half downed, I'd fetch her dinner. "Fetch" being one of those words, like "want," that didn't really translate, I realized as I rummaged around the fridge for the remainders of last night's chicken. Although I had interpreted Wallis' rebuke in human terms, she might as well have been saying I should hunt for the prey I sought. Or—it occurred to me as I pulled the foil from the carcass—that I should ask.

"Are you saying I should have interrogated the sucker fish about something?" I had her full attention, seeing as how I was pulling poultry flesh from bone. "Or Sage?"

"*That rat dog?*" Wallis grows impatient quickly. "*Pampered little runt.*"

"Now, now." I placed the dish on the floor, and Wallis dived in. Often, she'll join me at the table, but old habits die hard. "She had some kind of misadventure, and an animal her size doesn't have many defenses."

"*Huh.*" The dismissive grunt was muted by the sound of her lapping at the salty flesh. "*Pampered runt…*"

I was curious as to what had happened with the Chihuahua, but Wallis' reaction confirmed my suspicions. Wallis isn't psychic—not as a human would term it, anyway—but she can read the clues that other animals leave on me better than I can. If she didn't think that the little dog had been seriously endangered, then it was likely my initial take was correct. The dog had been "lost" somewhere safe, rather than outside in the wild as Ernest Luge had originally thought. Granted, Wallis wouldn't have lost any sleep if the little dog had been taken by a predator, but I didn't think she'd entirely dismiss my concerns—or what I did to keep us in roast chicken—if the dog's life had been threatened.

"*And then there's your boyfriend…*" The thought poked into my mind like a chicken bone as I finished my beer.

"I'm supposed to interrogate a cop?" I turned toward the tabby by my feet. "You know how Creighton gets when he's in that mood."

A low growl, though whether that was directed toward me, Creighton, or a gristly piece that was giving her trouble, I couldn't tell. Nor was I completely surprised when my phone pinged. Wallis isn't psychic, but she is a cat, and cats do pick up on things. Two texts appeared. The first was from Greg, telling me that the bear was in good shape and would be "re-homed"—what a word—soon. The second was from Creighton. I glanced over at the cat, who only flicked her black-tipped tail, before reading.

Pru—Can you see to the AOC tomorrow?

Creighton was texting about the animal control office. I replied:

Albert on a bender?

I imagined him driving the big man home, and realized I had no idea if Albert had retrieved his truck. Creighton might have had a say in that, of course. As I waited for a response, Wallis finished her dinner and licked the plate. She was busy washing her snowy white forepaws when I texted Jim again, a little peeved that he'd left me hanging.

What's going on?

Nothing. I knew that if Creighton texted me, it meant he didn't want to or couldn't talk. That didn't mean I had to play by his rules, so I called him.

"Hey, Jim." I ignored the disgruntled "yes?" with which he'd picked up the phone. "What's going on?"

"I need you to cover animal control." His voice was flat. "You can bill the city."

"I know I can bill the city." He wasn't getting away with this. "But why? Is Albert dug in over at Happy's?"

It wasn't simple curiosity. If Albert was seriously out of commission, I'd also be taking care of Frank, and I wanted some idea of how long I'd be on the hook. If Albert had been so shaken up that he'd gone on a bender, I would only need to look out for his mustelid companion until he sobered up. If something else was in the works, well, I had too much respect and affection for Frank to leave him abandoned in the office.

"Don't push, Pru." The warning note in Creighton's voice made the hair on the back of my neck rise.

"Jim, I have a right to know." I didn't. Not really. But this was as much a battle for dominance as any out in those woods. "You're already involving me."

A sigh of capitulation. "Albert's staying with us for a while," Creighton said at last.

"Albert still isn't telling you what happened with the bear?" I caught myself. Creighton wouldn't hold a man for illegal hunting, not someone like Albert, who wasn't a flight risk. "It's about the body."

Another sigh. "Pru…"

"Jim, you know Albert. He's not the sharpest tack, but he's not mean. If someone died—if there was an accident or even a fight…" A stray thought popped into my head. I looked over but Wallis had gone. "Did you talk to Paul Lanouette? He's a mean drunk when he drinks. You know that—you've picked him up a score of times. If the staties want to question someone, they should put the screws to Paul. He's the kind to hit someone."

"He might've," said my sometime beau. "That might be what happened, but I won't know until Albert starts talking. Paul's dead, Pru, and Albert's the last person to have seen him."

My boy scout of a beau rang off after that little bombshell, and even though I shared Wallis' intense curiosity—her lashing tail a giveaway despite her feigned indifference—I let him. I'd get more out of him in person, I figured.

Paul Lanouette. So that's whose body had been found in the shed. The reason for Creighton's mood. Yeah, it was horrible, and I felt a twinge of something I guess you'd call shock at the news. That didn't mean I'd mourn the man. Not much. What it did spark was my curiosity. Considering Lanouette's proclivities, his end could have come in a number of ways. I didn't think he had the looks to be a ladies' man, the kind to be killed by a jealous lover or her husband. Not anymore, with his beach boy hair thinning and the lines around that rakish grin grown deeper than any dimple. But I also wouldn't have been surprised to hear that he was hitting on someone he shouldn't have—or even dumped the wrong woman. And while I doubted it was the drink that had done him in, or my guy wouldn't have been involved, I wouldn't be surprised to hear that drunken misbehavior had played a part. No, the man I'd known in high school had made bad choices, and, beyond a momentary pang, I couldn't grieve his loss. His death was a waste, nothing more.

Besides, I'd soon learn more. It had been three nights now since Creighton had come by, and that was as long as we'd ever left it. Work was work, but appetites need to be sated, and Wallis' deep, guttural purr let me know she agreed.

Despite the dour news, the tabby and I spent a companionable evening. While I waited, I passed the time paying the bills that never seemed to stop coming and she alternated bathing and staring into an inner space beyond my comprehension. I started drinking around dusk. The bourbon helped—me, not her—but by ten, I began to question whether my beau was ever going to arrive. The bills weren't done, far from it, but I'd reached the point where I didn't trust myself to not simply write obscenities on the checks.

Still, I dawdled. Since Creighton and I had become a regular thing, I'd gotten used to him coming by every night or two, and I had simply assumed he'd want to make up for lost time after the last few nights. As the clock kept ticking, the famous aphorism about assumptions —what they make of "u" and "me"—kept surfacing, despite the bourbon haze.

Wallis didn't have to read my mind to know my thoughts. I could see her green eyes following me as I'd turn my head toward the window, expecting a pair of familiar headlights. She might have been waiting for him too. For once, she held her snark in check, pressing against my legs without comment as I stared into the dark. When he hadn't shown by eleven, I'd had enough. It wasn't another woman. I know men—or, at least this man—well enough for that. But I'm not the sit-at-home-waiting type, no matter what the reason.

"I'm going out," I said, unnecessarily, to the cat at my feet. "Maybe I can pick up on something that Creighton wouldn't."

She didn't even bother to respond to that particular lie.

Chapter Ten

Happy's wasn't full. Little in Beauville was, these days, unless the newcomers took to it. But a small crowd had gathered, drawn by the need for community if not for the liquid solace the bartender poured with a reasonably generous hand.

"Bourbon." I didn't need to say it. Happy, the bartender, had the heavy bottomed glass out already. He knew enough to pour the Maker's Mark, rather than whatever brown rotgut Ronnie was drinking. The poor man was nearly facedown on the bar, but I didn't think I could either console or interrogate him. Not yet. The first shot went down easily, and before the warmth had even begun to spread, the barkeep had refilled my glass.

"Thanks, Hap." It was habit. The original Happy—if there had ever been one—had passed long ago. The current owner, who also served the drinks, had inherited the name. As dour as a basset hound, he'd accepted it without comment. Then again, he rarely commented on anything. That was one reason people kept coming here.

Well, that and the lack of options. I checked out the room, nursing my drink. Beauville had changed since I first snuck in here, underage and eager for trouble. That Happy hadn't been much friendlier, but he'd turned a blind eye—and poured the well liquor—for me and my running buddies. In those days, this had been a workingman's bar. Anyone with the money, as well as couples, went over to Pittsfield to that place that served steak and had dancing. Some women probably went there as well, not that I would know. My mother had only ever graced Happy's to pull my father out. I didn't know if she ever sussed out that I had followed his lead here, or if, by that time, she had simply given up.

These days, the definition of a workingman was pretty loose. Money had come back to town in recent years, with the newcomers. But it flowed to those places that catered to them, rather than old-school watering holes like this one. Not that I could really complain. I'd grown fond of Hardware, our one good restaurant, opened by urban homesteaders who'd taken over the long-vacant store of the same name. And if today was any example, I was set to make some money from the latest arrivals.

Looking around, though, I was reminded that the rising tide was drowning some of my colleagues. Ronnie, for example, had a gig at the local condo development. I knew he was holding onto that by his fingernails, however, which might have explained why he hung out there in the woods, where I'd found Albert and the bear. And most of this crew hadn't done half as well.

One of Creighton's deputies—Chuck—was seated at the far end of the bar. He'd glanced up as I entered, and we'd nodded at each other. That's the way Beauville was—all of us cheek by jowl. Chuck had been a year or two behind me at school, and he'd had a reputation as a hell-raiser, too. A tough guy, quick with his fists, it was probably only luck of the draw that had landed him on Creighton's team, as opposed to Paul's—or mine.

Larry Greeley's alliances weren't as clear. He nodded to Chuck as he came in, too, and then took a seat next to Ronnie. From the way Chuck watched them, I thought he wanted to join them. They'd all known Paul, better than I ever had, and I could only guess what they'd all been up to during my years away. Ronnie slumped lower in his seat, once Larry was settled in, and Larry threw a collegial arm over his shoulder. It made me like the guy better, and gave me some sympathy for Chuck. The deputy had only recently joined Creighton's team—a part of the expansion to help the department service the new population—and he hadn't figured out that he no longer quite fit with the old crew, I guessed. One more reason for me to keep my allegiance to myself.

But that wouldn't get me any information. And so as I finished my drink, I slid over to a closer stool. "Happy?" I nodded to their glasses, and he filled them. Mine as well, which helped when the door opened again and my ex, Mack, walked in, making a beeline toward me.

"Pru." He nodded and held out his hand.

So it was to be handshakes, then. "Mack." His palm was callused and cool. He'd been working.

"I heard about Paul." He looked over at the other men. "I figured I should pay my respects."

"Albert tell you what happened?" I sipped my whiskey, hoping to cover my curiosity.

Mack's eyes strayed to the glass but snapped away. "Ronnie," he said. "I gather Albert's in for a while. He—they—have kept him locked up."

He licked his lips. That could have been because of my glass of whiskey. Mack was on the wagon. Then again, it could have been because he'd almost named Jim Creighton, who had replaced him in my affections.

"I'm kind of surprised Creighton is holding him." There, I'd said his name. The bourbon helped. What didn't help was how good Mack looked. Sobriety agreed with him, as did physical labor. He'd filled out a bit, with muscle this time, and his eyes were clear and dark.

"Me too!" Ronnie chimed in. "You're still buying?"

"One more." I nodded again toward Happy and raised my own glass. "So what happened?"

"I hear Albert wouldn't talk." His buddy stared down the bar, licking his lips before proceeding. "He said if they weren't going to—you know—charge him with something he didn't have to say anything."

"That wasn't—" I closed my eyes and tried again. "I told him to talk to a lawyer."

"Yeah, well, I guess it's the same thing." He downed his drink, the whiskey kicking in as certainty. "He knows what he's doing."

I had nothing.

"Anyway, I guess someone else wants to speak to him."

The staties. My head was becoming heavy. Mack reached over and touched my arm.

"You okay, Pru?" His voice was warm.

"Yeah, why?" Mine wasn't. This was old territory.

He shook his head. "I don't know," he said. "You seem, on edge, maybe."

"A man died." I was stating a fact. "And Albert is treating it like reality television." Truth was, I might have cared more about the bear, but at least the bear had survived. "Why are you really here?"

He laughed and stepped away. "I don't know," he said again. "I guess I should take off. Work in the morning."

"That's good." I put some lift in my voice. Suddenly, I found I wanted him to stay. "Contracting?" Those calluses.

He shook his head, but he was smiling. "Construction. I'm on a crew over in North Adams. That whole town is coming back." He looked toward the door. "I might take a place over there."

"Well, good luck to you." I swallowed hard and reached for his hand. But he only raised it to wave as he backed away and then turned toward the door.

"He's a smart guy." I'd almost forgotten Ronnie next to me. "Getting out of here, while the getting's good."

"You're not going anywhere," I growled.

"I know. Jim said if I didn't show up in the morning then he would arrest me. So, Pru?" He blinked at me with sad puppy eyes and raised his glass.

"Sure." I needed the company. "Happy? One more round, on me."

Chapter Eleven

It was barely dawn when I woke with a start, jostling Wallis, who'd been sleeping beside me.

"*Good morning.*" She snorted in derision as she readjusted, kneading the pillow beside mine in a rhythm that made my head pound. "*For some of us, at any rate.*"

"If you had unlimited catnip…" I couldn't go on. I rolled on my back and waited for the room to stop spinning. "I was upset." It was the best I could come up with.

"*You were unsettled.*" The accent she put on the last word made her meaning quite clear. Knowing she could read my thoughts as easily as I could the morning paper, I didn't hold back. Yes, seeing Mack had disturbed me, maybe more so because I wasn't sure what was going on with Creighton. Maybe it was just as well that he'd left when he did. I hadn't stayed that much longer, although the way I'd stumbled over a bar stool on my way out—only luck had kept me from wiping out entirely—meant that I'd already been in bad shape.

"*I gather you missed a step.*" Cats can be such prisses at times. There she sat, washing one white paw as if she'd never gotten it muddy.

"*Muddy?*" That mind-reading thing was really annoying. "*Well, then, maybe you should pay better attention. I gather it was a— hmmm—mixed crew?*"

I pulled myself into a seated position. She was getting at something, but I needed a shower and coffee before I could decipher her hints.

"*Hints?*" Another swipe at that paw and she settled down to nap. "*Like I'm the one who's missing the obvious.*"

Mack. "I thought you liked Creighton." Wallis may be spayed, but I'd swear that at times she flirted with the handsome cop.

"*You are slow today. Last night, too...*" Her internal voice started to fade as she drifted back to sleep. "*I didn't mean him. Not at all...*"

I wasn't going to waste my time trying to second-guess a cat, not with a head like mine. I blamed the hangover when I couldn't find my knife. My favorite blade is sharp, but small enough that in my current condition, it could be right in front of me. I had a vague memory of mumblety-peg at the bar, before Happy threatened to cut me off, but I was sure I'd sheathed it in my boot, as was my wont, before stumbling out the door. I didn't like taking off without it, but I had little choice. Making a mental note to turn the house over later, I gave the GTO a cursory once-over before heading into town.

For once, getting behind the wheel wasn't the answer to my malaise. Even as I drove, I found myself chewing over my tabby's parting crack. Wallis hates to be disturbed, so she could have been talking about my drinking, although if she really found my movements that disruptive she had plenty of other places to sleep. But it was possible she meant something else, like that I should have tried to learn more about Albert, who was on my mind even more than my missing beau. I didn't see his truck, as I rolled up to the office over which he was at least nominally in charge. I did spy Creighton's souped-up sedan, the one whose headlights I'd been searching for, before I'd gone out last night.

"Albert?" I unlocked the door and peered around. Nothing. So Creighton still had him. "Frank?" If Albert hadn't been released yet, then it was a good bet the ferret was here someplace. Frank might be more perceptive than his human, but I doubted Jim would take him in for questioning.

Grumbling, I poked at a dirty sweatshirt in the corner. Albert seemed to be living hand-to-mouth, using the office as a crash pad as often as the dinky studio he paid rent on a few blocks away, and I could feel my temper rising, irritation adding to the hangover that had only just started to recede. I wasn't overly concerned that Frank would starve. Ferrets are resourceful creatures, and between our leaky tap and the summer's crop of Japanese beetles, I figured he'd do okay. But that wasn't what an animal signs on for, when he—or she—agrees to be a pet. Besides, I wanted to speak to the sleek creature. Strategize, even, before the humans involved messed things up.

"You there?"

The triangular head popped up over Albert's desk, the dark eyes blinking in their distinctive mask. Frank had either slept through the night on the desk chair or retreated there after a night of exploration.

"*You!*" I seemed to have surprised the little beast. "*Find it? Find?*" As the ferret mounted to the desk, his nose twitched, giving him information faster than I could answer any of his questions. Still, I extended my hand for him to sniff. It was only polite. "*Cat! Know her. Not the dog? Not yet?*"

"No, I came here first thing." I felt the whiskers tickle my palm. "I'm afraid Creighton has detained Albert. I'm not sure, but he may be holding him for interrogation by the state police, at least for now." I didn't know how much would translate. Frank was intelligent, but his experience with human society was limited—more so than might be usual for a pet, considering that his human was Albert.

"*The uniform?*" The query was voiced with a level of anxiety that startled me, and I looked down into those wide black eyes. "*The cage?*" Animals like ferrets don't have the facial muscles that help humans show their emotions with smiles or grimaces and the like, but the droop of his whiskers echoed the concern I'd heard in his voice. I only wished I had better news.

"Kind of." I didn't say what I'd been thinking: that for Creighton to hold Albert overnight, it had to be serious. Men like Paul Lanouette are accident-prone—between the drinking and the generally ass— …well, let's just say arrogant behavior, it was a surprise he'd survived as long as he had. Creighton might not have run with the likes of Paul when he was younger, as I did. But he knew him as a cop would. And he wouldn't be holding one of Paul's buddies unless his death appeared to be more than a drunken accident. Albert was the farthest thing from a flight risk I could imagine. So, no, this was bad.

"I'll do what I can," I said to the defeated-looking creature before me. He sank down onto all four paws and hung his head.

"*Didn't do anything,*" he replied.

Poor beast. I had to restrain myself from reaching out to pet him. Another human—or Wallis, even—might respond well to my attempts at comfort. But although Frank and I had a better relationship than I had with most people, I needed to respect his animal nature. Plus, I didn't want him reading more of my thoughts than he already had. Instead, I watched as he poked his nose among the papers on Albert's desk, hopefully finding some comfort in his human companion's familiar smell. While his rooting didn't turn up a grub, it did spark my memory. Pulling the guest chair up once more—it only seemed fair to leave Albert's chair for Frank—I dug out the memo I'd retrieved only the day before.

"Mr. Walz?" I realized belatedly how early it was. Well, he'd wanted me to get on it. "I'm sorry if I woke you, but you had called about your fishing license?"

"What? Yes, yes, I had." The voice on the other end sounded a little peeved. Well, yeah, in my city days, I wouldn't have been awake at this hour either.

"I'm afraid I can't find any record of your application," I

continued on. After all, he had answered the phone. "But if you've got a moment, I can take your information and fill out your application now."

"What? What do you want?" Gruff, almost like a bark.

"Your information." I don't like being in a subordinate position, but this man was a client—of the office, if not mine, personally. "Let's start with your permanent address." I retrieved my pen—which I'd pocketed, for safekeeping—and pulled a flier toward me. Frank, caught off guard, glanced up.

"No, no, it won't be necessary." I could feel the warmth of the ferret's breath on my hand as I wrote. "*Treat?*" Maybe he was the reason so many pens went missing. "Good day." Walz was ready to hang up.

"It's no bother, really." I worked to keep my voice even. Nobody was going to say I'd alienated one of our all-important summer people. Especially not one who had already had an unpleasant run-in with this office. "I can take your info and enter it online. The license will be ready for you to pick up."

"No, really." He paused and I waited, wondering just how to broach the thought that was forming in my mind.

"You know, we take our licensing laws very seriously out here in Beauville." I put it as gently as I knew how. "Even if you're only planning to do some fishing for fun—"

"I said, I'd take care of it." That was definitely a bark, though I found myself thinking more of a noisy little toy Growler's size than of anything that had any weight behind it. "I'll do it myself, I mean." His tone moderated somewhat. "I've already started the application process. Online, I mean."

"Okay, then." I put the pen down, a dozen questions jostling to be asked. "If I can help in any way—"

"No, no." The bark had calmed down. "It's fine now. Everything's under control."

He hung up before I could say farewell, and I held the phone for a moment longer, wondering what had just happened. Granted,

I didn't like being woken too early. Neither did Wallis. But once he was up, I was trying to do him a favor. And if he was serious about applying online, why hadn't he done that in the first place, rather than bite my ear off about his lost application?

Maybe he hadn't known about that option when he'd first called, I told myself, as I took a deep, calming breath. Maybe he felt stupid that he hadn't thought of it. Maybe he just wanted to gripe at someone then—or to bark at me now. Summer people. Who knew what they wanted? I mulled this over as I walked over to the tiny kitchenette. Truth was, the ferret probably could have fared well enough on his own here. Albert's housekeeping encouraged just the kind of grubs that the little beast would love. But I'd grabbed two cans from Wallis' store—she considered commercial cat food a last resort—thinking I'd be responsible for this other carnivore, as well.

I managed to find a clean enough plate to suit my aesthetic sense. But before I could place it on the floor, I felt the brush of fur by my arm. Frank was on the dish rack, and so I simply left his breakfast there. He was cleaner than his person anyway.

Watching him chew the chunks of something called Turkey D-Lite, I was struck by how hungry he seemed to be. "Doesn't Albert feed you? I mean, real food?"

I hadn't meant to voice the question out loud, but the lithe little beast paused in his meal to glimpse up at me.

"*Busy!*" He blinked and turned back to the sticky stew. I did my best to squelch my anger. Busy, indeed. When a person takes on the responsibility of a pet, the most basic priority is keeping him or her fed. "*Busy!*"

The echo came through, and although I didn't know if Frank had picked up on my simmering resentment or was simply repeating himself, I knew I had to let the subject go. To distract myself, I turned and walked back across the office. I was supposedly covering for Albert, and the least I could do was check out the mail. A small bundle had come through the slot, and I took it over to Albert's desk to sort through. Junk, mostly, though how a city office address got on the mailing list for an adult novelties shop in Boston, I didn't want to know. Something about the upgrading of property values that touted brokerage services. "The time is right!," the firm logo—a smiling lion—appeared to be saying.

"Roar," I responded, leafing through the rest. Two—a notice about hunting and fishing licenses, and another on trapping—were from the state. By law, they were supposed to be posted, this being the Beauville Animal Control office, after all. I left them on the desktop as I rummaged through Albert's desk, searching for thumbtacks.

I wasn't optimistic, and finding the last few iterations of these notices on the desk, ringed with coffee stains, didn't bode well. The central drawer did turn up another pen I'd long missed as well as a book of Sudoko, which, if not Frank's, must have been left by some errant tourist, and a silver spoon of my mother's that I'd brought into the office one day for my lunch. Pocketing my pilfered possessions, I opened the right-hand drawer to find fast-food wrappers. I closed that one quickly, before anything could crawl out. Frank could deal with that. The drawer below was, I knew, where Frank preferred to nest, on the days when he stayed with Albert here, and so I turned instead to the other side. A pile of bills addressed to Albert's apartment made me wonder if he still had power or phone service there, while some B-grade girlie mags made me swear off wearing tight sweaters ever again.

The dented and rust-spotted tackle box in the bottom drawer was my last hope. If Albert didn't have any tacks in there, maybe I could repurpose an old lure. Its lid was stuck, half open, and a smack with the flat of my hand did the rest. But when I lifted out the top tray, crusty with what I hoped was old bait, I realized that Frank had been using it as his own cache. A chewed bit of cloth, the remnant of a cat toy, and a chicken bone looked to be the best of it. Some of the feathered flies had definitely been gnawed. I poked around and was surprised to find a lure of a much different sort. A gold disc—gold-colored, anyway—a little larger than a dime, with a sparkler set into its center that caught the light like a diamond.

I picked up the little circle and turned it over, curious to know more. Sure enough, it was marked 14k, which made me wonder about the quality of that glittering inset. But the only other marking on the disc's back was a circular stub, as if some kind of setting had been broken off. A pretty thing; if I'd found it in a woman's jewelry box, I'd have thought it was a broken earring, waiting to be repaired. Only I didn't see its like, among the flighty lures. Nor could I imagine Albert owning—much less wearing—anything quite so fine.

I stared at the shiny piece in my hand, cool and surprisingly heavy for such a small object. Could Albert have a rich girl-friend—maybe one of the newcomers in Pine Hills? *De gustibus…* But no, I couldn't see the bearded buffoon as a boy toy. More likely, it belonged to one of his friends, though whether a gift or payment or a bit of petty thievery was beyond me.

Another thought intruded, unwelcome though it might be. This piece might be broken, its mate missing. But the metal alone was worth something, and that could make it important among my little town's more hard-up population. Could this thumbnail-sized disc have been the cause of a fight between two old friends? Was such a tiny sliver of possible profit what got Paul Lanouette killed?

Turning the pretty piece over once more in my palm, I decided to pocket it. Creighton would want to know about it, and that meant I could use it as leverage with him as well.

Besides, Frank had scurried over and now sat, clawing at the edge of the notice.

"*Box!*" Now that he had my attention, his voice boomed loud in my head.

The urgency I heard didn't seem to pertain to the missing

Albert, no matter how concerned the ferret might be. That clawing at the paper, though…I looked around. "You mean, like, litter box?"

"*No! No!*" He grabbed at the paper and began to gnaw at it. The state notice about trapping, I saw. The top one on the pile. "*Box!*" His voice insistent and demanding.

He couldn't read. No animal could, but he might be able to pick up the meaning of the notice from me. "You mean, trap?"

I tried to visualize something appropriate, and my mind sped back to the bear.

"*Yes! Yes! Box!*" The ferret was jumping around with excitement.

"Don't worry, Frank." I slipped the notice out from under him and walked over to the board. Last summer's boating rules could go, and once that was down, I had what I needed to hold up the new notice. "Nobody's going to trap you or any of your friends." I pushed the rusty old tack in place.

"*Trap.*" That seemed to hit a note with the sleek creature. But even as he settled back on all fours, he reached down, as if to nose his way into that bottom left drawer.

Chapter Twelve

"You're lucky you caught me." Tracy Horlick squinted through the smoke of her unfiltered Marlboro. "I can't wait around all day, you know."

"I understand." I was late, and I knew it. I also knew I didn't want to waste any time sparring with this harridan. "Bitsy is probably eager to go out."

"*Come on! Come on!*" I could hear his sharp barks from the stoop. If I were kept locked in a basement overnight, I'd have a short temper, too. "*Out! Out! Out!*"

"Had me wondering" she drew deeply on the smoke, "what you were mixed up in. That nastiness out by the state road."

She was fishing, I could tell. Holding the dog—and my livelihood—hostage for some of the gossip that was as vital to her as those cigarettes. "The wildlife rescue, you mean?" Two can play at that game. Even as she exhaled toxic fumes in my direction, I did my best to stand there, wide-eyed with innocence. "We rescued a black bear, you know."

Her eyes narrowed to slits. "Animals," she muttered, but when I didn't respond she turned to free the poor bichon from his basement exile.

"*Animals…*" Growler could have been echoing the woman who'd held him hostage, but as I watched him sniff and then water a tree, I caught the difference in his tone. Unlike Tracy

Horlick, he was cataloguing the traffic out here by the edge of the development. In fact, as he raised his short snout, I realized I was mishearing him—or, as Wallis would tell me, misinterpreting what I'd heard. Not "animals," per se, but something more like "wildlife." We were standing on the edge of the scruff wood that led down to the river, and Growler was taking stock of the wider world beyond.

"You want to go down there?" I felt for the dog. Not only did his person saddle him with the degrading name of Bitsy, she didn't seem to recognize his essential nature. Except for letting him out back, to her fenced yard, to relieve himself at night, he only ever got outside with me. Dogs are social animals, and Growler lived in the equivalent of solitary confinement.

"*Huh.*" With an equivocal grunt, he began sniffing the ground. I waited. It wasn't like the petite dog to hesitate.

"*It's not like you to be so dense.*" His response came loud and clear, even as he continued to snuffle through the leaves. "*You're the one who's supposed to be able to hear what's going on.*"

That stopped me cold. "What do you mean, Growler?"

"*Stupid walker lady,*" he muttered, as the rich warmth of leaf rot filled my sinuses. "*Trusting walker lady.*" In his mind, that wasn't a compliment. "*No sense of danger, of the wild.*"

I had no answer to that and simply stepped back, letting him take his time with the leaves and trees by the edge of the road. Usually, this was an interim stop—most days, no more than a brief check-in—before the little dog would leap galumphing down the slope to the water. But after his comment, I wasn't going to question his sense of the woods—or of the other creatures who lived there. I'd seen that black bear, and I knew that many other animals made these hills their home. Most of them would be dissuaded by my presence, but clearly Growler had picked up on something I had missed. If he felt more comfortable staying within shouting distance of human habitation, I wasn't going to force him out further.

That didn't mean I didn't have suspicions, and as I followed a reluctant but silent Growler back to the house he shared with that woman, I made my plans to act.

●　●　**●**　●　●

"Greg? It's Pru." I know the laws about phones and cars. But my GTO pre-dated cell phones, never mind Bluetooth, and unlike most of my fellow Beauvillians, I was capable of doing more than one thing at a time. Besides, talking to voice mail is easy. "Mind if I join you?"

I was already on my way by the time he called me back, answering in the affirmative, as I was pretty sure he would. Greg's a nice guy. He might not have my affinity, shall we call it, with animals, but he gets that they have as much right here as we do—and he knows that I work to smooth things between our various species. What I was more concerned about was getting out to him before he had taken the black bear to somewhere deep in the preservation land and let him go.

He'd called me from the road, a few turnoffs from the county highway that my GTO was now eating up. As I'd thought, he was heading toward where the animal had been found, although I suspected he'd free him somewhat farther from the road than Albert's camp.

Greg—and his passenger—faced a quandary. Bears, like most mammals, are territorial. Release one in an area that it doesn't know and it's going to have a hard time. Just as you or I would fare badly if we were dumped in an unknown city, so too would Ursus find himself lost and alone, and possibly up against an affronted population that had already claimed the area as its own. Then again, as a young male, the bear we'd found was probably already wandering—on the prowl for a territory he could call home. Putting him right back there after his ordeal might throw him almost as much. If he'd been interested in the area, it probably had the resources—food and water—that would draw other bears. Disoriented as he was bound to be, the young male would be at a disadvantage battling for the area against all the other healthy animals out there.

There were no easy answers. Any relocation was largely guess-work, and I trusted Greg to know his field. And while there was an off-chance that my sensitivity might help the creature, once he was uncaged, to find his footing, so to speak, that wasn't why I was so eager to tag along. No, I had my own questions, and I was hoping that before he lumbered off into the trees, the black bear would be willing to answer them.

"Pru!" I saw Greg by the side of the road, leaning against his truck, before I heard him. He waved and I pulled onto the shoulder. "Climb aboard."

Leaving my GTO, I joined him in the cab. I didn't like leaving my car by the side of the highway—the engine alone constituted most of my savings—but the racing suspension wasn't made for the forest track I could make out under the spreading green. And as we bumped and rolled over the roots and rocks, I began to sense that I wasn't the only one with concerns.

"He's awake?" I turned to peer into the back. A tarp covered the cage, but I could sense the beast within waking and struggling to get to his feet in the enclosed space.

"Somewhat." Greg kept his eyes on the pitted track. "I didn't want him to be too out of it to take care of himself once we let him go. But, for the ride…"

I got it. A wide-awake and frightened bear could hurt himself. Plus, we had to take care that we could leave the scene of the release unharmed, too.

After another half hour of bouncing, Greg pulled up. I didn't question his choice of site. Greg's occupation involves knowing at least roughly where bears have denned in previous years and where older animals have died or been removed. The clearing looked pretty good to me. Old-growth trees, a few that had fallen in the winter storms, made for interesting topography—or at least some good back-scratching posts. I vaguely recalled that a stream ran through close to here, too. All in all, a perfect place to be a young bear—even if just as a starting point for his rambles.

It was a good thing the bear had been sedated. Greg's truck had a power lift, but we still had to do some shoving and pulling to get it set up, and the mechanical whine of the machinery had the forest on alert. To Greg—to any normal human—it probably sounded peaceful. The birds, in particular, had dropped their incessant—and often inane—chatter while they figured out what was going on. But there were other creatures besides the avian kind out there, and I was getting a constant barrage of questions—a kind of cosmic *what? What? What?*—as we maneuvered the cage and its sleeping occupant into place. Considering what we were doing, and what we were about to release, I did my best to stay open to the signals I was getting. I wasn't sure what I could do if I picked up another male bear in the area, but it couldn't hurt to be on guard.

"Earth to Pru."

I turned, blinking. Greg was smiling, even as he pushed his dark hair back to wipe the sweat from his brow.

"Sorry." I smiled back. Greg's the polar opposite of Creighton. Dark where my regular squeeze is sandy, with the hair at his collar line suggesting a pelt not unlike the sleeping bruin, Greg is barely taller than me, with the kind of build that could appear fat if he were wearing a suit. In t-shirt and jeans, though, his muscle showed, under a sheen of sweat.

I made myself turn away. I don't owe anyone anything, but Beauville is a small town. Besides, we were out here for a reason.

"You ready?" Greg had already told me how this would work. He wanted me well back, near the truck if not in it, before he lifted the cage gate. He'd be behind the cage himself, ready to bang on the metal backing in case the creature was slow to move. I knew the rifle by his side was loaded with bean bags, rather than shot, in case the bruin came toward us, but I didn't like it. More to the point was the emergency kit by his feet, complete with a heating pad, bandages, and more of the heavy-duty drugs that had been used to tranquilize the animal. If the bear had any trouble—if he got tangled up or was in medical distress—Greg would be ready to handle it.

What he didn't know, and what I couldn't tell him, was that I needed to be close to the drowsy beast, too. Not that I'd be of much help if there were trouble. My sensitivity doesn't work that well on truly wild beasts, and I suspect any attempts I made at calming the bear would simply feel invasive or, worse, threatening. I didn't even have my knife, in case he got caught up in the ropes. But I was hoping the bear could tell me—show me, rather, in his memories—just what had happened the other day, I was going to have to get close to him. He was going to be freed, one way or another. But a man was dead, and another man—for lack of a better word—was going to face the consequences.

"Let her rip." I had stepped back toward the truck, but as Greg began to pull on the release that would lift the door, I came forward. Quietly so as not to alert the man, I reached out with my mind, trying to phrase my questions in as basic a way as possible.

"*What did you see? What happened? Show me?*" It was no use. The hum and worry of the surrounding creatures was overwhelming me, filling me with their confusion and concern. "*What did you see when the net fell on you?*"

Clang! I jumped. But it was no memory. Greg was glaring at me from the other side of the cage.

"Pru, what the hell?" The bear, who'd begun to wake, appeared as startled as I was by the slamming gate.

"Sorry." I considered my own outstretched hands. For all the world, it must appear as if I'd wanted to touch the bear, which now struggled to its feet. "I guess I got carried away."

His dark brows lowered, Greg stared at me until I retreated once more to stand by the open cab door.

"*Cave…*" The word, more an image, really, came to me, and I realized I was seeing the world as the bear did. The idea of a trap was foreign to him. But a camouflaged net, covered in leaves and debris…

"How did you get here?" I muttered the query, all the while staring at the bear's black hide.

"*Rock—rock fall?*"

I didn't know if he was hearing me, or simply working to make sense of his drugged hours in captivity.

"*Them?*"

I blinked as it hit me: a wave of fear, as unexpected as a thunderclap. I struggled to stay upright as the blackness around me slowly gave up a sense of smell and then, yes, color and shape. This was it, I understood as my pulse began to slow, the bear's experience in what must have been a traumatic moment as the net came slamming down, pinning him to the ground. The shapes were vague, colors distorted from what you or I would see. But three things—vertical and bright—stood out.

They were people, I realized with a start, their clothes and coloring setting them off from the woods beyond. Three figures, which meant that Albert had not been alone with Paul—not at this point. I strained to differentiate them. It was hard: to the bear, they all stank like Albert. But then I caught their outlines. Albert, with his beard; his buddy Ronnie, nearly as fat but pink-cheeked; and one figure—taller and lighter—the ill-fated Paul. All three stood there, staring, as the net came down, and then a sudden dull pain in his hindquarters before sleep made the scene go dark.

"There he goes." The image broke, as I looked up to see Greg staring in wonder as the bear made his way into the woods. Ungainly, at first, he seemed to shake off the tranquilizer with each step, until he was loping into the shadows. "Beautiful creature."

Greg turned to me, and although he still affected a scowl, I could see his good humor had been restored.

"I'm sorry about that," I said, feeling my face grow warm. "Truly."

"I get it," he responded, a slight huskiness coming into his voice. "The attraction."

I could only nod and turned away. That's when it hit me. The bear's memory. He had seen the three men—our local layabouts, Albert, Ronnie, and Paul—before the tranquilizer dart hit. He hadn't had time to peer behind him as the drug kicked in. To see whoever had shot him—a fourth person, whoever it was, must have set the trap.

Chapter Thirteen

"So what are you up to, Pru?" Greg asked as we bounced back toward the highway. He had been all business as we packed up the cage, rifle, and emergency supplies that, luckily, we'd not had to use. I'd been so preoccupied with the riddles that the bear had presented, I'd been lost in thought.

I'd suspected Ronnie had been out there. He and Albert were two peas. Fat, soused peas. But although Ronnie was no saint, it's a far cry from being lazy and a bit of a sleaze to being a killer. Then again, that had been my automatic defense of Albert, too. And while I didn't know what had gotten Paul killed or even how, being inept wasn't much of a defense.

I was sorry then that I hadn't had more time with the bear. That one memory—the moment of realizing he was trapped— was etched in his mind. If I'd been able to focus, I might have seen more. Might have seen what had happened next. Or even—and this was the question I kept coming back to—who that fourth man was.

I stared at the greenery around me, hoping to read the answers there. But all I got was the frantic housekeeping of some jays and squirrels. And as the tree cover thinned, Greg's question brought me back to my day ahead—and to the hunk beside me.

"The usual." That was no answer, and I knew it. Whatever my interest in Greg, he was a friend and a valuable professional contact. "I've got cat-care appointments, and a dog that I'd like to follow up on. She got lost yesterday, and her owner didn't want to bring her for a checkup." I stole a glance at Greg as he drove.

He nodded. He knew how I made my living. "But in the larger sense. I mean, down the road?"

"Am I going to get my degree, you mean?" Until I figured out how I felt, it made sense to assume his curiosity was professional. Besides, Greg knew that I'd come this close to finishing my master's, the next big step in being certified as an animal behaviorist. "I don't know."

"You could get certified in wildlife rehab." He glanced over briefly, correcting as the truck hit a rock. "Come work with me, at least part-time."

"And poach on your territory?" I chose the word intentionally, hoping to raise a smile, but the man beside me was serious.

"I've got more than enough to do, and the district could use someone like you. We're going to be posting an opening soon. Officially, it's for an assistant warden, but..." Another look, this one a little longer. "You've got the best natural rapport with animals I've ever seen. They don't seem to be frightened of you."

I swallowed. This was getting a little close to home. When my sensitivity first manifested itself, I'd thought I was going nuts and had ended up checking myself into a psych ward. After my three-day stay was over, I swore I was never going back, and a large part of that was pretending to be as normal as the next girl. Problem was, I was as susceptible to a good-looking man as the next girl, too, and Creighton had already picked up on something unusual between me and Wallis. If Greg did too, that meant I was less good about covering it than I'd thought—or growing more lax with time.

I knew I was never going to voluntarily check myself back into a psych ward again. I really didn't want to have to worry about anyone else making that decision for me.

"There I am." As I struggled to find the right words, we broke through the trees to where my ride sat waiting. I couldn't help a chuckle of relief. Saved by the car. "And there she is."

His eyebrows went up at that, but he pulled up beside the GTO without further comment.

"Thanks, Greg." I was out of the cab almost before he'd come to a full stop. "I appreciate you letting me ride along. And…I'll think about what you said."

With that, I slapped the door behind me and nearly ran to my car. I could see him in my rearview, staring after me, as I gunned the engine and headed back toward town.

The talk about my future had one effect. I'd been thinking of dropping by Ernest Luge's place and checking on his Chihuahua. Animals are great at hiding their hurts—an injured animal is a vulnerable one, so it's a self-protective mechanism—and I wouldn't have been surprised if the little dog was showing delayed reactions to her misadventure. But I also had to admit I wanted the older man as a client. He had an active animal and, seemingly, the money to pay for her care. If he needed anything from a dog walker to some informal training to keep the little gal from running off, I could do us all some good.

Maybe I shouldn't have been surprised to see a familiar battered pickup turning into the same development. The pine tree logo on its side belonged to a slightly older—and less ritzy—condo development further down the hill. Ronnie called himself the development's manager, but his duties there were largely custodial. They also gave him access to the mower and other equipment bouncing around the truckbed, which I was sure were intended for use only on the condo grounds.

"Hey, Ronnie." Once he'd parked, in front of a McMansion with a lawn like a golf course, I pulled a U-turn and glided up beside him. "Doing a little freelance?"

"What?" The chubby janitor nearly jumped out of his skin, and I realized then that he'd been wearing earbuds. "Pru, I didn't see you."

"I gather." I leaned out my window. Sure enough, the same pine tree logo emblazoned on the truck had been stenciled on the mower. "The condo association know you're here?"

"You going to report us?" The voice at my passenger window caught me unaware.

"Larry Greeley." I showed my teeth. I don't like being frightened, and the lanky man—Larry had to be six-four—leaning over my car would scare anyone. "I should have known that Ronnie here lacked the initiative to hustle for extra work."

"Like you belong here?" His sneer revealed his bad tooth, chipped and gray. "What'd you come back to this town for, anyway?"

I should explain, Larry and I have a history. Growing up here, I was as bad as either of these two jokers. Even before my dad left for good, I began to take after the old man. As soon as I'd hit my teens, I was going full out—and all my mother's attempts at discipline only made me wilder. Larry had been close to my ex, Mack, one of the crew picked up for joyriding back in the day, and I knew he thought I got off light. Granted, the boys were probably roughed up more than I was, but then, they didn't have my mother waiting at home. And while Mack and I shared some good memories, Larry clearly harbored a grudge.

My return had only added to it, with a healthy dose of small-town resentment. I'd escaped—I'd thought I was "better" than Beauville, as he'd put it—while he'd been stuck here, labeled a loser from the get-go. His smirk, damaged as it was, showed exactly what he thought of me, begging for scraps on the rich side of town, same as he was.

I felt as vulnerable as that Chihuahua, only I knew to hide it.

"I've got a trade, Larry." I kept my voice calm as I looked up at that crooked grin. "A profession. You know, something other than mowing lawns? Who you working for, anyway?"

He scowled. At least it obscured the tooth. "You think you're so smart. But I've got something going on, too."

That was interesting. "Yeah?" I let him hear my doubt. A man like Larry wouldn't be able to resist showing off.

"Uh, Larry?" Before he could respond, we were interrupted. "Uh, help?" It was the thunk of metal, more than the plea that prompted him to turn. Ronnie was behind the truck, wrestling with the mower. With a sneer at me—and enough hesitation to make his point—Larry went to help his shorter, rounder colleague. Something else going on? I'd have to warn Luge to lock his doors, with these two around.

"Larry?" Ronnie is big, but not with muscle. "I think this is stuck."

"Hang on." With a glare that wasn't nearly as scary as that tooth, Larry stepped back, banging on the roof of my car for good measure. I waited to see that he really had climbed into the truckbed before driving away. I'd tell Luge to warn his neighbors, too.

"Miss Marlowe, good to see you." I hadn't thought to call first, but Ernest Luge was home. From the excited barking I heard from behind him—"*Who? Who? Who?*"—so was the dog he called Sage. "Would you like to come in?"

"Thank you." For a city person, Luge was very trusting. Then again, many of our vacationers mistake Beauville for Eden, only with mosquitoes. "I should have called to explain why I wanted to come by."

He nodded, and—I hoped—took the hint. "It's about Sage, isn't it?"

"Is she okay?" I caught my breath. That bark had sounded happy and welcoming, but the little dog could have been masking. "Are you noticing any ill effects?"

"No, none at all." A grin split the lined face. "But you were worried about her, I could tell."

"I was," I admitted. Either I was slipping or the men in my life were a lot more perceptive than I'd given any of them credit for. "You see, after an incident, an animal may have a delayed reaction..." As I followed his slow progress into his frosty house, I outlined the basics. "And so when you said you didn't want Sage to be checked out..." I left it open, as he motioned me toward an overstuffed sofa.

"Of course." He nodded as he carefully settled into a velvet recliner. As soon as he'd put his cane aside, the little dog rounded the corner with a scrabble of claws and leaped to his lap. "That's what Sage told me."

"Sage told you?" I was turning into a parrot. I turned from his face to his pet's. Sage was panting from the run, but her big eyes seemed clear. Joyful even, matching the waves of contentment emanating from her small frame. "*Is he right?*" I formed the question in my mind, just to be sure. "*Are you healthy? Are you well?*"

A short bark—"*Home!*"—was my answer.

"Sage!" Her person reprimanded him. "Don't bark at the nice lady."

"It's all right, Mr. Luge." I slid from the sofa to kneel by the chair and held out my hand once more for the Chihuahua to sniff. "I think she's protecting you."

"*You are, aren't you?*" I did my best to visualize Larry, as well as Ronnie and Albert, for good measure.

"*Treats!*" She barked once more, oblivious to danger and safe in her person's arms.

Chapter Fourteen

"*Now we're talking.*" Wallis settled into the cushion beside me, eyes half closed in a satisfied grin. We weren't, not really, but as I've learned to better understand the thoughts of the tabby before me, so has she become more colloquial in her communication. I believe it amuses her, to use human slang. At the moment, it did not amuse me.

"Wallis." My tone would have been enough with any of my clients. She only let her eyes close further, the spread of her whiskers serving to accentuate her self-satisfied Cheshire smile. "I am not bringing Greg Mishka home."

"*Pity.*" She lifted one hind paw and inspected her toes. The pads were perfectly pink between the tufts of white fur, and I suspected she was trying to avoid my direct gaze. "*Because, that other one...*" She meant Creighton, of course. "*If he's not going to come around anymore...*"

"What?" I was in no mood, and as I reached up to take a nonexistent tuft of fur from between my teeth, I realized why. "You know, I respect your privacy," I growled. "I do not plumb your thoughts to find out what you've been doing—or thinking."

She bit a toenail, and I stopped myself from once again reaching to my own lips. "Will you cut it out?"

Foot still aloft, she turned her cool gaze on me. "*I'm only pointing out the obvious, Pru,*" she said, without a word. "*You've finally learned how to listen, and you're making a hash out of it.*"

"Great." I left the room, ceding the sofa to the cat. In a way, she was right. It wasn't so much that she discussed my most private thoughts as if they were open for debate—anyone who lives with a cat knows they can read our minds—it was that she had identified what was becoming a very sore spot.

For starters, Jim Creighton. I didn't know whether it annoyed me more that he had not only not come around for several nights now or that he'd made no effort to reach out and explain his absence. He'd worked major cases before, even cases that I was involved in, and still managed to find time for a brief nocturnal visit. I'm a big girl, and I've made my own limits clear. I no more want to be owned than Wallis would. But I've no interest in chasing a man who covers so much territory for his work, and I've long gotten past the point of what in the city they'd call "ghosting." I saw the man often enough in our professional capacity. He wants it to be over, he could tell me.

"*Or you could ask him.*" I didn't need Wallis, sidling up beside me, to hear that thought. I consciously kept my mind blank as I poured myself a bourbon.

"*You think I care that much about your love life?*" The question surfaced, even as she lapped delicately at the bowl of water I'd left out. "*You have this gift, and yet...* The rest was lost as we both turned in surprise: Wallis at the sound of car wheels on my gravel drive, me at the headlights I could see turning from the road.

"Hey, stranger." I was grinning as I opened the door, rather to my own surprise.

"Hey." Creighton looked tired, with lines I didn't recall around his mouth and eyes. "I'm sorry, it's been a bad couple of days."

"You don't have to explain." I took his hand. And for once, Wallis held her tongue.

• • ● • •

It wasn't until later that all my questions came rushing back, along with that vague sense of outrage. I'm not so dim that I didn't recognize the latter for my own part in it—nothing like thoughts of another man to make me lash out in guilt. But the questions were real, and I figured my beau was probably in as good a mood as he was ever going to be.

"You'll never guess who I ran into today." We were lying in bed, and he turned toward me, brows raised. "Larry Greeley."

He nodded, settling back on his pillow. Not the response I'd expected.

"He was over in that new development—Pine Hills? One of the summer people has a Chihuahua. Nice guy, older. Larry and Ronnie were making the rounds. Ronnie's moonlighting, doing yard work. But I can't see Larry making that much effort."

I glanced over. Creighton's eyes were still open, so I kept talking. "I think he was casing those houses, Jim. You know Larry."

"Did you see him attempting entry?" His voice was light, but there was something in it I didn't like.

"No," I admitted.

"Emerging from someone's house or property in a suspicious manner?"

"He was in Ronnie's truck. Ronnie was trying to get this monster mower out of the truckbed. I think it belonged to the condo."

A nod.

"Come on, Jim. There are a lot of old folks there. They've got money, and they don't know Beauville the way we do."

"And you were over there—why?"

"A client, Jim." I was losing my post-coital buzz. I was also lying, at least technically. Ernest Luge wasn't a client. Not yet, anyway. I decided to take the offensive.

"And what's going on with Albert? You can't really think he killed his friend, can you?" Creighton didn't answer, but I could feel him shift. "I mean, if it had been a drunk driving accident or something, I could understand it."

"Pru, come on." His voice was still soft, still warm. "You know I can't talk about work with you."

"Never stopped you in the past." I rolled onto my side, facing him. He's good to look at, especially without his clothes. But right now what I wanted was to be able to read him. If only he'd been a cat. "You asked me to cover the office, so I've got a vested interest in what's going on—and what your plans are."

I was thinking about Albert, about the suspicion I had that he knew more than he was letting on.

"Pru..." He was beginning to growl.

"You think he knows something, don't you?" I had no facts, but I've learned to trust my instincts. "You think he knows more than he's telling you, and so you're holding him until he talks. Until he gives someone else up."

Bells were going off. Those same instincts were telling me I was pushing too hard. But I don't like it when anyone—a person or an animal—won't talk. "Come on," I tried to make it light. "You can't really think he's a killer. Do you?"

"All right, then." With a sigh that came from more than the exertion, Creighton sat up and swung his legs over the side of the bed. I started to reach for him, ready to make up and undo the damage I had wrought, but he was already standing. Already retrieving his clothes from where they'd been scattered around the room.

"Oh, come on." I was pissed at myself as well as at him. "Don't be like that. You just got here."

"And maybe I shouldn't have come over at all." He seemed focused on his pants as he stepped into them. "Not while I'm in the middle of an investigation. Not while people you know are involved."

"So you do suspect him." That was more than I'd expected. "Jim?"

Another sigh, as he zipped his pants. "Pru, come on." At least he was talking to me as he began to button his shirt. "I know you care about Albert. No—don't say it." He stopped me before I could protest. "I know you do, like you would for, I don't know, a turtle or some particularly dumb hound. But you can't get involved in this. Not this time. You can't help him."

"And you can?" He didn't respond, only squatted to retrieve his shoes from beneath the dresser. "Jim, he's stubborn. You know that. He's going to stick by his stupid story that he couldn't have killed Paul Lanouette in the camp shed because he didn't have his keys."

The stupid keys. I didn't understand how Albert could think they'd be an alibi. Maybe that was the point. "He's saying that, isn't he? And that's why you're holding him?"

"Stop." He held up his hand. "Enough. I care about you, Pru, and I know you have a tendency to, well, meddle in things you shouldn't. This time, though, you've got to stay out of it. I'll see you when it's over."

Of all the responses that flooded my head, none seemed particularly apt. And so I lay there, uncharacteristically silent, as my beau picked up his shoes and walked to the stairs. It wasn't until I heard the front door close behind him that another voice made itself heard.

"*Good work with the questions,*" sniped Wallis, as she jumped up to the bed beside me.

"Thanks a ton," I barked back. But she was already asleep.

I might've been silenced by Creighton's stonewalling, coming as it did when he'd already done his best to disarm me. But I'm no fool. He wasn't going to share what he knew, not yet anyway. That didn't mean I couldn't do some digging on my own. And if I found something that might interest my law-abiding beau, well, then, maybe he'd have to play ball.

I confess I was thinking of Ernest Luge as well as I dragged my laptop over to the bed and entered Larry Greeley's name. City folks might come out here expecting some kind of bucolic wonderland, but I knew better. And while gentle Helen Birman might have Tillie to look after her, to me the lame old man and his tiny dog were just the sort that Greeley and his chums would prey on.

As I typed, Wallis started to snore. She doesn't think she does, but she does—a faint sound, half sigh, half grunt with each exhalation. "Greeley," I muttered in response. Nothing popped up, so I tried again: Laurence. Lawrence. All I got was a blank screen and a blinking cursor.

With a louder grunt, Wallis woke and licked her nose. "*I don't know why you bother.*" Even her voice sounded sleepy. "*Prey animals that don't know how to save themselves...*"

She drifted off, and I stared at the screen. It wasn't like sleep was an option for me. I was too angry at Creighton. And, truth be told, at myself. I had no idea what had happened with Paul Lanouette. I got involved with this because of a bear—a healthy, young creature who was once again roaming free. Albert was not my concern.

No, a small voice that wasn't Wallis' piped up. *But you know he's in over his head. And if he's in trouble, then so is Frank.*

I closed my eyes and took a breath. This was it, what was bothering me. After that morning with Growler—when Tracy Horlick had been particularly horrid—I was more aware than ever of how my species victimizes others. Albert might not be my favorite human. But the fat man was essentially guileless. Witless, too, and that made him an easy mark for anyone who wanted to take advantage of him. Much as I might fight it, I did feel the slightest bit protective.

Not just of him, but of Frank. The ferret was more than a pet—a vulnerable animal. He was a friend. An ally. Hell, the slinky little creature had helped me out of some jams recently. And while I might not have more than a passing sympathy for the dumb beast who carried him around, I couldn't help but relate to Frank in his distress. My aid might not have been necessary to help out old Mrs. Birman or Ernest Luge. But Albert wasn't going to come home safely without my help. And Frank, his ferret, needed me.

Wallis sighed and rolled over, showing her tiger-striped back, as I went back at it, switching my search terms to seek out break-ins in the greater Beauville area. Rather to my surprise, I didn't find any—although that could have been our chamber of commerce at work. A search of the online police blotter was a little more helpful. No robberies had been reported this season—at least none that made it online—but there had been some little things. A lawn mower had been taken two weeks before. I thought immediately of Ronnie, but it wasn't the Evergreen condo association reporting the theft. More gardening tools—a hedge clipper and a trowel—had gone missing, as well. Hardly the stuff of a major criminal investigation.

Mindful of the cat, I put the laptop aside and tried once more to sleep. The night's exertions—and the bourbon—must have worked eventually, because the next thing I knew, the ceiling was dancing with shadows as the morning sun lit up the trees outside. And I was panting with panic, having dreamed myself trapped like that bear and unable to get free.

Chapter Fifteen

I waited until I was in my car before calling Greg. I suspected that like most people who deal with animals, the warden was an early riser. But dawn comes early in the spring, and I didn't need to wake a hardworking man from his slumber. Besides, I didn't want Wallis butting in with any snarky comments about my love life or the options I may or may not have.

What I did want was information about the illegal trap—and to hear if any progress had been made in the investigation. My dreams had been disturbing, disordered images of cages and snares, and this was one problem I could throw myself at. Anything else, I told myself, was besides the point.

"Hey, Pru." He was already in his truck. I could hear it running a little rough and remembered him saying something about the points.

"You check the condenser on that?" I raised my voice to be heard over the bark of a backfire. Behind him, the early morning cacophony of birdcall, undisturbed by the engine noise.

"You call to ask me about my truck?" He laughed, and I felt my face warm. Creighton had a lot of good qualities. He wasn't a gearhead, though.

"Maybe I should." I admit it, I purred. "But not this time." I gave it a beat, just to let him wonder. "I was calling about the bear, actually. I wanted to know if you'd found out anything—if you had any leads about who might have trapped him or why."

"No leads, though I've got some ideas." I waited. Greg wasn't given to idle speculation. Outside my own open window, the birds were getting busy. Food and childcare, love and rivalry playing out in trills and whistles. "So that's what I'm competing with?"

I blinked. Had I let something slip? "Excuse me? I think the connection went out for a moment."

"For you." He raised his voice, and I found myself hoping that nobody was in earshot. "I mean, are you thinking about Albert's job? I'm sorry, Pru, I know he's your friend." He didn't give me time to respond. "But I can't see him keeping it after this."

"You can't think Albert would actually be behind this?" I stammered, desperate to explain the certainty I felt in my gut. "He's too lazy and, frankly, too chicken. He's not the type to trap a bear—to trap any wild animal. I mean, he might steal your donut, but…"

"Pru, I'm not saying he's in it alone. But he was there. And who knows what else he's a part of?"

"What?" This was all new. "I thought, maybe they'd all been drinking or…" I didn't know what I thought.

"This is more than just missing paperwork." Greg's voice sounded more distant as he drove. Around me, the birdcall was increasing in volume. "That trap? The tranq? That was a professional setup, and you know as well as I do that there's big money in the dark wildlife trade. Best guess is someone wanted that bear alive for some reason, and none of the possibilities are good."

"How would Albert even know how to get involved in something like that?" The man I knew could barely function.

"I bet he was recruited." I was about to argue. Albert was no wildlife expert, and the only tranquilizer gun I knew of was in Greg's truck. He didn't give me time. "Face it, Pru, from all you've told me about Albert, he's got no problem with earning some bucks the easy way. From what I hear, he's not doing anything to help himself, either. Jim Creighton called me yesterday. Said Albert wasn't talking. That he clammed up whenever they tried to get a statement out of him. He's going to have to hand him over to the staties soon."

"But the idea..." The squawking outside was maddening. My temples were pounding.

"Maybe someone came to him. Made him an offer." Greg sounded very far away. "Maybe someone's got him scared. I don't know, Pru. But if he won't cooperate, he's going to be the one going down."

I had to stop at the edge of town and root around in my glove compartment for some aspirin. I knocked it back with the coffee in my travel mug, and sat there by the side of the road with my eyes closed, waiting for it to kick in.

Greg was guessing, same as me. But his speculation was informed and intelligent. A for-profit scheme that required a live bear—and Albert had been roped in as well. I didn't know what I'd thought. A prank, a case of mislaid or misunderstood paperwork. A misdemeanor, nothing more. Add in money, though, and everything got more serious. Not to mention that this all made it more likely that Paul Lanouette's death might not have been the result of some drunken accident.

One thing Greg had said struck a chord. If Albert were removed—arrested or even simply fired—I stood a good chance of being named his replacement. Never mind that I did it already or that I was more qualified than Al or his predecessor, a glorified dog catcher who had been someone's crony back in the day. I was a local girl come home. Plus, Creighton would put in a word for me, no matter where we stood as a couple. He was honorable that way.

I had to confess, the idea had some appeal. It would make my life a lot easier, not having to hustle for every stupid gig. Even if I converted Ernest Luge into a client, I'd probably lose him once the autumn foliage was gone. In fact, with the cold weather, even the locals cut back. The Chinese restaurant would probably put me on every other week like last winter, as their business dried up. Heating my old heap of a house wasn't going to get any cheaper, of that I was sure.

It wasn't only winter. The GTO needed a new exhaust system, but I'd been holding off, hoping to put some money aside. Having a steady job meant a paycheck year round. And with Albert's gig I'd be my own boss, more or less, with only the city to answer to—and the occasional call from Greg.

The idea was looking better and better, especially if I didn't have to do anything much to stop it from coming my way. It wasn't like I'd be leaving a lot behind. I'd probably even still walk Growler. I couldn't abandon him to Tracy Horlick. And then there was Frank…

I closed my eyes and leaned forward, resting my forehead on the steering wheel. Frank. No, I couldn't. I remembered too well the visceral thrum of fear as the sleek little creature waited for his person to return. I took a deep breath and let myself linger, for just a moment more, on the fantasy at hand. And then I started the car and continued on my way. I had work to do, and—if I could—another big, dumb beast to set free.

Chapter Sixteen

Frank. I needed to find out what the ferret knew. He'd been there, when the bear had been trapped, and even if he'd not witnessed most of the day's happenings, he'd have picked up thoughts and memories from Albert and possibly from the other men as well. I could tell Creighton that Ronnie had been there; he probably had figured that out already. The two fat men were thick as thieves. But I didn't yet have any proof that another man—Larry, most likely—had been there as well. Nothing I could take to a cop, anyway. What I did know was that two other men had been there, with Albert and Paul, and that Paul had been alive when the bear was trapped. As for what happened after? Well, that remained a mystery.

I also was beginning to suspect Albert's pet of being more than an observer in this particular tragedy. When Creighton had said that the fat man's defense hung on his keys being lost, it had struck me as both odd and appropriate to the burly animal control officer. He would think that losing his keys would absolve him of being implicated in anything locked up with those keys. But Albert isn't anything if not lazy. Being unable to drive seemed a bit much for him to do willfully. Add in that Frank, for his own reasons, was protective of the bearded man and had definitely been hinting at something that I couldn't yet decipher—and that ferrets had a propensity for stealing bright, shiny objects, and I had to wonder. Was Frank behind the loss of the keys? Did he think he was protecting his flannel-clad person by making some piece of evidence disappear?

Preoccupied with these questions, I probably wasn't at my most alert as I pulled up to Tracy Horlick's split level. If I had been, I'd have noticed that her lips were more pursed than usual, her silence even more loaded as she drew on the ever-present cigarette and regarded me.

"Back on time today." The way she said it, I knew I couldn't win. "For a change."

"I try to be prompt, Mrs. Horlick." For Growler's sake, I kept my voice neutral.

"Maybe you should be." She flicked ash into her own sad boxwoods. "Now that you're not the only game in town."

That startled me, I'll admit. But I wasn't going to give her the satisfaction of seeing it, and so I kept my poker face on until she relented, once again freeing the small white dog in her care.

"What's that about, Growler?" As soon as we were around the corner, I put the question to the bichon, using his name for his jailor. "Is old smoke teeth going to hire someone else?"

"*Nobody else coming around.*" He snuffled, digging his nose under last fall's leaves. "*Not for what she's offering.*"

I caught my response short. Growler had reason to disparage the old lady. If he wanted to interpret my question as more personal, so be it. Besides, this was the bichon's time, and I tried to let him enjoy it. I wasn't worried about competition—not for the white fluffball's affection, rough as it might be—but I was aware of the inherent inequality between our two species. Just because I could scoop him up with one hand didn't mean I shouldn't respect his privacy.

"*Thanks, walker lady.*" As he trotted up the concrete walkway to the Horlick front door, he turned to me with a soft bark. "*You've always been a straight-shooter—unlike some.*"

I know that what I hear is translated—I couldn't really imagine the tiny dog knowing what a straight-shooter was, even if he wanted to use the phrase—but I still had a smile on my face as I turned over his lead to the scowling Tracy Horlick and went about my day.

•• ● ••

In some ways, I'm lucky. Not only in terms of my basic health, considering the years I spent abusing it in the city—and the fact that I probably still drink more than a human should. Not even in that I cohabit with a cat who has seen fit to fill me in on some of the subtler points of my strange sensitivity. No, I was thinking of my career, such as it was, and how through no fault of my own I have a leg up on any competition that might be out there.

Take my other morning appointment, for example. Karen Fell's aged basset hound Louis was acting oddly again. Karen had taken my advice and brought Louis in for a checkup, and Doc Sharpe had given him a clean bill of health. So it was up to me to find out why the floppy-eared hound was behaving strangely, falling over in the garden whenever she let him out, apparently deaf to her calls.

In a way, it was child's play. Even as I went through the motions, asking Karen about the dog's habits and diet, Louis was spilling the beans.

"I'm worried about Rascal," Karen was saying, using the rather undignified name she had given the hound. "I know he's getting on, but we always used to take such brisk walks. Now he never goes past the corner, and when I let him out—well, look at him."

I did. Lying on his back, the pink showing through his white belly fur, he might have appeared to be ailing—an aging pet. What he was letting me know, however, was just the opposite. Louis, despite his geriatric status, was in love—madly in love—with the Persian cat two doors down. A Persian who, unbeknownst to Karen, returned his canine affections by coming by the yard on her nocturnal ramblings and marking this particular patch of dirt.

The challenge, for me, was reconciling the species-crossed lovers in a way that their people would understand.

"Sometimes, animals act out because of a need to socialize," I ventured. There was some evidence for this in the discipline. Not that I needed that. "We love our pets and, of course, they love us," I was quick to add. "But animals—dogs, especially—are social creatures. Have you noticed Lou—I mean, Rascal reacting to any particular houses when you go out on your walks?"

"Well, now that you mention it." Karen nodded, her face thoughtful. "There is one house that always has a cat sitting in the window."

"*She's so beautiful! So beautiful!*" Louis started to howl.

"Have you considered talking to the cat's owner?" I did my best to suppress a grin. "Asking if she could come out to play?"

It would take some tricky footwork, being the intermediary between the cat's people and the aging dog's, but by the time I left the appointment, I believed something had been accomplished.

It was as I was leaving that my earlier concern came to mind again.

"If this works," Karen was saying, "I'm going to call you the basset whisperer."

"Thanks." I wasn't going to let her know how on target her compliment was. "By the way, have you heard of anyone else doing training or—you know, animal services?"

She shrugged. "No," she said. "I mean, it's not like Beauville is that big."

"Well, thanks." Curious, I thought, but even as I walked back to my car, another idea had suggested itself. Or been suggested, rather, by Louis and his smitten scent. The black bear was long gone, and I had to hope he'd never come near humans again. But before he disappeared—while he was trapped—he must have left some scent trail. Saliva or even urine, in his panic, that would have seeped into the rope or the framing device that had held the confining net in place. Something that would carry pheromones from what had undoubtedly been a stressful time. Maybe there would be something in those traces that could help me fill in some blanks.

Chapter Seventeen

"I'm sorry, Pru." Greg sounded genuinely bummed. And not, I couldn't help thinking, simply because he had to disappoint me. I'd called him back as soon as I got into my car. Even if he had no leads, that trap might, or so I'd thought.

He'd had the grace not to bring up his earlier speculation—or the job offer that still hung between us—and I'd been quick to tell him why I'd rung. My excuse was that I was intrigued by the idea of a net snare and wanted to check it out, just to see what kind of knots were used. I'd spent a few minutes trying to come up with a rationale—I mean, what was I going to say? Was I going to tell a state fish and wildlife warden that I wanted to feel out what psychic clues I could get from some old bear spit? Partly, well, it was a nice change to talk to a man who wanted to please me, even in something as small as letting me examine an illicit trap, simply because I was curious.

"You see, it's evidence," he finished. Still, I was taken aback. Was everyone out to block me? I mean, yeah, he was a state official, but still... "I don't have it anymore."

"Ah, thanks." I was driving, which always helps my mood, but Greg's explanation sweetened the pot. He wasn't holding out on me. And he did sound honestly sorry to disappoint. "Well, it was just a whim," I kept my voice light.

"You should talk to Jim Creighton," he was saying. "You two must know each other, right?"

"Yeah." I left it at that. Plausible deniability. But he had just clued me in on something I hadn't realized. I'd thought that perhaps his department had someone doing what I was claiming I was going to try—examining the trap for some indication as to where it had come from or who had purchased it. Clearly, the bear was part of the larger investigation—animal cruelty subordinated to a murder case.

The hunky warden had also cemented my resolve. I'd not had a chance to tell Creighton what I'd learned from my all-too-brief encounter with the confused bruin, not that I had figured out how to explain it. But now I knew, I had to make sure he knew about Ronnie, although I would need to come up with something concrete to explain my knowledge to my straight-arrow beau. As for the keys—well, I am an animal behavior expert. If I could suggest that maybe Albert's pet was responsible for the missing items, maybe I could win the bearded suspect some slack.

I'd been planning on swinging by County. Doc Sharpe had left a message about some clients of the canine kind that he wanted to discuss. Our local vet had been a solid ally, and besides, his consults usually ended up in paying work for me. Beyond that, all I had on my schedule was Jeanine Cooper's Siamese, and the prissy little girl would be just as happy to wait for her weekly nail-clipping. Midday was her prime nap time, and she got annoyed when that was interrupted. But before I went about my own duties, I'd see what I could about saving someone else's.

With a slight flutter in my belly that I couldn't quite explain, I veered off the Pike and back to Beauville. It would be good to beard this particular lion in his den.

"Pru." Creighton was standing behind the front desk, talking to his deputy, Chuck, over a sheaf of papers, when I came in. "You just dropping by?"

Chuck must have mumbled something, because Creighton handed him the file they'd been looking over as he slunk away. Just as well, seeing as how the young deputy had witnessed my debauch at Happy's the other night. Over by the phones, Kayla, the desk clerk suddenly became very busy.

"Hey, Jim." I said, and nodded at Kayla, but she turned away. I didn't know how word had gotten out, but clearly Creighton's staff had heard we were on the outs. "Can we talk?"

His eyebrows rose a fraction of an inch, but otherwise his poker face held. "Of course." He buzzed me in. "My office?"

"I'm here in a professional capacity," I said, as soon as we were back in his office and he'd closed the door behind me. I didn't want him to think I was trying to make up—not this way. "I mean, about the bear."

"Please." He gestured to a chair and sat himself down behind his desk. We're not an overly affectionate couple—not in public—but usually he at least offers me coffee. "Coffee?"

I blinked. No, I was the one who could hear things. Me and Wallis. Still, I had to smile.

"No." A flood of warmth—could it be relief?—rushed up me, and I could feel my cheeks grow warm. "No, thanks. I've got—well, I'm supposed to be meeting with Doc Sharpe out at County."

He nodded, waiting. Being a cop isn't that different from being an animal trainer. I knew what he was doing, staying quiet like this and leaving the space for me to fill it. Right now, that was fine by me.

"Greg Mishka told me you have the trap—the net the bear was held in." I jumped right in. "I thought I should take a look at it. I might have a better sense of where it came from or who built it."

Creighton's eyebrows went up, though whether that was because I'd mentioned Greg or because of what I was suggesting, I couldn't tell. He has good instincts—too good for my comfort level—and so I went for the distraction.

"I've also heard that Albert isn't talking," I said. "And I have some ideas. If he's here and I can—?"

I started to stand, when a cough from Creighton stopped me. "Pru." Forget command voice. This was cop voice.

"Please, Jim." I couldn't believe I was pleading. I figured it was a step up from pestering him with questions. "We both know Albert wasn't the one in charge out there and that he wasn't alone. He and Ronnie work as a unit, and you know maybe they've got half a brain between them. Plus, neither would turn on Paul Lanouette. They'd be afraid to. I mean, clearly booze was involved, and I'm guessing Ronnie took off before Albert passed out—and that somewhere in there, Paul—well, something happened. But it's pretty clear Albert wasn't the only other person there, besides the dead man. And..."

Those blue eyes had gone cold. I might as well have tried grilling him again. He wasn't giving me anything, and this was the tricky part. I had no hard evidence. Nothing that I could explain to Creighton, anyway, and I didn't want to say anything Albert would deny later. Then again, he was fuzzy under the best of circumstances. That realization gave me my in: "Albert wasn't too clear on this, when I drove him back. But I'm pretty sure there was a fourth man out there, too. Larry Greeley, I'd say. I bet if you'd ask Albert, or let me—"

"Pru..." This time, there was a growl in his tone. Still, I figured I might as well get it all out.

"Also, about those keys?" I licked my lips, my mouth suddenly dry. This was a little close to my own secrets for comfort. "I think—well, I don't know how much you know about ferret behavior." I focused on the facts. "They can become possessive of toys, shiny things, and the like. I think it's possible that Albert is telling the truth. That he really can't find his keys. He had his ferret in the truck, and it's quite possible that Frank—his ferret—stole his keychain. It was shiny and it might have smelled of Albert, so it would be fairly normal behavior."

His guffaw stopped me this time, laugh lines around his eyes softening that cold cop stare. But before I could capitalize on the burst of humor, he put a hand up to stop me.

"I knew it," he said. "I was right. You're not the tough case you'd like me to believe, but this confirms it."

"What?" I didn't like this.

"We found the keys, Pru. In his truck. Albert tucked them under the mat, thinking we wouldn't find them. But I'm kind of touched that you were trying to cover for him."

"Just because you found them doesn't mean—"

That hand again, like a traffic cop. "Please, your loyalty is admirable, but it doesn't matter. The state lab has them. That and the snare the bear was caught up in. They're looking for residue, so it doesn't matter how it 'got lost,' really." At this, he made air quotes, which normally would piss me off. Only now I was intrigued.

"Residue?" Drugs, I was thinking. Maybe Albert had taken a hit of whatever had knocked the bear out. I was also thinking of the ropes that had held the bear. I'd have given a set of radials to be touch whatever residue that poor creature had left.

But Creighton's mouth had set in a hard line and he shook his head. "You don't want to know, Pru. And to lock a man—a friend—up as he bleeds out..."

I had no words, but the question must have been clear in my face.

"Paul Lanouette was beaten to death, Pru. His face and body were a mess of contusions. And the back of his head—well, it wasn't pretty. Maybe his death wasn't intentional, but somebody wanted him to hurt, and he did. To me, that means anger or a premeditated punishment—or someone who was drunk or high enough not to care."

I swallowed, my mouth suddenly dry. This was more concrete than I had imagined, conjuring up images I didn't want to see. The men we were talking about liked their drink. I didn't want to think they were capable of something like this.

"But Ronnie couldn't..." I stopped. He was a large man, and he frequently drank to excess.

"We know Ronnie was there." Now the man before me just seemed sad. "But he'd already left—I'm sorry, Pru, I've already said too much. I appreciate you coming in, especially after—well, what I said."

"That's not..." I stopped. This was becoming untenable. "Jim, I understand that this is your job, and I'm not trying to interfere. But I work with Albert, and Lord knows, I'm not usually going to defend him. He drinks too much, and he's careless, and yeah, he's a big guy, so, yeah, maybe he doesn't always know his own strength."

I stopped myself. If I kept going this way, I'd make the case for the prosecutor. "Jim, you know Albert as well as I do. He's sloppy, but he's not violent. He's a screw-up, that's all. I'm sure he was just following someone else's lead, and I thought, if I could just take a look at that trap..."

I searched my beau's face for clues. He gave up a sad smile. "Is that why you're trying to drag Larry Greeley into this? Or do you really think I wouldn't have spoken to him? That I don't know Beauville as well you?"

"Larry Greeley wasn't there?" I couldn't draw any other conclusion.

"Pru." He was shaking his head again, the smile gone. "What's going on here? You can't really be worried that he's competition for you, can you?"

Kayla was absorbed in paperwork as I walked out. Chuck had fled the scene. Not that I cared any longer. Creighton no longer had the trap, and he wasn't doing to pull any strings to get me access, either. On the other hand, in terms of who was out there, he knew what I knew—no, he knew more. In fact, I realized as I stepped out onto the pavement, in addition to confirming what I'd already known about Ronnie, Creighton had given me a couple of pieces of valuable information. First, that Larry Greeley must have given Creighton some kind of an alibi. Second, that Paul Lanouette had been killed in a vicious and personal manner, and, finally, that what Greg had hinted at was true: Albert wasn't only being held because of the trapping of the bear. Despite all my protestations to the contrary, the bearded official was a suspect in a murder.

Chapter Eighteen

I looked in on Frank. Literally, through the glass door from the foyer that animal control shared with the Beauville cops. He was napping on the desk, and I didn't have the heart to wake him. If he had taken his person's keys and hidden them, he probably had a reason. But until he was willing to share that with me, I needed to pursue other avenues to get at the truth—and to get the slinky beast's person out of the box—as he'd envisioned it—that he'd trapped himself in.

Creighton was a good cop, I told myself as I walked back to my car. He might be holding Albert, but he wasn't going to charge anyone until he knew for sure what had happened. Even if the state was getting involved, Jim would still be the point-man for the case. And well, maybe Jim had a point. Maybe I did have a soft spot for so-called dumb animals—and the burly man my beau had in custody was certainly one of the dumbest.

At any rate, there was little more I could do for Albert now. And at least until I replaced him as the one behind that desk, I needed to earn my living the best way I knew how. It was time to pay Doc Sharpe a visit.

"Well, look who the cat dragged in." I adore the old vet. He's been a staunch supporter ever since I returned to this two-bit town. Pammy, his assistant, who now eyeballed me from County's front desk, I'm less fond of. "Late night?"

"You should watch it, Pammy." I brushed by her with scarcely a glance. "Your face might freeze like that."

It wasn't nice, and from the little squeal I heard as I walked by, I knew she'd make me pay for it. I didn't care. As grateful as I am to Doc Sharpe—and as much as I respect what he does—visiting the combination hospital and shelter is hard for me. He does good work, I know. And even Pammy is only really guilty of negligence—her cage-cleaning skills needed some work—and awful taste. None of the spring's kittens or returned puppies would complain about the pink geegaws that held her hair in check or the way she popped her gum. True, the good doctor should speak to her about the fragrance—what Pammy thought was floral would register as a chemical assault to anything more sensitive than the iguana who now paced in his box. And all he cared about was the rival he'd glimpsed in the mirror last week, which was the reason he'd been off his lettuce and plum slices.

But for me, the waiting room was a battlefield. Animals who came here were likely either in pain or lost. They picked up on the emotions of the children who cared for them, who were often as scared as they were, because Spot needed an operation or Fluffy had to go to a new home. On occasion, I'd been able to step in and alleviate some of the worst of these fears, but the overall impact of all that terror was hard to bear.

"Pammy." I growled. She knew I had clearance to go back and see the good vet. She wasn't buzzing me in as punishment. When the door still refused to click, I turned to see the back of her head. But as I did, I also heard another voice.

"*No, no. Can't go.*" A dog, a small one, but without the usual note of fear. "*Must stay. Stay! Stay!*"

I looked around until I saw a skinny little thing—male, about eight years old. Human, too. The thoughts I was hearing—in the form of sharp yaps—came from the box on his lap. "*Stay! Stay!*" The boy shifted, and I knew something was wrong.

"Hey, who do we have here?" I turned and knelt by the little lad, reaching my hand out to place on the box.

"Scout." His voice, barely a whisper, was drowned out by the dog inside the box. "*Guard! Guard! Guard!*"

"Are you bringing Scout in to see the vet?" I scanned the boy's face as he nodded, revealing the green of a fading bruise along his collarbone. He'd been crying sometime recently—more recently than that mark—and was struggling not to let the tears start up again. Under my hand, I could feel the box vibrating with tension. But the puppy inside seemed healthy. "*Stay!*" Another yap.

"Has Scout been misbehaving?" I looked from the boy to his father, who scowled and turned away. "Has he done something he wasn't supposed to?"

My questions were purely for the father. Animals don't misbehave. They also don't lie, cheat, or steal. What they do is act according to their natures. And domestic animals—in particular, dogs—have been bred to respond to us, their humans. They take their cues from us. They do what we tell them to; it's in their genes. Too often, though, we give them contradictory messages. We reward the unwanted behavior—rough housing with the puppy and then complaining when he bites, much as he would his littermates. Stroking the kitten until she is overstimulated, and not heeding the warning signs before she finally hisses at you to go away.

The little boy shook his head—and then stopped, going suddenly stiff. I waited for the man by his side to respond. "Sir?"

He glowered, and I saw my opening.

"My name is Pru Marlowe, and I work with Doc Sharpe as a behaviorist. A trainer." I pitched my voice to be clear and authoritative, but not threatening. In this, my pose—I was still crouching at the boy's feet—would serve as an advantage. I wasn't entirely sure what was going on with this family grouping, but I had my suspicions. "I may be able to help with your son's dog."

"That's not his dog." His bark was rougher than the mixed breed's in the box. "He can't have no dog."

I didn't respond, not verbally. I did meet his eyes, though, and I didn't blink.

"Is there a health issue here? An allergy, perhaps?" I waited a split second, not long enough for him to form an excuse. "Because if not, I believe this is a mistake. I'd say the boy and the dog have bonded, wouldn't you?" My voice was as smooth as a spaniel's coat. "And pets are wonderful for helping children learn about responsibility and empathy."

He might've known that first word—the second stumped him, as I knew it would. And then I stood. I'm tall, and most men find me easy on the eyes. In this case, however, I used my height, standing a little too close for the man before me to be comfortable.

"What's your name, sir?" He had to have heard the pause before the honorific. "I'm thinking you and your son are prime contenders for County's home services program."

"Wagner." The boy spoke up, a note of hope in his voice. "I'm Billy Wagner, and this is my dad. And Scout is my dog. My mom gave him to me. We live real close by."

I nodded, but I didn't break eye contact with the seated man. "Then why don't you go over to Pammy at the front desk then, and give her your name, address, and phone number. I'll finish up with your father."

Billy was off like a shot—with the box. He wasn't leaving that dog, and I'd wager that puppy—loyal beast—would do his best to never leave the boy, either. I didn't turn to watch them. Pammy wasn't great, but she was competent at taking down basic information. Besides, the kid was adorable—and he hadn't antagonized her like I had.

Instead, I leaned in until I could smell the older man's breath. "Now, let's get this straight." I spoke only for his ears. "You're not going to touch that kid or his dog in anger again. You hear me? You've got some beef in your life—or with your wife—you work it out. But that kid deserves something to love. Something that takes care of him, and I bet that dog does a lot better job of it than you do."

He shifted and I thought he was going to start in on me. I didn't want to hear it. I'd seen enough. "I'm going to be dropping by," I said. "Animal abuse is a felony. Same as child abuse. I'm guessing something went wrong for you—but you've got a kid. You can be a hero, or you can go away. It's up to you."

"Pru?" From behind me, I heard Doc Sharpe calling.

"Are we clear?" I wasn't leaving until I had my answer.

"Yeah." The man lowered his head, but before he did I thought I saw a slight blush rise to his cheeks. "Yeah, I just—I had a bad day is all."

I nodded, letting him have the last word, and then I went off to do my job.

Chapter Nineteen

"You might also be getting a call from a Mrs. Felicidad—Susan Felicidad, I believe." Doc Sharpe was leafing through papers. He'd already outlined the few tasks he couldn't get to—the ones he didn't trust Pammy to take proper care of—as we walked back to his office past the warren of examination and cage rooms that made up the bulk of County's space.

I waited. I'd been picking up what I needed along the way and now held three files in my arms, and the leather gloves we use for handling unfamiliar or aggressive animals. He'd stood at his office door, scanning the notes written in his indecipherable hand. "A cat issue, I believe. She lives near you—but on the newer side of town."

"Thanks." I said. I meant it. The vet was too much of an old Yankee to refer to money directly, but I got the hint. He'd steered one of the summer people my way. "Any idea what kind of issue?" I wasn't worried, but it never hurt to have a heads-up.

The vet only shook his own shaggy mane, his lower lip sticking out in a pout. "No idea." He was holding the page further away and squinting. "I can't make out my own handwriting."

"Everything okay?" Usually, the old man was as sharp as his name, but nobody's immune to age.

"Fine." He snapped and then caught himself. "Thanks for asking, though. I confess, I have been thinking about the future."

I waited, my heart sinking. If he retired, I'd be in trouble. So would the whole county. Doc Sharpe was not only one of the few remaining generalists around, he was a marvel at administration, basically keeping County running single-handedly.

"I hear Greg Mishka might be looking for an assistant." He blinked up at me. "Might be right up your alley."

"Really?" I tried to sound surprised. The doc thought he was doing me a favor. "Trouble is, I'm developing a clientele right in Beauville."

"Hmm." A noncommittal sound. "Beauville, yes, well. Beauville is a small town."

I thought of Larry Greeley and what Creighton—and Tracy Horlick—had said. "Doc, are you saying I've got competition? Is there someone else setting up as a behaviorist?"

"What? No." His protest a little too forceful. "Only, Pru?" He glanced up and then immediately turned away, the diffident Yankee to the end. "It might be good for you to get out there. In the wider world again, you see."

"The wider world." I waited for more, but the good doc was already opening his door. Creighton—it had to be. Though how the old vet was clued into Beauville gossip was beyond me. Granted, anyone in his office might have figured out that something wasn't right, but I'd always figured Creighton's staff was too loyal to gossip. Then again, their loyalty would be to him—not the raven-haired dogwalker who wouldn't settle down. I pictured a line from Kayla to Pammy—and then to Doc Sharpe? Or was Jim Creighton himself airing his woes, and—just maybe—getting the word out in an indirect manner?

Whatever. I had my reasons for keeping some distance. And, just maybe, I had some options, too. I thought of the hunky warden. More reason not to start working with him. Unless I really was in trouble...

"Pru?" I realized I was standing there, staring into space. Doc Sharpe too polite to close the door in my face.

"Sorry." I shook off the cobwebs. "Maybe I do need a change—but, Doc…?" The question I'd been about to ask evaporated, as I saw the web of metal and leather on the desktop behind him. "What's that?"

"What?" He turned to follow my gaze. "Oh, yes. The large animal muzzle." He lifted it, turning it over in his hands.

I reached for it—I couldn't help it—and got an immediate shock of panic that caused me to drop it onto the files. "From the bear?"

"What? Oh, yes." He peered at the leather-and-metal contraption through his spectacles, a note of pride creeping into his voice. "I am rather the expert around here."

"Of course." It made sense, and I saw my chance. Creighton—or the staties—might have the trap, but this piece of state-owned equipment had been in close contact with the bear as well. "Greg brought the bear to you for the blood work."

An assenting nod as the vet deposited the papers onto his desk. "Healthy animal, on the whole. Not poisoned, as I'd initially feared."

"Why would someone poison a trapped bear?" Caging it was bad enough.

He shook his head. "Not intentionally. Not likely, anyway. But you hear things." He peered at me over his glasses. "Private zoos—private hunts—they don't want a healthy animal. One that could fight back. And this fellow was certainly out of it. Still it was a bit of a risk taking that off." He peered up at me. "Greg really could use someone like you, you know."

I answered with a close-mouthed smile. Right now I didn't want to ask what he meant. Doc Sharpe saw more than he let on.

"Private zoos?" The hunts I'd heard about. They call them "canned." Basically, they're an excuse for fat, wealthy men to slaughter creatures that are far their superiors.

He nodded. "I've been getting advisories. Better than the alternative, but still."

I had to agree. I was also getting so mad, I knew I had better change the subject.

"You probably need this cleaned." I did my best to keep my voice level. Nonchalant. "I mean, we don't want to give some poor Saint Bernard a heart attack the next time we have to use it."

"True. I'd been meaning to return it, but..." He looked up, his gray eyes large behind his thick glasses. "Maybe you could take care of it? After you're done?"

"Sure," I said. At that point, I simply wanted to be gone. The muzzle lay on the files before me. It might as well have been radioactive. "I can do that."

"Call Mrs. Felicidad first, please, Pru." Doc Sharpe's voice sounded very far away. "I remember now—I believe her cat has gone missing. She sounded a bit scattered. These summer people don't understand the environment here, and I fear a feline who has gotten into the woods may be at risk."

I did. This was important to Doc Sharpe, and besides, the principle was sound—if I could help an animal, that had to be my top priority. I'd taken the muzzle, along with the files and those gloves, back to the main storeroom. I'd have privacy there, not only from Pammy—she wouldn't come back here unless her paycheck depended on it—but also from the hubbub of the cage rooms, three big rooms stacked like dormitories with animals in various stages of quarantine, recovery, or awaiting adoption.

Don't get me wrong. County is well run and its animals are in good shape. But between the pets who are up for adoption and those who've been picked up from the streets, there's a ton of confusion and miscommunication. Even walking down the hall, I'd picked up the sleepy emanations of a new mother. A calico shorthair, she had let herself be trapped knowing she was about to go into labor. She was purring and content now, lying on a bed of toweling in the cat room. But her squalling brood—five kittens, all doing well—were as noisy as any nursery as they took turns napping and wrestling, and their kittenish tumult was disturbing to an elderly Siamese who had dental issues and wanted everyone to know.

Stepping away from the muzzle, I dialed the number Doc had given me, working to clear my mind as the phone rang.

"Mrs. Felicidad?" The phone was answered on the first ring. Par for the course for a worried pet person. "I'm Pru Marlowe." I introduced myself quickly and explained the services I could offer.

"Thank you." A sigh of relief. "I've been—well, I've been distracted. I know having a pet is a responsibility, but I've been busy."

I bit my tongue. A worried pet owner didn't need a lecture, even if her excuses seemed to invite it. Luckily, she didn't seem to notice my lack of response. "I've already made up fliers," she was saying.

"That's good." I nodded, wondering if Doc Sharpe had suggested this. This Felicidad—what an unfortunate name—didn't seem to have a clue otherwise. "Stay by your phone, and maybe we'll get lucky. But I'll be by in about twenty minutes."

I looked around. This took priority, and I could come back to the training and, yes, the cleaning tasks later in the afternoon. The good vet would understand.

After I took down his information, I washed my hands. I should leave everything till later. Only, it was right there—the muzzle. And I'd already had a hint of what it might reveal.

I licked my lips and eyed the storage room door. Doc Sharpe had already hinted that he'd seen something unusual in me. I didn't need him to know any more. Still, locking the door would be suspicious.

I was stalling. Afraid of—I wasn't sure what. And that's not who I am. And so I took a breath and reached out, grabbing the leather of the muzzle with both hands.

Move! It hit me right away, that nightmare feeling of panic, when you want to run but you can't. It was physical, as much confusion as fear, and it dawned on me. The bear had been drugged when Greg put this muzzle on. Half-awake at best, and unable to process what was happening. Well, so much the better, then. The panic I had gotten at first would be muted—softened by the soporific effects of the tranquilizer.

What I needed was something deeper. Access to the bear's memory, some trace of what had happened left in the saliva. Gripping the leather tighter, I closed my eyes and asked, as I would the animal himself: "*What happened? What did you see?*"

Black. I got nothing. The drugs, I thought. Or maybe too much time had passed. And then—noise? Yes, noise. A roar of unfamiliar sound adding to the bear's disorientation. Greg's truck? Albert's? No, another vehicle, its engine well maintained. But over that sound were voices. Talking normally and then, yes, dropping lower. One wheedling, almost a whine. Asking for what, I couldn't tell. Only the other wasn't having it, and they both grew louder until one silenced the other—a command? A fight? Was one hunter directing the others, or was I eavesdropping on Paul Lanouette's last moments? It was all too distant, too foreign to the bear. And he was growing so sleepy. The voices too faint and far away.

"Pru?" I jumped, but it was only Doc Sharpe, standing in the open doorway.

"I'm sorry." I could feel my cheeks flame as I dropped the muzzle back onto the counter. "I was just heading out."

"I'm glad I caught you, then." He looked over to where my cell phone lay blinking beside the folders. "Mrs. Felicidad was trying to reach you. She says you don't have to come over. Someone's already found her cat."

Chapter Twenty

"These people are certainly careless with their pets." The words were out of my mouth before I had a chance to process. The expression on Doc Sharpe's face reminded me that they were, perhaps, inappropriate.

"I'm sorry." Doc Sharpe was a good guy—and always on my side. "It's just that I seem to be getting a lot of calls for pet rescues that turn out not to be necessary, and all from the other side of the cobble."

"Really?" Brushy white eyebrows bunched together like duelling woolly caterpillars.

"I didn't mean that they were negligent…" That was exactly what I meant, actually. But no way did I want the good vet to think I was badmouthing clients.

"No, I'm…concerned." He chose the word with care. "So many of those residents are new to the area, and it must be very different from what they know."

His brow cleared as he looked up at me. "This might be an opportunity for you, Pru. You lived in the city. You might be able to talk to these people. Perhaps offer a seminar, here, after hours." He cleared his throat, usually a sign of embarrassment or discomfort. "I'll find financing for it, of course. Maybe you could sound out the community? Gauge what interest there might be?"

"Sure." I didn't see it, not really. But I did want an excuse to head back over to the new development. Something odd was going on—and, besides, I wanted to see Sage again, as well as Reina.

But Doc Sharpe's requirements weren't all busywork, and once the urgency had been removed, I made myself useful. Before I took off, I gave the vet a hand with a squirmy puppy. It helped that I could commiserate with the poor pup's discomfort. Passing the toy truck—eaten in haste the day before—was necessary, but not fun. I also picked up some of Pammy's duties, grooming new arrivals with a flea comb. With high summer coming on, an infestation could spread fast. I also sat with the new couple, ostensibly guiding them through the care and feeding of the tabby littermates they'd be taking home. But while I had, in fact, led them through Feline 101—gently explaining the benefits of keeping their new pets inside, both for the cats and for the area wildlife—I was also doing my best to sell the couple to the tabbies.

"*They mean well,*" I'd said. "*But they may need some training.*" Cats don't mind condescending, as long as they're asked politely.

All the while I was in the back, I kept my eyes open for that father and his son. I was pretty sure Doc Sharpe would pick up on the dynamic between them, even once that bruise had faded, and he was in a good position to notify children's services if he thought there was abuse. Physical, that is. I had no doubt that poor child was not being loved or appreciated the way he should be. But when they didn't come back—as they would have to if, in fact, they were surrendering the dog, I dared to hope. Maybe I'd scared the father. Maybe the boy would be able to keep his pet—his ally. Maybe I wouldn't have to drag that man in for the punishment he deserved.

By the time I was finished with my duties and had washed up, Pammy was ready to go. The waiting room was empty. Even if it hadn't been, her posture—back to the door, phone at her ear—signaled that County was closed.

"We're open till five." I breezed over to her desk. She looked over her shoulder, her usual pout puckering further as I reached for the papers on her desk. "In case you forgot."

"Can I help you?" Her tone did not invite an answer.

Not that I cared. "Yeah, there was a man here with his son. They were supposed to leave their phone number and address for me?"

A snort, which must have sounded worse to whoever was on the other end of that phone call, and she retrieved a pink Post-it. I was too busy deciphering the childish scrawl to catch what she said next. But when I looked up, she was mouthing something to me. "Good luck," it might have been, though as I walked away, I realized she was more likely to be saying, "he's mine."

"Charming," I said to nobody in particular, once I was out in the fresh air. The grackles had their own family drama going on. Someone was really ready to fend for himself, and his parents were squabbling over how to give him the proper push. They must have sensed the fox lurking nearby. Nobody wants their offspring to be in danger—at least, nobody besides us humans—but at some point, we all have to go solo.

That boy, though—he wasn't ready. Even as I drove, the wind bringing a multitude of voices in with the breeze, I found myself thinking of his haunted face, his shadowed eyes. Creighton had hinted at marriage and a family, back when he thought we might settle down. I've never been keen on the idea. There are too many of us on this planet as it is, and I can think of a dozen species that deserve our space. That didn't mean I wanted the children already born to suffer. I'd do what I could for him, much as I would for any kit or pup endangered by some brute of a man.

I'm not good at compartmentalizing. That's one reason Wallis can read me so easily. I made the effort, though, as I pulled once more into the new development. Susan Felicidad might not think she needed my assistance any more, now that her cat had been found. But there were just too many pets going missing over here on this side of the cobble. I wanted to find out why.

"Ms. Felicidad?" I parked at the curb, where the starter trees were already high enough for the robins to have nested, and greeted the dark-haired woman kneeling by a flower bed. I could already hear the demanding mew of her pet—"*do your job!*"—coming from inside the screened front door. "I'm Pru Marlowe."

"Miss Marlowe." The woman turned and rose with ease. A sprigged poplin shirt, with the folds still fresh from the package, and jeans with a crease on a muscular body nearly as tall as mine. But when I extended my hand, I saw that hers were gloved. In one, she held a small spade, in the other what might have been a dandelion. I'm not good with plants. "How nice." She removed one glove and extended a hand free of rings. Her manicure, I noticed, was short and workmanlike, and her voice was calm. "But—you got my message?"

"I did." I nodded toward the house. "And I hear that someone is home safe."

"*Of course, safe. Safe!*" A loud near-caterwaul. The unseen feline might have been echoing me, but I thought it more likely that he was also alerting me that this was his territory—the feline equivalent of "don't come near here, there's a guard cat on duty."

"Yes, Spot seems to be angry with me." The brunette deposited the weed in a bag I hadn't noticed, and brushed off her knees. "Usually, I'd let him out while I work."

"Ah, maybe that's the problem?" I scanned the profusion of foliage and flowers, all things that my mother would have been able to identify—and would have sweat over, during her days off. The result looked like a landscaping portfolio, but it was still only yards away from the woods. When I turned back toward my new acquaintance, I saw her eyeing me curiously. "Not that it's not a gorgeous garden." I'd get to cat care later.

"Thank you." She turned to survey the plants once more. "This is why I moved here. Now that I'm retired, I wanted to be able to get my hands dirty again."

I smiled. My mother would have liked that. What I didn't say was how rare that was—especially in this neighborhood. Though as I followed her up to the house, I couldn't help wondering. She seemed young for retirement, and also fit, but still… "Do you ever hire anyone to help? I mean, with the heavier work?"

"What heavy work?" She turned to scan the yard, as if the idea were new to her. "Well, maybe I will in winter, if we get the snow we're promised. I'm a widow, you see."

"Good idea." I didn't comment on her marital status. I doubted any of the husbands in this section of town would shovel their own snow. It didn't matter. I'd find a good service to recommend. Not Ronnie and his buddies.

"So, who do we have here?" The cat waiting inside the screen door stared up at me expectantly, his serious mien accentuated by the black spots ringing the base of his white ears.

"*Yes?*" He lashed his black tail once in acknowledgment, but as I crouched beside him he bristled slightly. Most people must immediately reach out to stroke the big, black patches on his creamy back, but I knew better, and he relented when, instead, I presented my palm.

"Pru Marlow." I muttered under my breath. He sniffed, cataloguing the animals at County—and the scent of Wallis beneath them all.

"*Bunbury Bandersnatch.*" The answer came back with all the dignity a feline can muster. "*At your service.*"

"Bun—" I caught myself. "*Spot* looks to be in good shape."

"Bun?" This woman was sharp. I would have to be careful. Luckily, she chuckled, rather than waiting for an answer. Up close, I could see the lines around her dark eyes, but Susan Felicidad wasn't much older than I was. "I like it. I might have to start calling him Bun. Short for Bunny, of course."

I nodded, forcing my own smile while silently apologizing to the feline at our feet. Spot was a stupid name, despite his cow-like markings. But what kind of pet person changes her animal's name once it is grown? Sure, pets accrue names throughout their lives—but, as T.S. Eliot once remarked, the naming of cats is a serious matter.

"*It matters not.*" Bunbury dismissed the affront with another flick of his tail. "*All part of the gig.*"

I didn't know how to respond. "You know, it might not be the best idea to let a house cat out around here." I considered the placid feline face. "Of course, some cats can be taught to walk on a leash."

I got a flicker of interest from the cat. Part of the gig? I wondered if Wallis saw me as more of a responsibility than a companion.

"Well, I don't know." Susan Felicidad regarded us, a touch of humor playing around her lips. "I do like having him around me, but it seems sort of unnatural. I mean, isn't it?"

"Depends on the cat." I watched as the serious feline turned to take in his person. "But then you wouldn't have to worry about him getting lost."

"I was worried," she echoed back at me, the fear obviously past. "But it all worked out."

"Would you tell me what happened?" My query was to the cat as much as his person. But the stately feline wasn't giving me much more than the woman. "Please?"

"*Inspecting the perimeter.*" That's not what Bunbury said, of course, but that was the intent. I smelled the perfume of freshly turned earth, and the small burrowing creatures who had been in it, at the yard's edge. "*Doing my job.*"

"And you—he—got lost?" I modified my question to appease the woman standing above me.

"*Please!*" I had offended. I reached forward, both to make my amends with a friendly rubbing of the ears and to strengthen the connection. "*No!*" The cat reared up slightly, lifting a white forepaw as if he would strike me. "*Hands! Stranger!*"

"I'm sorry." It didn't take my gift to know that it was time to back off, and so I did, taking a step back to stand by Bunbury's person.

"And I told the young man how grateful I was." She'd been talking, I realized.

"Excuse me?"

"The young man who found him." She laughed. "I gather Spot ran off—probably thought he was protecting me from something."

"*Hands!*" The cat at my feet grumbled, and I had to wonder. Maybe he was.

Chapter Twenty-one

"Have you gotten to know your neighbors?" We were outside, walking around the block by then. I had snapped a spare lead on Bunbury's collar and he was taking it rather well. Professionally, almost. "*Part of the gig.*"

"Some," said the woman beside me, her long legs setting a pace that I'd use with an energetic dog. "They seem like nice people, though I was hoping it would be easier to get to know them. You know, outside of the city."

"Oh?" I turned toward her, and immediately caught myself. I should have been focusing on the cat. This wasn't a casual stroll; it was a first training session. And although it is important when leash-training a cat to be aware of his or her human, even when that human is distracted—or being gently interrogated by a total stranger—it is even more essential for the trainer to stay focused on the animal. A cat is more likely than a dog to get tangled up in a leash, for example, and that could lead to trouble.

As if reading my thoughts, Bunbury leaned forward, mouth open, as he took in the scent of—could it be?—a wild turkey who had crossed the yard. Yes, I got the trace of feathers and leathery feet, as the feline filed away the sensory perception. Turkeys were a new phenomenon for the city cat. But even as he bent again, cataloguing the dinosaur-like creature's traces, he also picked up a small stick, which wedged itself into his collar and which, with proper feline hauteur, he ignored.

I made a mental note to tell the dark-haired woman at my side to get a breakaway collar for any future walks. I doubted she would bother. There was something distracted about her. And although that fit with her pet's custodial air, I silently apologized to the spotted cat, even as I watched to see if his human companion would notice his plight.

"I don't mean that in a negative way." She knelt to pick the twig from the cat's collar, almost as if she had picked up on my anxiety. Well, preoccupied then, if not distracted. "Just—I thought people might be more open out here. Let their hair down, if that makes sense."

"Yes, I think it does." She was lonely, I figured. Maybe hoping to snag another husband, out here in this moneyed enclave. Well, that's how some women survive—and she was younger and more fit than many of her neighbors.

"In fact, if you know of any—" Before she could follow up, I put out my hand to stop her. "Wait," I said, holding onto her arm.

The questioning expression on her face matched her cat's so closely I could have laughed. But this wasn't only my aversion to setting up my clients. This was work. "Call him," I said.

"But he's…" A nod. She understood. "Spot!"

"*Yes?*" Bunbury's ears pricked up in acknowledgement. And before I could stop her, Susan Felicidad threw the stick. She had a good arm—all that digging in the dirt—and it went flying, end over end, just topping a boxwood hedge that had been sculpted within an inch of its life.

"*Shall I?*" The cat watched with curiosity, and then began trotting toward the hedge as Susan played out the lead behind him. Bunbury, looking for all the world as if mimicking a dog's role was—what was his expression?—all just another "part of the gig" made me laugh. The scenting, the retrieval: I've known doggish cats in my day, and even Wallis liked to fetch at times, but this cat could out-canine most of the pups I worked with. I was about to comment—I had a feeling the woman beside me didn't know what an unusual cat she had—when it hit me.

"Come on!" I didn't wait, but took off after the feline. Responsive and responsible. The master of his territory until now—

"What is it?" Susan called, even as she ran, the extra length of lead dragging behind her. I had no time to come up with an excuse. All I knew was that I had sensed danger—a deadly threat. I tore around the hedge—and I saw it. A tall, older man, blinking wide-eyed in surprise, an expression mirrored in the posture of his dog, a husky whom he held on a tight leash as the spotted cat stared up unafraid into his wide, furry face.

"Good, Bun—Bunny." I exhaled, shaking, as I scooped up the unprotesting cat. "Good cat."

At that he turned, with a blink that called my judgment into question. "All is well," I repeated, and his eyes half-closed with satisfaction.

"Oh! Oh, my." Susan Felicidad had caught up. She took the scene in quickly and took the spotted tom from me, squeezing him tightly enough to induce a slight huff of protest. "When you took off…"

"I thought I heard something." I improvised, elaborating on the truth only a little. The cat stared at me, affronted. "And this close to the woods…"

"Excuse me?" The dog walker had recovered from his shock. He pulled the lead in, causing the dog—who still seemed stunned—to back up.

"I'm sorry." I took a breath. That moment of fear, more than the quick dash, had drained me. "We're training Bun— Spot to walk on a leash."

The man stared down his long nose, his mouth set in a disapproving frown. Not a cat man, clearly. The husky merely blinked those blue eyes, so much like Creighton's and seemingly similarly thoughtful.

"He wouldn't have attacked," I said, and the corners of that mouth twitched. I could see why—Bunbury would barely make up a mouthful to the big dog, but I wasn't joking. Clearly this man wasn't a regular cat person, either, or he'd have known how often cats go for dogs, especially if they view them as a threat. In fact, just to make sure we didn't have an incident, I turned to make sure Susan was holding Bunbury close, and was pleased to realize that her fear, along with his displeasure with me, had dissipated. Instead, Bunbury was viewing the larger beast with curiosity.

"That's a beautiful animal," I said. It never hurts to compliment someone's dog. It also makes a good opening. The man only grunted, but the husky looked up with those soulful eyes and wagged his tail. I took that as invitation and held out my hand for him to sniff. "*Bear.*" The word as clear as if he'd spoken it in my ear.

"He's got a fine pedigree, although I've never shown him." The man's voice interrupted my question for the husky, as gruff as a bark and almost as distinctive. "Those eyes, you know."

"I see." Blue eyes aren't uncommon in huskies, but why burst this man's bubble? Besides, something else was going on. The dog was curious. Too well behaved to strain at the leash, he had that husky urge to explore. I was getting a stream of thought that could only translate as questions: "*Woods? Forest? Bear?*" Beyond that, I was hearing—no, it was the man.

"Excuse me." I withdrew my hand, to the husky's dismay. I needed to focus and held it out to the man instead. "I'm Pru, Pru Marlowe."

"Jack Walz." He took my hand with his own. French cuffs, I noted, the nails buffed to a smooth glow. The city had come to Beauville.

"Finally." I nodded, more to myself than to him. I knew I'd recognized that voice. "I'm the woman from animal control. We spoke about your fishing license."

"Yeah, right." He brought his hand to his mouth, almost as if he was registering my scent. His own was more cologne than dog, a faint spicy musk that might have confused an animal not used to it. It went with the gold bracelet and designer shades.

"Did you ever finish the application?" I didn't really care, and both Bunbury and Mrs. Felicidad were standing by, waiting.

"No, not yet." He turned from me to the woman by my side, and I realized how rude I was being, particularly in light of the dark-haired woman's half-voiced request.

"I'm sorry." Sometimes human graces elude me. "Do you two know each other? You're practically neighbors."

"Susan Felicidad." My new client set her own pet back on the sidewalk and stretched out her flower-bedecked arm. He took it, and they eyed each other carefully. Well, every creature mates in its own way.

While the two humans made their introductions—her background seemed to shift as she talked, and I wondered if she was modifying it to match his—I watched the two animals. Bunbury was still on alert, his muscular little body tense with excitement, but he was silent now. Watching. The husky—to whom I still had not been introduced—was typically low-key. Distracted, I would have said, which can be typical of a service dog bred for intense physical labor. Until he was called for—or hitched to a sled—he'd probably continue in this dreamy state, fantasizing about the tundra and, yes, the bears out there.

Unless, it hit me, he was picking up a scent or, more likely, something from me. "You scenting that muzzle, big fella?" While the humans made small talk, I dropped into a squat and finally placed my hand on the thick, rich fur. Sure enough, I was rewarded with that strange musky scent, undeniably wild. But not, I thought, first-hand. The husky was curious, and some ancient memory had been triggered. But he was not sensing a bear this close to the new development.

Still, I reminded myself, Beauville was not the city, and Bunbury could be at risk. His fearlessness combined with his size could get him in bigger trouble out here than it ever would have back wherever Susan Felicidad used to garden. That would be reason enough for leash training.

"Excuse me," I murmured to the two pets, and stood to broach the subject. They weren't focused on us anymore, however. Instead, they were both looking toward the street, where a familiar truck—dark green with a pine tree logo—was cruising slowly. Ronnie.

"Hey, there." Ronnie, uncouth as always, pointing to the far side of the hedge. "Is this your house?"

"No, I'm sorry." Susan, her voice polite, appeared puzzled. "May I help you?"

"Get out of here." Walz was less so, his cultured voice growing gruff. "Quit bothering the lady."

Ronnie blinked but drove on.

"The temerity of those hucksters." Walz sniffed. "Shilling on the street."

"I think he's simply offering lawn services." I couldn't believe I was defending such a loser, especially as Ronnie was quite openly using his employer's truck. Then again, what I was doing wasn't that different. Sure, I'd lived in the city once, but to these people, I was another Beauville hick.

"No, it wasn't that." Susan shook her head, an unlikely champion of the man in the truck. "I have no problem explaining that I enjoy yard upkeep. It's just that—that truck. The young man who found Spot for me." She turned to me. "I thought he was in a truck like that. Maybe it was simply parked up the road."

"Ronnie and his friends are doing a fair amount of lawns in the area." I wasn't convinced. "Maybe it was one of them?"

"I don't know. I don't think so." Another shake. "I've never seen that man."

"You lost your cat?" Walz's voice softened.

"He likes to explore, I've discovered." Susan glanced down and shook her head, as if the cat were a stranger. Well, animals will exhibit different behavior in new circumstances.

"I was thinking we should talk about that." I was suddenly a bit reluctant to discuss my services. "Whether or not you stick with the leash, I would advise training him not to bolt and to stay inside unless you're with him."

"You can do that?" Her voice lifted, and I smiled in return.

"I can, and Spot can too. He's a smart cat." At our feet, the cat began to purr. I didn't add that my special sensitivity gave me an edge when it came to feline behavior. Or that I was consciously buttering him up. "He only wants to learn what rules to follow."

"*Yes!*" His eyes closed at the compliment. "*That's my job!*" The spotted cat wasn't going to need much training at all, and I almost felt guilty. Well, I couldn't exactly call what I did translation services, even if that would be more accurate.

"You work with animals?" Walz's gaze was coolly appraising, but, I thought, interested.

"Yes, I do." I stood up straight, shoulders back, and did my best to look him in the eye. So much of communication is non-verbal, no matter what we humans try to tell ourselves. "Although I consult with the Beauville animal control office, and often help them out with routine matters, I also have private clients."

"The nice vet in charge of the animal hospital recommended her." Susan Felicidad had picked up on our dynamic as well.

Walz took this in, along with a sniff of our green and grassy air.

"Are you having issues with your husky?" I wasn't going to suggest anything. Not until he let me know what he wanted. I could read men, too. But I would bet that any problems came from boredom. Huskies, like so many of the larger breeds, are fundamentally working animals. That made them even-tempered, but it also opened them up for behavioral issues if they weren't properly engaged.

"Not exactly." He sounded taken aback, as if I'd insulted his dog. "But I may need some help from time to time."

"Of course." I don't have a card, and he didn't seem to have a cell phone with him. "You can reach me through the animal control office, at any time. Mrs. Felicidad?"

We made our way back toward her garden, pausing every few feet to wait for Bunbury—Spot—to catch up. He was an intelligent animal, but as intent on cataloguing the area as if he were in fact a sentry. Still, he seemed content to follow after his person.

"*Of course.*" The thought reached me on a chuff. "*She's my person, and I'll protect her. I'd protect you, too, if you'd let me.*"

"I'm sure you would." I spoke softly as I crouched down. His silky fur was eminently pet-able, but after I gave his ears a good rubbing, I reached for the lead and unclipped it. Now we would see if he'd stay by his person—or bolt.

"Are you sure that's a good idea?" Susan spoke softly, but her eyes were on the hedge, which once again hid Walz and his dog from view.

"I believe he's ready," I said. What I didn't tell her was that her cat had already assessed the big husky and dismissed him as a threat. And that the husky was dreaming of much larger game.

Chapter Twenty-two

I would've done more. Bunbury—and Susan—were quick learners, and it was gratifying to teach them both how to better communicate. Not that I called it that, of course. Susan Felicidad might be a little more hands-on than your average Beauville newcomer, but I still wouldn't go that far. Instead, I called it training. Bunbury and I knew that his person was really simply learning how to clarify what she wanted the spotted cat to do and what not.

Besides, I could still feel Jack Walz watching, staring down his patrician nose like a judgmental hound. They can be quite proud, you know—it comes from knowing they have the best sense of smell in the woods. I didn't give a damn if he approved of me. I was used to his type from when I lived in the city and, truth be told, tended to play up my rougher aspects, just to get their goat. But I had liked his dog, even as I wondered what was going on beneath that thick fur, and I thought he loved the shaggy beast, too, which spoke well of him. In truth, I might have been looking for a redeeming feature in Walz. I could sure use his money, if the snooty New Yorker would ever come around to admitting that the big husky needed more time and attention than he was willing to give. At least I could meet him halfway on the dog.

The first time my phone buzzed, I ignored it. Creighton could wait, especially at this point. And if it were any of my clients, well, it didn't do anybody any harm to think that a service provider was busy.

"Now, you try it." I waited while Susan walked off. Bunbury squirmed a bit, flicking his tail as a sign of impatience, but he waited too, aware all the while of my eyes on him. Aware of Walz, too, who had come back around the hedge with his magnificent dog and stood silent, his mouth set in a serious line. Bunbury glanced at him, his dark-ringed ears up to catch any movement from the man. Had the husky done anything, he might have tuned into him as well, but the big dog was dreaming again, his sky-blue eyes gazing off in the distance. Maybe it was this disconnect that had piqued the cat's interest.

"Spot." The cat sprang to attention, every fiber of his being focused on the woman before him. "Come."

The cat took his time, strolling like a proper boulevardier. But he did make it up to his person without trying to run or pull at the leash, or other untoward behavior.

"Very good." Susan reached to stroke the cat, from those alert ears to the sensitive base of the tail.

"You're impressive," said Walz. From him, this was probably high praise.

"Thank you." I turned away. Susan was my client, and besides, men like that need to be reminded that they're not always the priority. That's when my phone began ringing again.

"Do you mind?" My question was for Susan. She looked up at me and nodded her permission. I didn't have to see Walz to feel him recoil, slightly, in response. And so, in a rare conciliatory moment, I turned and offered him a small smile as well. Hell, I've dealt with worse in my day, and I'd be happy to work with that husky.

"Pru Marlowe." I didn't recognize the number, but it was local.

"Pru, thank God." Albert, sounding like he'd just run a four-minute mile.

"Albert, catch your breath." No matter what I thought about replacing him. I didn't want it to be because he'd keeled over from a coronary.

"Pru, no— " If anything, he was breathing heavier. "You can't let anyone know it's me."

I opened my mouth to respond to that one and then gave up. Calling from the cop shop, I gathered. Or a burner phone. "Okay," I drew it out, letting my hesitation ask the question for me. The heavy breathing the followed had me both worried and annoyed. "So?"

"Pru, Jim is saying there are other people who want to speak with me. He said, like it could be serious." His voice was still worryingly wheezy. "And what I want to know is—can they make me?"

I told him what I knew—fast and sweet. There was a limit to how long Creighton could hold him without charging him, and he should lawyer up. He seemed unclear about whether he was going to be arrested, and even why Creighton had been holding him.

"I think he's worried about me," he confessed. "He keeps asking me to talk to him. But, Pru, I can't."

All I could do was repeat my advice, and I made my exit after that, promising to get back to him with whatever I could find out. This was not the kind of conversation I wanted to have in front of a client and a potential client, never mind their pets. As it was, Bunbury was on alert. His sensitive ears had picked up the tension in my voice before he even tried to make sense of the words. The husky, meanwhile, had woken up a bit. Maybe the company—and the cat's lesson—had sparked something for him. At any rate, he now regarded me with those strange blue eyes, his head cocked at an inquisitive angle.

"I'm sorry," I apologized to the two humans, whose expressions were frankly just as curious as their animals'. "I'm afraid a colleague is in a situation." That was as vague as I could be. "Anyway, I need to help him out."

"It sounds like you're the person to know." Susan made it sound like a compliment, though I suspected she had her own needs in mind. "I'm glad we met."

"I am, too," I almost meant it. She would be an interesting client, at the very least. "I'm glad that Bun— Spot was found, and I look forward to working together again soon."

Walz, meanwhile, was watching me. I don't like to kid myself, but I felt that I'd made an impression. At any rate, he nodded slowly and held out his hand to me. "I may be in touch as well." He almost sounded impressed.

We shook, and I ducked down. In part, I wanted to take my leave of his dog, but I'll confess, I also wanted to hide my own satisfied smile. Men like that, once they realize you're competent, they start seeing you as an equal.

"Hey, big guy." I held out my hand once more.

"*Bear*," said the husky once more, sniffing my palm, and I realized what I had missed before. The sled dog was gifting me with his name. "Bear," I repeated quietly, my voice intended for only those fuzzy ears. As I stood, I saw Jack Walz regarding me curiously. One eyebrow rose in question and his thin lips pursed.

"Something about your dog," I said. I'm used to covering. "He made me think of a bear."

"That's his name." Walz nodded slowly. "I don't believe that I told you, but we call him Urso."

My smile felt a bit tight as I drove away. It's not that surprising clients is a bad thing, not usually. But I have reason to be protective of my secrets. When I first developed my sensitivity—or, as Wallis would have it, discovered the latent ability all of us have—I'd been sure my mind was shot. I'd been feverish for days, when I first heard Wallis, telling me I had to drink some water if I wanted to live. That's when I'd checked myself into the hospital, hoping the voices would go away.

They never did, and Wallis had been furious that I'd run out on her, leaving her to fend for herself locked in a city apartment for three days. What I did learn, however, was that I never wanted to be locked up again, for any reason. And I could not see any way in which having my sensitivity made public would not lead to—at the very least—a court-ordered evaluation. No, I needed to keep this part of my life private. And something about the way Jack Walz checked me out made me think that he was smart enough to see that something else was going on.

Wallis, of course, thought I was worrying needlessly.

"*He's a man.*" She purred as she made figure-eights around my legs. It had been a long day and, while she would never admit it, I believe she missed me.

"It wasn't that kind of look, Wallis." Granted, the fact that I was opening a can of tuna—the good stuff, packed in oil—probably helped. "Besides, he's at least twenty years older than me."

"*One-track mind.*" The purr didn't let up, giving her words a kind of rolling rhythm. "*Maybe you need to get out more?*"

I didn't respond, other than to empty the can into a saucer for her. She jumped neatly and nearly silently to the counter and began to eat, as I opened a second can for myself. "Well, what did you mean, then?"

"*Oh, please.*" I couldn't tell if her expostulation was in response to my dim-wittedness or because I was spooning mayo into my bowl. "*It's you.*" The answer was immediate, and tinged with the sharp fishy taste of the oil. "*What you should know is that the male of the species is always a bit slower on the uptake. They think 'We're the hunters; we're the ones who call the shots.'*"

I didn't argue with this, and if Wallis read any disagreement in my silent thoughts, she let it be. Instead, she worked on finishing the fish, licking the dish clean before proceeding to wash her whiskers until they glistened.

I ate my own meal, washing it down with a beer from the fridge, as various thoughts rumbled through my mind. I hadn't tried to call Albert back, partly because I wasn't sure Creighton or

Kayla or whoever answered the main line would put me through. Partly, because I didn't know what to say. Should he get himself an attorney? Of course, but I'd already told him that and been ignored. What he wanted was for me to fix it, I suspected, either through my connection to Creighton or simply because I was a woman, and thus the magical mommy archetype that men like him were always seeking.

That didn't help me figure out what role I wanted to play, though. Did I even want to insert myself into his particular mess? Did I care that with every misstep Albert was apparently digging himself in deeper? And what had the usually laidback town official so scared he wouldn't talk, even if it meant his liberty? These were questions that I still hadn't answered when Wallis looked up at me, licking her chops, before jumping down to the floor. I realized then as she made her way, tail high, to the door, that she knew the conversation would be continuing. The gravel of my driveway rattled under Jim Creighton's wheels.

Chapter Twenty-three

We have a pattern, Creighton and me. We don't talk, or not much. And when we do, we keep it light. I don't mean to say we don't care for each other. That wouldn't be accurate, not after this long, not considering some of the adventures we have shared. I mean, sure, there's a physical connection, but that's not all. It's more like we respect each other's privacy—a deal-breaker for me.

So it must have surprised my blue-eyed boy when, for the second time in a week, I began grilling him. We were lying in bed, sated by then, and Wallis, with her usual disregard for human modesty, had joined us.

"What's up with Albert?" I saw no point in beating around the bush. Besides, Creighton was drifting toward sleep. My window of opportunity was closing.

"You're thinking of Albert?" He flipped on his side and reached for me, a drowsy grin on his face, and nuzzled my neck. "Is it the beard?"

"No." I pushed him away, so I could look him in the eyes. "I'm serious, Jim."

His brows went up but he showed no signs of wanting to talk. At our feet, Wallis began to wash quite noisily. "*Real smart.*" Her comment had me reaching for an imaginary hair between my teeth. "*What? At least I know how to take care of myself.*"

"What you said the other night—you were right. I'm worried

about him." I propped myself up on one arm. I doubt Wallis had meant it that way, but her comment gave me my in. "That's why I've been pushing. He called me. He's scared."

The surprise on his face registered as real this time. I thought it was at my confession, until he started to speak. "Funny, he didn't want a phone call when we offered," he said, though he might have been covering. "I thought he was embarrassed in front of the guys. But, Pru, you know what he's got to do."

"I do." I sighed, falling back. Creighton meant Albert had to talk. I thought he should too—to a lawyer. And despite my confession, I still wasn't sure why I was getting involved exactly, except that I knew Albert hadn't been alone. "He's just kind of lost."

A grunt, and I pulled myself back up. "Come on, Jim. You know it, too. And I don't know what you're playing at by keeping him locked up. He thinks you're going to charge him. Or—I don't know—hold him indefinitely."

A storm must have started someplace up in the mountains, because suddenly the room grew chilly. Even as he continued to stare at me, those blue eyes inches from my own, I felt the wall of ice descending. Creighton was freezing me out.

"Jim." I didn't want our encounter to end like this—not again. I also thought I could still get something out of him. Old habits die hard. "He asked for my help, okay? I told him to get a lawyer, but you know Albert. He's…" I broke off, unsure how to describe the oblivious mess of a man. "Clueless," I said at last.

"Complicit is the word I would choose." His tone was as cold as his eyes. "Pru, there's a lot going on that you don't understand. That I don't either, come to think of it, but I'm trying. A man was killed, Pru. And I know you didn't think much of Paul Lanouette or his friends, but he was a human being."

Before I could protest, he was pushing the covers back and reaching for his jeans. "I get that you're loyal. That you work with the man. But this time, Pru, you've got to trust me. Just accept that your—ah—understanding of some of the animals out there only goes so far."

With his back toward me, it was hard to tell if he was talking about Albert or about himself. "Pru." He was buttoning his shirt. I could see his face in the mirror, but in the dark, his features were shadowed. "I don't ask you about how you do what you do. Do me the same courtesy, all right?"

My mouth had gone dry, and besides, I had no words, the memory of what he'd told me about Paul rushing back to my mind. Still it was a relief when my beau bent over and kissed me before leaving. "Early morning," he said, as if that explained everything. Even before I heard the front door close, Wallis had risen and taken his place on the pillow beside mine, where she resumed her evening toilette.

"*Good work.*" She slurped out the words, as she tamped down her white belly fur with a zealous tongue. "*If I didn't think you really took what that creature said seriously.*"

"Albert?" I watched as she extended one leg for inspection. "Or, no, do you mean Frank?"

"*Clueless.*" Working with her teeth as well as her tongue, she set to work on the curved claws of her left hind paw. "*Don't know why I bother...*"

I was missing something, at least Wallis thought so. She and I have lived together long enough for me to read her innuendo. But whether I really had overlooked information or she just decided to lord it over me that I'd sent my bed partner off out of concern for a bearded lout and his pet ferret, I couldn't tell. Besides, even as she concentrated on that paw, I needed to figure out what I'd just learned.

Creighton had wanted to freeze me out but he was too nice a guy—and I knew him too well. Looking back not only on what he'd said but how he'd said it, I could see that he'd decided to trust me—at least with a few confidences. Namely that he was trying to configure a larger scheme, one in which Paul Lanouette had been a player. And that whether my beau was going to charge Albert with his role in it eventually or not, he hadn't yet—and, boy scout that he was, he'd released the animal control officer to the wild. It had taken me a moment, but what'd he'd told me about Albert turning down the chance to make a call while in custody revealed that. Finally, in everything he'd said—and also in what he'd refused to say—my straight-shooter of a boyfriend had clued me in on another secret, letting me know that he had definitely sussed out more about me and my special sensitivity than I had previously been willing to admit.

Chapter Twenty-four

Wallis was snoring in the morning when I awoke, and it was a relief not to have to explain myself as I slipped out of the house and headed across town. If Albert was indeed out, I wanted to see him. Plus, I had questions for Frank. The ferret had been avoiding me, and I needed to know why.

"Wake up." I pounded on the door of Albert's apartment, my mood not improved by the bad takeout coffee I'd fetched from the gas station. "Come on, Albert. Open up."

"Hang on." The bleary mess who opened the door didn't inspire confidence. He had donned a robe, thank God, but neglected to tie it and the stains and tears on the t-shirt and boxers beneath did not bear close examination. I shoved one of the insulated cups into his hand and pushed my way into the room.

"Hoo boy." I reached for the shade, partly to let some light in but also so I could open the window. The room was close and smelled musty. And no, I did not think the ferret was to blame. "This isn't healthy."

Albert stood there blinking in his bathrobe, and I saw my chance. "Get dressed," I told him. "We've got to talk. In the meantime..." I looked around and saw the familiar masked face peeking up at me. The ferret knew my words were primarily for him, and I held out my hand. I couldn't resist a smile as the limber creature scurried up my arm to nestle around my neck. Maybe I had missed the cuddling last night, after all.

"Frank and I will wait outside," I said to the man who stood blinking in the light as I took the ferret, my own coffee, and a number of unanswered questions out to the street.

"*Sweet?*" I'd walked back to my car, the better to have a little distance from Albert's beastly lair. Our animal control officer is far from the brightest bulb in the closet, but I didn't want to risk anyone asking about why I was conversing with a non-human creature. Frank had scampered down my arm and was sniffing at the insulated cup. At least, that was what I think he was getting at, as his wet leather nose moved around the lid.

"No, I take it black," I said. "But Frank, we've got to talk."

The sinewy mustelid didn't answer, but I could tell from the way he had raised his head that he was listening.

"I'm on your side," I was pushing. "You should know that. But—you were hiding Albert's keys, weren't you?"

"*Sweet, juicy.*" He clambered around to where I leaned on the GTO, his claws finding no purchase on my car's flawless finish. "*Shiny. Open up.*"

"Frank." This was exasperating. I wasn't sure how to proceed. Animals don't lie, per se. That doesn't mean they are all forthcoming. Smaller animals, for example, are great at misdirection. You ever see a bird fake a broken wing to lure a predator away from her nest? But this act—

"Frank, is he feeding you?" It hit me, maybe the ferret really was searching for food.

"*I get what I need.*" The answer came immediately, along with an image of a fat grub that, frankly, put me off breakfast. "*Shiny.*"

I sighed. If the lithe beast didn't confide in me, I didn't know how to proceed. "Frank, you probably didn't mean to, but you may have made things worse. Creighton thinks Albert hid his keys—that he didn't want anyone to find the body in the shed." Even as I said it, I realized what a boneheaded move it would be. And perfectly in keeping with Albert's usual behavior.

"But that was you, wasn't it?" It also occurred to me that

perhaps Frank had intentionally sabotaged the man who, after all, was not the most conscientious caregiver.

"*Hungry!*" The retort came so swiftly I drew my arm back from where the ferret stood, alert, thinking I'd been bitten. He dropped back onto all fours, and began sniffling around the hood of my car, clearly distressed.

"You were hungry?"

"*No, he's the one. The one wanting.*"

"Yes, he is that." I was still confused, but I was also touched. Clearly, the ferret had feelings for the fat slovenly man. "But he gets what he needs."

"*Not the box!*" This time the response was physical. He was up on all fours, his back arching like a cat's. "*Can't let him!*"

I paused, unsure of what I was missing. "I know you don't want Albert to go to jail, Frank. But you're not helping him—"

"*He wants the shiny.*" The ferret was agitated now, jumping from paw to paw. "*He doesn't see the beast!*"

"Wait, what beast?" I know Wallis thinks I'm slow-witted but usually I can keep up. "The beast in the box?"

"We're getting something to eat?" I spun around and saw Albert, dressed now in his customary flannel and jeans. How long he'd been standing there, I didn't know.

"I was talking to Frank." The best defense is a good offense, but a cold trickle of sweat rolled down my spine. "Animals respond to our voices, you know. "

"Huh," Albert grunted as he waddled over to the side door, a torn knapsack in his hands. "Creighton still has my truck."

"You don't have an extra set of keys?" I nodded up at the apartment.

"I don't—I mean, this place is safe."

I didn't respond. Truth was, I doubted security was Albert's main concern. Besides, I had more pressing questions. I tried to make eye contact with Frank one last time as his person sidled awkwardly into my car and dropped the knapsack at his feet. The ferret had settled down by then, but the black eyes that met my own were opaque, the thoughts silent. However, when I opened my own door, he scurried inside, curling in Albert's lap like he owned the man.

Maybe he did. I might not understand what the supple little creature had been trying to say to me. I did get that he was as protective of Albert as any one of us would be of a beloved pet. And that meant that if I was going to help Frank, I needed to try once more with Albert.

"You going to tell me what's going on?"

Albert squirmed, as much from the ice in my voice as the acceleration as I put my baby-blue baby into gear and peeled out.

"Me?" His voice squeaked as he was thrust back into his seat. But if he thought he was going to flip my question, he didn't know me. Or, for that matter, the ferret, who dug his little claws into Albert's thigh. "Ow."

"You're making your ferret nervous." It was true. And my saying it also unsettled him, which was to my advantage. "Talk, Albert."

He shifted again in his seat and played with his beard. "Jim wanted me to talk to him, you know. But, I was thinking…"

"Don't think, Albert. You're not good at it." Silence. I corrected my course. Breakfast was out of the question until I was served some truth. "Albert?" I waited until he turned toward me. "Just because Creighton let you go doesn't mean this is over. I don't know if Creighton is preparing a warrant for your arrest or if the staties want to talk to you or what. I do know that you know more about what happened out there than you're telling him—or me, for that matter."

"I told you." He was trying for aggrieved and ended up sounding simply sulky. "I got a nuisance call about a bear."

"You did not." I wasn't having any of this, and my window of opportunity was closing. "Even assuming that you didn't log the call, which would be a dereliction of duty…" Another squirm.

"…there's no way that a bear out in the conservation land was bothering anybody. If anything, people would be bothering him.

"And besides, what about Paul? Are you going to deny that Paul was there with you, when you trapped that bear?"

"What? No." He shook his head, and I got a quick flash of how Frank saw it. How tempting it was to reach up and grab at that cascade of dirty fur. "I mean, I don't know anything about that."

"Uh huh." I'd known, of course, from the bear's vision. But Albert had just confirmed that at least he was aware of the presence of his late friend. "You guys weren't hanging around, drinking?"

"Well, maybe a little."

I didn't want to speculate on how much that might be. "Who was with you?" Silence. Frank had settled back down, but whatever he was thinking he was keeping from me. "I mean, besides Ronnie?"

"Yeah, Ronnie." I waited. "Me and Ronnie and—and Paul."

"And?" I was trying to prime this pump to flow on its own, but I was almost at the center of town and I'm congenitally incapable of driving slowly. "Was Larry Greeley with you?"

"What? No." A bit too fast, I thought. Creighton had downplayed Greeley's involvement, and Creighton is a good cop. But that didn't mean that Greeley had an alibi—only that Creighton hadn't fully interrogated him yet. And Creighton hadn't seen Greeley lurking around the moneyed side of town, like I had. I wasn't sure what the tall man with the ugly teeth was up to, but I knew it was to no good.

"No Larry?" I was a block from our destination.

Albert snorted. "He wishes."

I stopped at that—hitting the brakes with a squeal that nearly threw Albert out of his seat—and turned to him. "Because one of your friends ended up dead?" Sometimes, I swear, the man amazed me.

"No, I didn't— that wasn't what I meant." He sounded so

flustered, I kind of believed him. At any rate, I started to drive again. "I still can't believe that's true, Pru. I mean, Paul was—we were just hanging out."

"Ah huh." I was sure that was how it started. "And drinking and then?"

"And then I must've passed out. Honest, Pru. I don't know what happened."

"So you passed out, and Ronnie and Paul were still there." I figured Creighton had to know this much.

"No," Albert was shaking his head again. "I think Ronnie had taken off by then."

"Not Paul?"

He shrugged. If he were a turtle, he would have tucked his head inside his shell. "Paul was—you know, Paul." I did, but I wasn't letting Albert off the hook. "He had a plan," he said at last. "You know, one of his—deals."

"Deals?"

Another nod, another shrug. "To get some dough."

"With the bear?"

Albert frowned, as if confused.

"*Not* with the bear?"

I thought of Frank's agitation—all his worry about "the beast."

"I don't know. Honest." When someone says that, I know he's lying. "But, I don't think so. I think it was—" He broke off as we passed Beauville's lone bus station. "Pru, do you think—?"

"No." I held up my hand. "Finish your sentence."

"I don't know nothing." He addressed the ferret in his lap. Frank was strangely silent.

I was done. "Have you spoken to a lawyer yet?"

"Me?" Another squeak. "No, I don't—I mean, those guys are expensive. Anyway, I thought, you know, maybe because you know Jim?"

"Forget it." I growled. That was an even worse idea than he could ever know. "Look, Albert, if you're charged, the state has to appoint a public defender for you. But it still makes sense for you to talk to someone first. I'll see if I can get any referrals. There's probably a legal clinic in Amherst that might be able to help."

"Amherst?" I could tell from his voice that the reality was beginning to sink in. I had pulled up at the modern brick building that housed animal control by then, and he shifted in his seat to face me. "Pru, maybe I'll just—you know—turn things over to you for a few days?"

"Albert—" I didn't know how to break it to him. The man had some serious deficits.

"I mean, I've got my things with me. Maybe, after we get something to eat, you could give me a ride back to the bus station?" Even Frank appeared to be waiting on me, his ears pitched forward in hope.

"Albert, no." I parked the car and, as a precaution, pocketed the keys. "In fact, we're not going to breakfast. And you're not coming into the office. You're going to do the right thing and go back and tell everything to Jim."

There was some squealing after that, both from Albert and from Frank, who was probably more upset at his person's sudden bolt for the door. But I'm a lot more limber than my portly colleague, and I was there to take his arm when he finally managed to stand and extricate himself from both the seat and the ferret.

"Look," I said, "maybe he'll just take your statement and let you go." I didn't believe it myself, but I hadn't gotten that much out of Creighton the previous night. "Don't you want to find out what happened to Paul?"

The whimper I heard in response told me more than Albert intended. Creighton was right—the bearded man I had hold of was in the thick of it.

"Pru, Albert." Creighton was talking to Kayla when we walked in, me with my hand as firm on Albert's arm as if I were guiding any large animal into a cage. "Thanks for coming in."

"Oh, I'm just the taxi service." I kept my voice level, my

eyes on Creighton's baby blues. "In fact, I'm going to take off now. Got mouths to feed, you know. But Albert here has had a change of heart."

I was rewarded by a flash of Creighton's dimples. "Come on in, Albert. You've got some more to say?"

The expression on the bearded man's face was much less amused. If I had to categorize it, I would have said, he looked in fear for his life.

It wasn't until I stepped outside that I realized he'd left Frank behind. As I walked toward the GTO, I saw him, standing on his hind feet, craning for a view through the passenger window, and watching the man who was the center of his existence as he was led away.

Chapter Twenty-five

"I guess it's you and me." After a moment's hesitation, I started the GTO and began to drive. Partly, that's my default mode: when in doubt, step on the gas. Partly, I couldn't see any other option. I didn't necessarily want the ferret accompanying me on my rounds. But he'd been left alone in the town office too often recently. Besides, I had a strong sense that he wanted something from me.

What it was, I didn't know. As I pulled away, Frank leaped from the passenger seat into the tiny backseat of my car. In my rearview I could see him peering through the rear window until the cop shop was out of sight, his obvious longing tugging at my heartstrings as no mere human's could do.

His presence—especially standing on the back upholstery, holding himself up with his tiny hands as I accelerated—also pulled at my sense of responsibility. Under normal circumstances, I wouldn't have let any animal roam my car as I was driving. It certainly wouldn't do to have any of my clients see us riding around together, like this. But these weren't normal circumstances and Frank was not any animal. Besides, I felt for him, seeing his person taken away like that—another beast to be caged. "Albert must know you're with me, right?"

The advantage of my sensitivity is that I knew the dark-eyed beast could understand me. The disadvantage is I could also tell that he was now ignoring me. "Frank?"

Nothing. As I drove, he slipped back into the passenger seat, slinking between the two front buckets so smoothly I barely felt the brush of his sleek fur. But all I got in response to my repeated queries were muttered chirpings of anxiety and despair. Even without a clear answer, I had a good idea what was bothering him. He was worried about his person, and at some level, I suspected, he blamed me for not coming to Albert's aid.

"Hey, I tried to help him." I was getting defensive. I didn't need to justify myself to the ferret. I wasn't the one who had trapped a bear and—just maybe—been involved in a murder. And I had given Albert my best advice. But here I was, making excuses. Wallis would have a field day, but I couldn't help but be moved by the little creature's loyalty and distress. "He's got to tell me—or, better yet, Jim—what happened out there."

"*The beast.*" The mutterings formed a word in my mind—a feeling of dread and threat—but they didn't provide an answer. "*He's in danger.*"

That wasn't what I had expected, having walked Albert into the local precinct—or "box" as the ferret had dubbed it—and for a moment I doubted my special sense. "*Danger*" was different from "*cage.*" Then again, perhaps in the ferret's experience, the two were connected. After all, Frank had been in Albert's car all that day, and I didn't know what his experience of the bear had been. Between the trapped animal's panic and fear, there must have been heady mix of menace and pheromones in the air.

All I did know was that the ferret's day out in the woods had deeply unsettled him. I resisted the urge to reach out and stroke his silky fur. To soothe his mind as I smoothed his glossy coat. I wasn't sure how such a, well, human gesture would be received. Better I should be honest and straightforward.

"Albert's not in danger from that bear." I put it as plainly as I could. "Not anymore."

"*Bear?*" The question caught me off guard, and I glanced down. The black eyes that met mine were bright with curiosity, and I bit back my usual sarcastic retort. Animals don't dissemble. It's one of the reasons I prefer them to most humans. Clearly, I had confused him, thinking in words that might not have any meaning to a ferret. Instead, I tried to conjure up an image of the bear, as I'd first seen him.

"*Danger, danger...*" It was too much. Frank was growing agitated —and I had arrived at Tracy Horlick's house.

"It's okay," I said, and this time I did reach out to pet him, hoping he would sense my good intentions through my fingertips just as I picked up the tension in his muscular body. I looked up at the Horlick house. "I promise. Hang on for a bit, and we'll talk some more."

And leaving the window ever so slightly ajar, I went off to start my rounds.

If I hadn't known better, I'd have thought Tracy Horlick could smell something on me. Frank or, more likely, Albert, whose funk had permeated my car during the brief drive. The woman's ever-present Marlboro bobbed below her snout, however, and so I went with the assumption that the audible sniff with which she greeted me was in response to that smoke, rather than any olfactory insight.

"Good morning." It would take more than a nonverbal slight to faze me. "And how are we this morning?"

"*We* are exhausted." Her voice did sound more hoarse than usual. "I don't know what you did to Bitsy, but he was up half the night, barking and carrying on."

"Is he okay?" As soon as the question was out of my mouth, I realized how pointless it was. This was a woman who locked her dog in the basement overnight. "Have you taken him to a vet?"

"*He's* fine." She sneered, her eyes narrowing further, although, again, that could have been in response to the smoke. "*I'm* the one who's suffering."

I bit back my response. There was no winning here, and I didn't want to cause Growler any more hardship than he already had to bear.

"I understand." I managed to get the words out. I really wanted to see the bichon, to find out what had actually happened. But the way to the dog was through his person, and clearly the old harridan wanted some sympathy. "Would you tell me what happened?"

Another sniff, and she reached up for her cigarette, flicking the ash into the long-suffering boxwood. We were standing on her stoop—or I was, she leaned on her doorframe like a gorgon standing guard. And although I was doing my best to appear interested in whatever she had to say, I was listening intently for any sign from behind her—any clue at all to what was happening with the little white dog.

"*Growler?*" I tried to think a query—visualized us walking down to the river. I could almost hear his sharp exclamatory bark.

"...what you did that left him so riled up." The image disappeared into one of pursed lips, the caking lipstick sinking into the cracks.

"Excuse me?" From the way those lips tightened, I knew she was waiting for a response. "I'm sorry." I gave her that. "I thought I heard Growl— Bitsy, and well, I'm worried about him."

"He's *fine*." She growled, exhaling smoke. "But I thought you said you could socialize animals. I mean, what do I pay you for?"

To exercise your dog, I could have said. But this confused me. "I'm sorry." I was repeating myself this morning. "I didn't know Bitsy had any behavioral issues."

"He didn't." She took a long drag. "Before. That's what I'm talking about."

"Yes, his disruptive behavior." I didn't have to have heard her whole story to echo back the part that mattered.

"All day, after you left." She nodded. "And I was trying to entertain."

I could only imagine. "Maybe he was reacting to your guests?"

Her eyes narrowed and so I rushed to follow up. "Like a guard dog." It was easier than explaining territoriality—not to mention the frustration of an animal who can smell and hear new creatures in his space but cannot interact.

"Guard dog." Another sniff, and it occurred to me. Maybe she simply had a sinus condition. However, whether she was dismissing my theory that Growler was trying to protect her or—more likely—that he could, she seemed to have vented enough. Without another word, she turned and walked back into her house, and I relaxed. She would release Growler from his basement imprisonment now, and I'd get to the bottom of what had happened.

"*Took you long enough!*" The white fluffball bounded down the hall. But despite what Tracy Horlick might think, he was too well disciplined to set off on his own. Instead, he stood at attention, his tail vibrating with eagerness, as I clipped on his lead. "*Letting that weasel lead you around like that....*"

"Now don't go getting him riled up." His person's voice had a hint of a threat in it. "I won't stand for that kind of behavior from an animal. Nor will my friends."

I pasted a grimace on my face and hoped it would pass for a smile. Threatening me was one thing. I was almost used to it. But threatening a dog? No, Tracy Horlick was pushing too far.

"I'm sorry, Growler." I waited until we were down the walk and near the corner, where the bichon stopped to sniff a tree. I didn't know what had happened. I was simply empathizing with his plight. "And about Frank—the ferret. I work with his person."

"*Huh! A ferret.*" I got a wave of animals and their associations as he took in the scent, and then watered the tree to add his own. "*That little weasel is hunting way out of his league.*"

Did Frank blame the bear? It was an interesting take, and one that would be worth pursuing. Only just then, Growler locked in on a new scent. "*Louis, you've got to stop chasing after her. She's spayed.*"

I stifled my amusement—and my curiosity. The bichon deserved his privacy, as well as such social interactions as his situation would allow. The thought did spark another one, though.

Who had Tracy Horlick been entertaining? And why had her dog reacted as he did?

"*You get it, right?*" The question startled me. Of course, Growler had picked up on my thoughts. He was the dog in question. "*That I had...concerns?*"

"I figured." I glanced down, but the bichon's black button eyes were focused on a squirrel, frozen in place across the street.

"*Prey.*" I heard him mutter, as if to himself. "*Wild...prey.*"

Notwithstanding what the old lady had said, I let him take the lead—and he made a beeline across the street and down toward the river. The squirrel was long gone by the time we trotted across. It didn't matter. Growler was in his element—a creature of scent and sound immersing himself in an environment so much richer than the one he had at home. No, Tracy Horlick was dead wrong. If Growler had any issues, they were caused by a lack of stimulation. Just because he was a small dog, didn't meant he was made to live in a small world

"*Small world, heh!*" With a snuffling grunt, the bichon once again inserted himself into my thoughts. "*Very small, isn't it?*"

"I know." I thought of the basement and of the bare, fenced-in yard—more dirt than garden—where Tracy Horlick let him out to relieve himself. Beauville might feel claustrophobic to me, but at least I was here by choice. Plus, my mind drifted to the night before, I had more social options than poor Growler did.

"*Small world, indeed.*"

I stopped, and he turned to lock eyes with me. But there was more than the expected reprimand in those shiny black buttons. Yes, I had interrupted our passage down to the water. That wasn't all, though. "What?" I asked.

"*Clueless.*" He dug his nose under the last fall's leavings and I got a strong sense of rot and leaf mold. "*No sense at all.*"

"Sorry." I was just out of it today, clearly, and so even as we walked on, I began to backtrack. "Small world?" I asked finally. "You don't mean—Creighton?"

I was under no illusion that Tracy Horlick was a threat to me, not in that way. But could my favorite local cop have come by to question to the chain-smoking old harpy?

"*Beast,*" was all I got back "*Wild beast...*" Growler, at least, was at peace.

On the walk back uphill I had more time to think. The little dog was sated, his nose and mind full of the wonders of the outdoors. I got images of squirrels and rats. There was a fox who had caused some confusion—he was attractive to the bichon but also, somehow, threatening. That was when it occurred to me—that the "small world" comment and Tracy Horlick's "guests" might be joined in another way: Albert, for example. Or—more likely—Larry Greeley. I'd seen him cruising around the moneyed neighborhood, but I didn't put it past him to prey on his own. As we made our way up the walk, I made a mental note to check out Tracy Horlick's lawn. She wasn't the sort to throw money away—she had driven a hard bargain with me for my services, and only my sympathy for Growler had kept me coming back—but I could imagine her falling prey to flattery from a younger man, even one with bad teeth.

Then again, maybe they deserved each other. I watched as Growler's pace changed from a happy jog to something slower and more resigned. Well, at least the old shrew would think I'd tired him out. Still, I felt my own heart sink as I prepared to hand his lead over to the evil woman who waited by the door.

"*Beast,*" said Growler. I had to agree.

Chapter Twenty-six

I extricated myself from Tracy Horlick as quickly as I could. "I don't want to keep my other clients waiting."

Growler had frozen at that, halfway down the hall, and turned to take me in with his large dark eyes. *"Clients?"*

"The ferret." I let myself picture the slender brown creature, the mask over his eyes, and his cream-colored snout. It was too late, though, and I realized I should have questioned the bichon more when we had the chance. Now I had only his inquisitive glance, and his human gatekeeper exhaling smoke in my face.

"Interesting to see that you care about some of your clients." She took a deep drag, her eyes almost closing with the pleasure. "The ones who've bought up all those new houses, I'm betting." She let it out, and I stifled a cough.

"I try to be courteous and professional with all my clients." I didn't know why I bothered. She wasn't going to fire me. She enjoyed tormenting me too much, and besides, I was a more reliable dog-walker than any kid left in the neighborhood would be. "And loyal," I added for good measure. Call it a hint.

"Lot of good that'll do you." The corners of her mouth turned up, like she'd just eaten a tasty bug. She knew something, that much was clear. And I thought once again about the rumored competition. What I didn't know was how to get any information out of her, short of asking—and I'd be damned if I did that. It didn't matter. I'd provided enough amusement for her to start her day. Either that, or she had other plans—the much-vaunted "entertaining" she'd spoken about. Because as I stood there, blinking in the smoke and trying to conjure up a comeback, she closed the door in my face. A moment later, I heard a sharp yip—"*Watch out!*"—and I could only hope that she hadn't vented her spleen on the white bichon as well.

One of these days, I'd come up with an excuse to remove Growler but not until I could find another home for him—and certainly not without his consent. Still, it was with a heavy heart that I walked back toward my car. I'd parked a few houses over, where a mature oak cast its shade on the street and far enough away so I didn't have to worry that old lady Horlick would get a glimpse of Frank inside. As I approached my GTO, I realized I needn't have worried. The ferret had enough sense to stay out of the window, now that he was no longer pining for his person. In fact, I didn't see the slender brown animal at all as I walked up to the car and opened the door.

"Hey, Frank," I slid into my seat and started the engine. No sense in risking funny looks from the old harridan's neighbors either. "I'm sorry to have left you so long."

Despite the shade and my precaution of leaving the windows ajar, the inside of the car was steamy. Automobiles are sweat boxes, and can be lethal for animals, and I knew I'd been breaking most of my own rules by leaving him here. When he didn't respond right away, I felt a clutch of fear. "Frank?" I craned around in my seat. "Are you okay?"

A moment later, I had thrown the emergency brake and was on my knees, peering under the seats and dashboard. Only after I'd checked the glove compartment and then the trunk not once but twice did I collapse against the side of my car and admit the truth. The ferret was gone.

Chapter Twenty-seven

"Frank!" I kept my voice low, hoping that the urgency of my plea would serve to amplify it as I walked around the car. "Where are you?"

This had never happened—not to me. I'd never lost an animal in my care. I'd certainly never lost one whom I had a relationship with—whom I thought of as a friend. With everything that had been going on recently, I had to consider the possibility of foul play. Would someone have stolen the ferret? Or could a non-human predator have grabbed the agile little beast?

No, both were unlikely—at least as long as Frank had remained in my car. Frank was a sociable little fellow, but he'd be quite capable of biting anyone who reached for him when he didn't want to be picked up. And although ferrets are small, as predators go, and would certainly be at risk out in the wild, I couldn't imagine a coyote or bobcat poking through the gap in the window to claw the poor fellow out.

The gap in the window. That was the only other option: Frank had taken off on his own. I'd known he was upset, and that he'd felt that I had failed him somehow. Now, despite all our projection, animals aren't vengeful—they don't hold grudges. So I didn't think he'd taken off to scare me or to punish me somehow. No, he'd left for a reason. Frank was going to do whatever it was he'd thought I should have done. But short of breaking Albert out of jail, I wasn't sure what exactly that was.

I also realized I had to leave. Up the road, I could see Tracy Horlick, now in what looked like a velour track suit, fumbling with the keys to her own car. I couldn't see explaining to her why I was leaning against my own ride with a dumbfounded expression on my face. I certainly didn't want her speculating on her own. And so, with a last muted plea—"please, Frank, let me know where you are!"—I drove slowly around the corner and waited until she passed by before parking, once more to think.

Specifically, to think like a ferret. Yes, I know, I can "hear" what animals are saying. But too often, as Wallis is quick to remind me, I put my own cast on their thoughts—interpreting them in terms of my own desires or fears. Clearly, I had been doing this as I drove to my morning appointment. Frank had been agitated, and I'd assumed he was worried about Albert—and infuriated that I wasn't doing enough.

In truth, that may have been my sense of guilt—some vestigial feeling of community or social obligation—pasted on top of what the ferret was really trying to let me know. In fact, the more I thought about it, the likelier it seemed he'd given up on me. Why else would he have gotten so upset? I know animals well enough to be pretty sure I'd gotten that right, and why else would he have run off, while I was working?

Unless his disappearance had nothing to do with me. I took a deep breath and made myself consider that once again I was wrong. Maybe Frank had gotten bored or felt caged. Maybe he had spied a fledgling fluttering about and thought he could snag a quick meal. Maybe a female had passed upwind. Frank might have been neutered, but the urge never really goes away. Or maybe the lithe creature didn't care or understand that I expected him to wait for me, seeing the open car window as an invitation to adventure.

"Frank, where are you?" The one thing I could count on was the little animal's instincts for self-preservation. Surely, he would have enough sense not to, well, hare off into the wild. Wouldn't he?

I was trapped by my own indecision. Part of me wanted to remain in place, certain that Frank would come back eventually and expect to find me there. Part of me wanted to run into the woods. For surely that was where he would be in the most danger—and thus in the greatest need of any intervention I could provide. What I didn't consider was going on about my day. Not with Frank missing.

Which was why, the first time Susan Felicidad called, I let it go to voice mail. Yes, I'd arranged to work with her cat today, but I was in no mood for training an already quite self-reliant feline, no matter how much fun it might be. The second time she called, I did the same, although this time I started formulating excuses. Telling a potential client that I'd lost someone's beloved pet was not going to cut it. Not that I had any better idea of what to do, besides waiting here and wondering what had gone wrong.

Then it hit me. As my phone pinged through the sequence of numbers, calling the cat's equally self-possessed person back, I worked on my spiel. Felines have an excellent sense of smell. In fact, it was likely Bunbury's nose that had gotten him in trouble in the first place, luring him off with the promise of adventure, if not game. And tracking was a team effort—one that required coordination between human and animal. Discipline, too, because the tracking animal had to remain aware of his person and not run off, no matter how tempting the scent might be. The spotted cat and I had already developed an understanding, and now I saw how I could put it to work. I would tell Bunbury's person that I was going to take her cat for a walk—and then utilize the feline's sensitive nose to trace Frank.

It was perfect. Even neutered, Frank had a bit more scent than your average house cat, and so following him wouldn't be that much of a challenge. Besides, although Bunbury would be able to track Frank, the ferret wouldn't necessarily see him as a threat—nor, what might be just as important, my working with him as a betrayal. And the cat would get some training and a bit of exercise as well. All I needed to do was convince the human involved to let me drive off with her pet.

"Mrs. Felicidad?" I was so eager, I was nearly panting. And while my human clients might not be as sensitive as their animal companions, I knew I needed to tamp my excitement down lest I alarm her. "I'm sorry I missed your call. But I'm on my way over now. In fact, I have an idea."

"Oh, well, actually—" She paused, and my heart sank. If I didn't have access to her cat, I wasn't sure what I would do. Break into Tracy Horlick's house and recruit Growler?

"I'm hoping today still works to continue our training," I cut in before she could go much further. "In fact, I've set something up that I think will be wonderful—and that Spot will enjoy immensely." I was selling it hard and had to work to keep my voice level. "Do you realize that felines have an excellent sense of smell?"

"Why, yes, dear." She chuckled, but there was something a little off about her laughter. She was nervous, or tense. I'd pushed too hard.

"I'm sorry." A large part of what I do is listening to the humans who pay me. That's more difficult than communing with their animals. With a sinking feeling, I asked the obvious question. "Would you like to tell me what's up?"

Please don't cancel, I was thinking. Please don't even ask if you can reschedule. Not today. But even as I pleaded with any benevolent deities out there, I could picture Wallis. Cats don't roll their eyes. They don't have to. The dead stare she'd give me if she heard me like this would carry enough scorn to freeze a kitten in its tracks.

"Well, it's kind of funny that you should be talking about Spot's hunting abilities." Strain and worry, too, tightened her voice as she spoke, but also—was it?—a note of pride? "In fact, I was calling to see if you could come over a bit earlier today. Dear Spot seems to have cornered an animal of some sort. Right now, they're facing each other. I thought I'd simply grab him, but he growled at me, and I'm not sure what to do."

That was it. My dilemma resolved. I was worried about Frank. Terrified that he might have gotten himself into trouble. But all I knew for sure was that he was gone. Bunbury—Spot, as she called him—was facing a real threat. Although the dark-haired widow couldn't describe exactly what her cat was facing, the brief description of the feline's behavior—"he's growling, you see, and his whole body is all tensed up"—suggested a predator of some sort. A threat, at least in the cat's mind, to his person and to his home. And while Bunbury could probably hold a few smaller predators at bay—a fox, perhaps, and maybe a fisher—he was not going to keep anything else back for long. I needed to get over there and fast.

I was grateful, for once, for the location of the new development. It might not have made sense to put these luxury homes right around the stone outcropping from old Beauville, but it did get me there fast, even though I—unlike the noisy crow who greeted my arrival—had to get back on the county road and off at the new exit, rather than climb directly up the hillside.

"Mrs. Felicidad," I called to her as I jumped out of my car, the engine hot and ticking. "Where is he?"

"There." She pointed, her hands shaking slightly. "We were out gardening, and he was being so good. I wasn't using the leash." She looked at me, as if expecting disapprobation, but I nodded, willing her to go on. "Then he started growling and his fur stood on end—and he dashed off. I called, like you said. And when I went to see..."

I cut her off, not wanting to waste anymore time. "Please, wait here." If there was carnage, I would deal with it. What a bobcat or coyote could do to a cat was not anything that his person needed to see. Instead, I followed her gaze toward the hedge where the feline had challenged the husky, only the day before. At that memory, hope flared briefly—but, no. Susan Felicidad had seen some kind of wild animal in there. Not the big dog.

"Bunbury?" My voice, level and deep, would alert him of my presence. I reached out, hoping to pick up a sense that the cat was alive and well. "What do we have here?"

"*Danger! Danger! Danger!*" I didn't need any special sensitivity to pick that up. The cat was overexcited to the point of spitting.

"What is under there?" I approached slowly. I didn't have any tools—no net, no leather gloves—a lapse I was kicking myself for now. "Hello?"

As I've noted, I'm no good with wild animals. Their minds may not be that different from their domestic peers, but they haven't spent generations learning to read us. Still, I tried to reach out—to take in whatever was out there, as the spotted feline must have. And what I got was fear and confusion. That was normal for a forest creature, coming face to face with a yapping domestic dog. And also—could it be embarrassment?

"Frank?" I sat down on the lawn, hard. "Is that you?"

"*You didn't—you didn't understand.*" Yes, although I could barely see his masked face beneath the hedge, I could now clearly hear him. "*I had to go!*"

"Yes, I gather you did." Relief washed over me, draining me of whatever energy I had left. But a quick glance back at Mrs. Felicidad reminded me that simply introducing these two small creatures would not suffice. "Bunbury? You need to calm down."

"*Danger!*" He was trembling, he was so tense.

"Yes, I know." I reached out gingerly, all the while aware that if I was bit, it would be my fault. "Good boy. Good."

"*Suspect?*"

"Of course you did, but everything is safe here now, Bunbury." I was speaking softly, using low and calming tones. My voice, as much as my words, were pitched to comfort him. "There is no danger now. No threat."

A squeak from under the hedge. Frank was standing, his body arched in alarm. "*But there is!*"

Chapter Twenty-eight

"Frank, stop it!" I was practically hissing. Wallis would have been proud, but the ferret only stared. "This is nonsense. Bunbury is a friend!"

At this, the cat—who had stopped hissing when I sat down beside him—turned to look at me. Considering me in a new light, he titled his head at a quizzical angle.

"*You know this…this…?*"

"Ferret." I provided the word. "Frank, Bunbury. Bunbury, Frank." It wasn't the most gracious introduction I'd ever made. Then again, by that point, I was on my knees in the dirt, leaning under the hedge to better intercede with the agitated mustelid and painfully aware of the worried woman behind me. "Now, will you two cut it out?"

The cat gave a soft, final whine, and the ferret settled, resting his long body on the ground as he waited for my next move. "Hang on." I was still speaking softly, but forcefully. This was a command, not a request.

"Everything's fine." I turned and called over my shoulder. "In fact, Spot has done us a favor."

"Are you sure?" The woman took a step forward.

"Of course." I snapped back. I couldn't help it. I needed to settle this before the other human on the scene got too close. "Now, Bunbury, chill, okay? And, Frank, come here."

He stared at me—they both did—but I wasn't taking no for an answer. I needed to be able to explain the feline's behavior to his person, and I sure wasn't letting the ferret out of my sight again. "*Now!*"

With a whine of annoyance that Wallis would surely have recognized, the slinky mustelid came out from under the bush. Making a wide circle around the still-bristling cat, he came toward my hand and climbed my arm to the shoulder. "*You didn't listen...*" His chittering right by my ear made the cat's ears twitch.

"Later," I whispered, as I stood and turned to the waiting woman. "Spot is a hero," I said. Keeping one hand on the ferret, I walked toward her—only to see her stumble backward.

"What is that?"

"Not what, who." I kept my tone jovial and light, all the while silently asking Frank to just bear with me. "This is Frank. He's a masked ferret—and a friend."

Out of the corner of my eye, I could see Bunbury. His round face stared up at us, full of pride and excitement. He understood praise, in any language, and as his fur settled, he had begun to purr.

"Frank got out." I left the details vague. "But he's as much a house pet as, well, Spot here." The ferret on my shoulder began to whine, and I clamped my hand down further. I knew what I was saying was insulting and that he was bothered. "Please," I tried to direct my thoughts, "let me deal with this situation first."

The woman before me didn't appear convinced.

"You can imagine how relieved his person will be." *If he knew that Frank was missing*, I supplied the missing words silently. "After all, think of how you felt when Spot got lost."

"Yes, I—I guess so." A smile and the hint of a laugh. We were over the hill. "And I guess I should give Spot a little reward for all his good work."

"That's never a bad idea," I said. It isn't. Positive reinforcement not only works better in training, it tightens the bond between a human and her animal. I was preparing to expound on this—along the same lines, it helps when clients understand my training philosophy. You could say that by bringing them in, I give them a little treat too. Only as I did, I felt Frank begin to get restless. Tiny claws were itching to climb over me and down...

"But I think we'd better reschedule our session." Fishing my keys out of my pocket with my free hand, I nodded toward the ferret on my shoulder. "I should give Frank a ride home first."

"Of course." Susan Felicidad appeared relieved. I know that Frank is a well socialized and thoughtful companion. To her, I feared, he resembled a weasel a bit too much for comfort. "Maybe tomorrow?"

"That would be great." I needed to get out of there. The ferret was fussing, a low, anxious whine right by my ear. "*No, not done, not done...*" I clamped down tighter as I reached my GTO, angled up toward the neat lawn in my haste. Well, all's well, I turned once more to say my farewells.

"See you tomorrow, Spot," I called, wanting to leave an impression with the cat as well as his mistress. He had begun to knead the ground in joy. "*Treats!*"

"Mrs. Felicidad?" I stood, the question popping into my head. "If I may, did you post a reward when Spot went missing?"

"No." She shook her head, the smile growing broader. "There wasn't time. Though I might have."

I turned back to my car. It had been a random thought, the result of too much input and too little time to digest it all.

"But I did give a little something to the young man who found her." A confession, touched with embarrassment. City people, not knowing the rules. "It seemed only right. Don't you think?"

Chapter Twenty-nine

"You are going to tell me what's going on." I wasn't taking any chances. I had the windows rolled up as I drove, never mind that the vent air only amplified the musty aroma of ferret and scared human. "What all that was about."

"*Don't you see? Don't you see?*" The ferret was still agitated. Although he remained in the front seat, he was pacing back and forth, reaching up to stare out the window as I drove. "*There's a threat! Danger!*"

"There's danger out there, all right." I had smiled and reassured the woman that, indeed, her generosity had been justified. After all, it was quite possible that my suspicions were more a result of my own dark psyche than of anything nefarious going on. That didn't mean I wasn't going to follow up. "But I don't think it involves you."

"*Not me!*" The agile little beast was growing frantic. "*Not about me! Beard...*"

"Albert." Of course. I should have realized. The ferret was worried about his person. After all, he had seen him taken away—caged, a concept any animal could understand. How that tied in with what I suspected, I didn't quite understand.

"Do you think he's tied up in some kind of scam?" I didn't want to take my eyes off the road. I didn't need to. I could feel the ferret's agitation subside slightly as he considered the question and—just as important—realized that I was taking his concerns seriously.

"*He's not...*" More chittering and then that anxious whine again. "*He means well.*"

That wasn't what Frank was saying. Not exactly. But I was getting a sense of affection. Of food and warmth shared between the two, and of time spent enjoyably in each other's presence. In its way, it was a relationship, as companionable and mutual as anything Jim Creighton and I shared. No wonder the poor beast was worried.

"But what were you trying to do?" I would put aside my own fear. The horrible panic I had felt when the ferret had gone missing. Clearly, Frank had his own reasons for going AWOL. "What were you trying to find?"

"*The beast.*" The whine was revving up, as the ferret grew more alarmed again. "*Danger. Danger!*"

"It's okay." I needed to calm him down and find another way in. "You're safe."

"*No!*" Frank wasn't buying it. "*Trap!*"

"Wait." I pulled over to the curb. I needed to understand what was going on. And if anyone saw me talking to a ferret, well, I would deal with that later. "Frank, what is it? What did you think you could do?"

"*Trap!*" Frank was so upset that instead of the usual phrases, I was getting pure emotion. Combined with the whine and his agitated hopping, this was the equivalent of him yelling at me—or having a panic attack.

"Is this about the bear?" Surely, the little ferret couldn't have been thinking to find the bear in the woods. What would he have done? Did he expect the wild animal to come and, well, bear witness about what had happened that day?

"*No! Not the bear!*" Frank was positively screaming. "*The man! The man!*"

"I understand." He was scared, but I didn't dare reach out

to touch him, as much as I wanted to smooth his fur. Instead, I tried to pitch my voice in a reassuring tone. Calming—steady and low. "I'm going to take you home, to Albert's place," I said.

That only set him off again, hopping and, yes, hissing like a cat.

"Please, Frank. Calm down. Believe it or not, Albert's safe." I knew he picked up on my meaning. Whether he shared my confidence was another matter. To try to soothe the harried beast, I thought about Creighton. Yes, he and I were often at odds, but I had no doubt he was an honorable man. He would treat Albert fairly, and he wasn't likely to do anything until he had a good command of the facts. "In fact, after I take you home, and I'm going to see if I can find out what exactly is going on."

A low whine interrupted me, and I looked up confused. That's when it hit me. Frank didn't necessarily understand the difference between an investigation and an indictment. He probably didn't care if Albert had been arrested, or simply brought in to answer questions. Maybe the ferret wasn't concerned about Albert getting a fair trial. Maybe Frank was worried about Albert because he thought his person was guilty.

Chapter Thirty

There was no point in trying to hide my surprise. The sleek creature in my passenger seat probably read me better than most other humans, including my own mother. But I couldn't help turning over my newfound realization in my mind as I pulled back onto the road and began—rather slowly, for me—to drive.

"I thought you didn't see what happened…" It was a statement, rather than a question. Still, I waited for an answer. "That you were worried, because Albert was asleep."

"*Hungry.*" It wasn't the response I expected. But Frank was already moving about, obviously frustrated by my inability to understand. "*The man…the box.*"

And maybe I was reading the ferret's signals wrong. "He's not in a cage." I tried to explain. "Not exactly. And they'll feed him." Not as often or in the quantity he was used to, I was sure. But that might not be a bad thing, considering the animal control officer's girth.

"*No! Hungry…*" I was definitely missing something, and Frank was growing increasingly upset again. Then it hit me. Animals, unlike us, live in a continuous present. It means they can survive despite terrorizing odds. It also means they have problems communicating tenses.

"You're saying Albert was hungry?" I thought back to the scene. He hadn't trapped the bear for food. And he certainly hadn't killed his friend for—"Wait, you mean, he wanted some-thing." Hunger would be a catch-all word to an animal. Although ferrets are known to covet toys and shiny objects, they would still, like any animal, think in terms of food. "You mean, greedy?"

My passenger turned away, though whether in frustration or dismay I couldn't tell.

"Albert wanted something." I tried again. The flash of warmth that came in response convinced me I was on the right track.

"*Fear! Trap!*" The ferret was standing, at this point, his front paws in the air as if he could explain through gestures.

Maybe he could. "You mean that Albert wanted something— and this led him into trouble?" This seemed like the obvious conclusion, and Frank appeared to accept it, settling down in the bucket seat as I turned off toward Albert's apartment.

I'd given some thought about where to take the little mustelid. In some ways, the office might have been a natural choice. Frank was used to hanging out in the desk, and I could visit him regu-larly there. Besides, when—or, if—Albert got out, he'd be right next door and could pick up his pet himself.

But the ferret had been through a lot, and I couldn't see camp-ing out in a desk drawer once more as ideal. Besides, I had no idea how long Albert would be this time, especially if he'd begun to talk. And with all of this talk about "traps" I didn't think it would be healthy for the little animal to be anywhere where he might spy Jim Creighton or, really, anybody with a badge. I'd hoped to communicate my confidence in Creighton, but to a ferret who had seen his person taken away, I didn't know how long that would last.

There was also the question of the legality of having a ferret on city property, but considering that Albert and I were animal control—and this was Beauville, after all—such punctiliousness wasn't top on my list of concerns.

No, I wanted to get Frank back into a safe place where he could wait in comfort. And if Albert was detained, it would be easy enough for me to drop by, although I suspected—having seen my colleague's lair—that the ferret could easily find enough to eat and entertain himself, either among the provisions that Albert had laid in or those that made their own way inside.

Maybe that was why I slowed further as I rounded the corner on Albert's street. Even at that speed, I feared that my turn had thrown the ferret off balance. Although he had ridden the sway and movement of my GTO admirably, I heard him scramble to regain his footing as I swung onto Albert's street. I let up on the gas and was about to voice an apology, when I realized that, no, he hadn't fallen. He was simply scrambling up to get the best view of what he must consider his own home.

"Here we go—" I caught myself in mid-sentence, suddenly struck dumb. I'd expected to be able to pull up right in front of Albert's place, much as I had that morning. Only now a trio of cars stood out front: Beauville's two police cruisers and the powerful sedan that I recognized as Creighton's.

For a moment, I feared the worst. More violence. Another murder. Then I remembered that Albert left his place unlocked. Could someone have taken advantage of the open space? I didn't imagine Albert had much of anything to steal, but still, years in the city had taught me that some people will see any open door as an invitation.

As I pulled up, I saw Creighton coming down the front steps. He saw me, as well, and so there was nothing for it but to roll down my window and call out.

"Hey," I leaned out and called, aware all the while of the animal on the seat beside me. "What's up?"

"I could ask you that." He stood back and squinted in the sun. He looked handsome enough to eat, which might have explained the distance.

"I've got Albert's pet ferret." I nodded to the creature on the seat beside me, who now stood upright and was stretching his pointed nose toward the window, eager to pick up any scent. "I thought I'd bring him back here. You know, while Albert's busy with you."

"You've been driving around with that in your car all day?" The hint of a smile, though it could have been sun.

I shrugged. Better not to lie if you don't have to.

"Well, you can't go in there." He glanced back up at the apartment. I couldn't see who was in there. If this was now a murder investigation, the state would have sent its own people. I eyed two other vehicles parked nearby and suspiciously nondescript. "And we can't have an animal running around in there."

"Afraid he'd destroy evidence?" I made it sound like a joke. In truth, I was trying to find out what was going on.

"Nice try." He backed up a step and turned, the interview over. "Can't you bring it over to County? Surely Doc Sharpe would let you use a cage for a few days."

"A few days?" I wasn't deaf. I wanted to confirm what he'd said.

"Most likely." He turned to go. "We'll see."

With that, he walked to his car, leaving me to do the reckoning. Creighton could hold Albert for up to seventy-two hours before the state charged him, but I didn't know if the earlier detention would count into that. Then again, he could just be keeping the portly official while he executed a search warrant. Figuring in that "few days" comment, odds were good that my cop boyfriend was still investigating, and this was a fishing expedition, though what he hoped to find was a mystery to me. Of course, it was also possible that Frank's protector had been arrested, and that Creighton expected him to make bail. Either way, the window of opportunity for me to clear my fat colleague was closing.

Plus, I had a ferret in my car who needed a place to stay.

"Frank, what are we going to do?" I turned toward the masked animal and met his black eyes with my own.

"*Fish?*" His face, like most animals, maintained its serious expression, but I couldn't help smiling.

"No, that's an expression," I explained. "When I said a 'fishing expedition,' I just meant Creighton was searching for something."

"*Let's fish then. Go hunting! Fish!*" He repeated, with more emphasis. And after a moment's hesitation—was I giving the lithe creature too much credit for abstract thought? Was he, in fact, hungry?—I realized that I was the one being dense.

"Yes," I nodded in agreement. If Creighton could investigate, we could too. The question was, where to begin.

"*Hunting ground?*" The answer was so obvious, I had to laugh. Frank seemed to enjoy this too, as he chirruped in a satisfied manner. I put the GTO in gear and began to drive away, when another thought hit me. Frank had seemed so panicked before. Afraid of the man who would trap Albert. Who would put him a cage. But he hadn't reacted to Creighton at all. He was afraid of someone else.

Chapter Thirty-one

I couldn't bring Frank home. That was not even an option. Part of being able to communicate with Wallis was respecting her preferences and her boundaries. As much as I would have liked to pretend otherwise, she and I both knew that I could hear her loud and clear—and that she would have very strong feelings about my bringing another animal into the house we both shared.

"*A ferret?*" I could imagine her rearing up, baring her teeth as she took in Frank's faint, but distinctive scent. "*You expect me to share my home with a stinking weasel?*"

No, I tried to wipe the image from my mind. Frank had curled up to nap on the bucket seat beside me, but I didn't want him to take offense. I did need to find a place for him to stay, however. He'd had an exhausting day, and he deserved some peace and quiet.

As I drove, I thought about Creighton's suggestion. It was true, I could lodge Frank at County. A crate—I prefer that term to "cage"—wouldn't be the prison that it might seem to us. Some animals enjoy being in a confined space. It's comforting, after all, to know you have a secure place to call your own.

What I didn't like was the idea of bringing him in, even on an unofficial basis. I'd had friends, back in the day, who were in and out of trouble with the law constantly. The ones from my teens, up here in Beauville, soon became known to the local chief of police. Creighton's predecessor was pretty much the law here then; before we all became wired together, the state police were only called in when it suited him. But he knew whom to pick up, whether or not they were responsible for whatever the complaint. During my days in the city, the crimes I heard about tended to be bigger—less joyriding and more drugs, not to mention the occasional trade in ill-gotten goods. But the same idea held: once someone was in the system, he—or she—had a target painted on his back. You became known, you were more likely to be picked up. And once picked up, you were more likely to stay in that cage forever.

No, I wasn't going to put Frank in the system. On the very real chance that Albert did some time, I didn't want his pet relegated to the shelter system—or worse.

I looked over at the sleeping ferret, now a sleek and peaceful disk of fur. Damn, Wallis. I mean, I'm as territorial as the next creature but…no, there was no way around it. I turned toward the animal control office. Frank was going to have to bunk down in the office once more overnight.

"*It's not my fault, you know.*" Wallis didn't sound repentant. The fact that she was explaining herself, however, suggested a modicum of regret. "*You act like we're all alike, but we're not. I mean, how would you feel if I asked you to room with a mountain gorilla?*"

"Frank is hardly a mountain gorilla." I was making us both dinner: meatloaf for me, and, well, meatloaf without any of the additives for her. "You sure you don't want some catsup?"

"*Huh!*" She reared back in disgust. Onions, I understood. They're poisonous to cats. But I'd thought everybody liked catsup. Especially…

"*Oh, please.*" Wallis didn't appreciate my humor. "*And those …things…*"

She meant the onions, and it hit me that she wasn't talking only about herself. It didn't matter. I knew that it was only going to be the two of us that night. Wallis and I and some old blues discs I'd taken with me when I'd left the city. Those and the bourbon almost kept me from listening for the sound of a car coming up my drive.

Chapter Thirty-two

I woke with a head like the clouds that had gathered outside. Not even Wallis, leaning her soft fur against my legs, could make me feel much better.

"It's just that I've gotten used to him," I said. She knew better than to reply. She did, however, leap up on the counter as I poured my coffee and I realized she was staring at my phone.

"*Well, that's interesting,*" she spoke, as if talking to herself. "*Aren't you going to answer?*"

"Am I—?" The phone rang before I could finish the question, and Wallis jumped to the floor, her tail set at a smart angle as she sauntered over to the doorway. "Good morning?"

"Jack Walz." The caller announced himself as if he were claiming a prize. I looked over at Wallis. She'd meet her match in attitude with this one. "I'm following up on our conversation."

"Yes, Mr. Walz, I remember." I had been waiting for a more gracious greeting. I don't believe any dog is too old to learn new tricks, but I also wanted this man's business. I straightened up, the better to convey my own stature as we spoke, and pulled my diction up accordingly. "How may I help you?"

"I would like to hire you to work with my husky." I remained silent. I wanted his custom, but I wasn't going to beg. After a moment, I heard a very restrained huff of acknowledgement. Of course, he could simply have been clearing his throat. When your nose is up in the air, it tends to collect dust. "I have an opening on my schedule this morning," he said at last. "I'll be home until eleven. Would you be available at that time?"

He was asking for an appointment, only he made it sound like he was doing me a favor. Clearly a dominance play, but that was probably the behavior that had made him the money for Pine Hills. I've worked for worse—I did work for worse, I corrected myself: Tracy Horlick.

"I've got one appointment this morning, but I can swing by afterward." Besides, it didn't hurt to let him know that I was in demand. "I should be there by ten."

"Grand." He didn't repeat his address. Men like that know that you've noticed them. He was right. I had. Wallis, meanwhile, seemed to take note of my raised eyebrows. Sometimes I think she resents how mobile my face—like any human's—is. Right now, she simply looked smug. Before I could question why, the phone rang again.

"Hey, Pru. It's Greg." Wallis had wrapped her tail primly around her forepaws. Was this the call she had anticipated? Does everyone's cat play matchmaker?

"Hey, Greg." I heard the trepidation in my own voice. I missed Creighton more than I had thought. But there was no denying that relationship would always have its challenges, and I had to admire Greg's timing. "What's up?" Of course, he might simply have called about the job. Not that I'd made up my mind about that, either.

"I was wondering if you'd heard anything more about that trap."

"The trap?" That hadn't been on my list. "You know Creighton's holding Albert, right?"

"I heard." A sigh. "But I'm looking ahead."

I didn't understand, and I let him know. If he thought I had insight into the criminal investigation because of Creighton, he should know better.

"No," he said. "I really was thinking about the bear. I mean, we got lucky with that one."

"Yeah," I nodded as we spoke. If I hadn't been trying to track down Albert, we probably never would have known about the trap. Or, maybe, Paul Lanouette. "But the animal was healthy, right? He's got a good chance now that he's free."

"I'm not worried so much about him as the next one."

He heard the question in my silence.

"Pru, I've been thinking." I waited. "That bear was trapped for a reason. I mean, someone wanted it."

"You said, maybe for a private hunt?"

"I've been doing some reading. That's still a possibility, but the trade journals have been noting a growing number of private zoos too."

"Here?" There had been a case, recently. I had thought it was a one-off. "In Beauville?"

"I doubt anyone here would care about a black bear." His voice sunk into a growl. "But there's big money in it internationally, and a growing domestic market. It fits with the animal being taken alive." He paused. "That's why I'm worried."

"You think there's more of this going on." If I hadn't taken that call…

"At the very least, I think it's likely that animal was trapped for someone—for a client. We managed to free it. But if someone ordered a live bear…"

"If they have any sense, they'll hire a more competent crew." I couldn't help it. The words just slipped out.

"That's what I'm afraid of." I heard him sigh. "So, Pru, I'd appreciate it if you hear anything…" Another sigh, and a pause a bit too long. "If you do, if you'd let me know?"

"Of course." Then it was my turn to pause. The silences had told me something more than the warden's words. I took a breath, unsure of how to phrase what I needed to say. "Look, Greg. I grew up around here and I know—well, I know a lot of people."

Sometimes the best approach is a direct one. "But you've got to know that I'm always going to put animals first. I mean, I've got no loyalty toward anyone who would hurt an animal."

"I get it." To do him credit, he sounded somewhat abashed. "And I'm sorry if I misread you. It's only—I heard you were defending Albert, and it seems to me, this has the hallmarks of a local operation."

That caught me up, and I waited.

"Think about it." He sounded sad. "Someone knew about the camp. They knew who would be open to that kind of work."

"You don't think Paul was behind it?" Albert had referred to one of his running buddy's "deals."

"Paul might have been a middle man, but Paul's dead. And Albert's in the thick of it."

"Yeah, he is." I thought of Frank and my heart sank. "Only, he's much more a follower than a leader, and he certainly didn't kill anyone."

The silence on the other end of the line spoke volumes. I waited it out, though, and when Greg spoke again, it was clear he was weighing his words carefully.

"Maybe you're right," he said. "But keep in mind, the illicit animal trade is big business—and big money will make a lot of people do things they wouldn't ordinarily consider."

It didn't even have to be big money, not with the way things were going in Beauville these days. Jobs were scarce, and too many locals were barely scraping by. I counted myself in that category, and after Greg rang off, I found myself staring out the front window. The trees were green now, but soon enough they'd be bare and cold—and I'd have this old heap to heat again. What if Albert went away? Would I be happy taking over this gig? The regular hours would be odd, but I suspected I could keep my freelance clients and nobody would complain. The regular paycheck would be welcome. That was for sure.

What other options did I have? Greg hadn't mentioned the

posting in his department again. That didn't mean it didn't exist. The man was sensitive enough to have picked up on my reluctance. Still, if I did choose to pursue it...

"*Or pursue him...*" Wallis twined around my feet. "*Or entice him to pursue...*" The way she rolled the "r" left me in no doubt about her intent.

"I don't know, Wallis."

"*You don't want to think about it, you mean.*"

She was right, and I let her have the last word. Besides, I had clients to see to. I was heading out the door when my cell rang. Susan Felicidad's name showed up. For a moment, I considered not answering. I'd see her and Bunbury only the day before. But then I remembered why our appointment had been postponed. I owed her and her feline, whether they knew it or not.

"Good morning." I locked the door behind me. A city habit, but it no longer seemed so strange. "Are you calling about our appointment?"

"Oh, no, no." She sounded breathless and I paused, fearing that something had happened to her smart little cat. "It's Coco."

"Coco?" I could do little more than repeat the word back to her in my confusion. The woman had introduced her cat as Spot. When she'd caught me using Bunbury's real name out loud, she'd seemed amenable to changing it. Had she revised it yet again? If so, it was a wonder that spotted cat was as stable as he seemed.

"Oh, yes, Coco. My neighbor's toy poodle. She's gone missing."

"Wait, what?" As relieved as I was to hear that poor Bunbury hadn't been given yet another moniker, this was alarming. City people didn't have much sense, but how many pets had gone missing? "Did she let Coco out?"

"Yes, but there's something else." She paused, and I got the distinct impression that she was steeling herself to say something terrible. "Merilee—my neighbor—well, she fears something happened. She says—she swears—that a few minutes after she let Coco out, she heard a yelp."

"I'll be right over," I said. Not that it would make a difference. If a coyote or some other predator had grabbed Coco, there was precious little I could do about it. Susan Felicidad knew it too. I could hear it in her voice—a steeliness I didn't associate with the average garden-happy widow. Well, one of the reasons we hire professionals is to break the news we don't want to have to speak aloud ourselves.

I was trying out various phrases as I drove. If I said, "I'm afraid," would that give her too much hope? Should I be more direct: "It's most likely..."

Before I got there, though, I had less trying logistics to work out. Tracy Horlick was on speed dial, but I still took a deep breath before I hit her name.

"Mrs. Horlick, it's Pru." I began to talk before she could start with the complaints. "I'm sorry to call so early, but I'm going to be delayed today. I have an emergency."

It wasn't that early. I would usually be heading over to her place now, but it seemed politic to offer her a sop. "I'll be there as soon as I can." I rang off, catching her in mid-complaint. She'd let loose with both barrels when I saw her, but that was the least of my worries. One way or another, Coco's fate would be clear by then.

The next call was more challenging. Scrolling down the numbers on my phone, I found Walz's and hit dial.

"Mr. Walz." I had him on speaker. "I'm afraid I will need to postpone. I've had an emergency call—"

"Well, really!" His voice rose in surprise and, I suspected, annoyance.

"Yes, I'm sorry, but I'm the acting animal control officer, and we've had an incident." I was explaining, not apologizing. He might choose to be dominant, but I didn't want to give a man like him too much.

"This is unacceptable." That shut me up. Usually, normal human beings understand things like emergencies.

"I'm sorry. A dog has gone missing, and that takes precedence." I was about to hang up, when I heard him begin to backtrack.

"Wait, wait, I'm sorry." He did sound bothered, I'd give him that. "It is simply that—well, I've structured my whole morning around your visit. But put that aside," he grumbled. I waited, curious to hear what he'd offer. "I've already arranged to be at home all morning. Why don't you drop by whenever you can manage?"

That was, I suspected, as gracious as he could be. "That sounds perfect, Mr. Walz. I'll give you a call when I'm on my way."

Chapter Thirty-three

I slowed as I pulled into the new development. On the off chance that the missing dog was running loose, I might be able to pick up her confusion or fear. Over time, I've learned how to shut out some of the ruckus around me, and as I drove I intentionally tuned out the noise of nesting birds—"*we're here! We're here!*—and smaller mammals already looking ahead to the end of summer's bounty—"*Quick! Quick! Eat it up!*"

Despite Wallis' claim that the ability to do this comes quickly to the youngest kitten, I still found it a challenge. There was so much urgency in these short lives, and I was afraid of missing something that mattered.

"*Quick, here!*" I jammed on the brakes, only to find myself face-to-face with a startled squirrel. Only after I realized the matter of great import involved acorns and a greedy possum did I relax, and let the fuzzy-tailed creature go about his day.

"*What are you doing? No! No!*" A robin warning off a blue jay, her angry defense fortified by her mate, who chose that moment to dive-bomb the marauding invader.

Maybe it was just as well I hadn't finished my coffee. I was clearly on edge. In large part, that was because of my errand. I didn't have a good feeling about this poodle, based on what Susan Felicidad had said. What Greg had told me was also weighing on me. A client. I hadn't thought through what had brought Albert into the woods, nor what kind of "deal"—that had been Albert's word—had gotten his buddy Paul killed.

I flashed back to my time in the city. I'd lived in a kind of iffy neighborhood for a while, the kind of place where my nocturnal ramblings weren't taken much note of. Even though I was there by choice, I knew a lot of people weren't. I was a newcomer—a tourist, in a way—and that insulated me from much of what was going on. But I'd seen the kids on the corner. Too young to do hard time if they were arrested, they weren't too young to fall victim to violence, when someone else wanted that corner for their own. Albert wasn't a child, far from it. In his own way, though, he might be as innocent. One man was already dead. No, when big money wanted something, it was best to stay out of the way.

"*Let me go! Let me go!*" For a moment, I thought the cry was a memory. I remembered one boy, no more than ten, who'd been grabbed up. I couldn't remember if he was taken by the cops or by a rival gang, and I realized how much that bothered me. How I wished I had gotten involved or intervened. "*Home!*"

That did it—that cry wasn't a memory. I braked and jumped out of the car. If what I'd heard was the poodle, she was still alive—alive and struggling. The question was: where?

I'd come to a halt on the edge of the development. To my left a block of new houses stood, their lawns allowing little cover for a hunt. To my right, however, lay the strip of woods that gave the area its name—scenic greenery that would also hide a hunting animal and his prey.

"Coco!" I called. Perhaps the poodle had run off seeking adventure and even now was holding off something larger and, most likely, confused. "Come, girl! Coco!"

Nothing. I made myself breathe, taking heart in the silence. Surely, if a death blow had been dealt, I'd have heard a last cry. Unless the poodle had been carried off, beyond my hearing but not beyond scent.

I looked over at my car. If I drove over to Susan Felicidad's house, I could borrow Bunbury. Maybe even get Walz's husky—Urso.

Only whatever I had heard was close by, and that cry had been urgent. As much as I wanted the use of a better nose than my own, I didn't dare risk losing the trail, so I began to walk up the street, flanking the woods—and to whistle. Domestic animals respond to human voices. It's something about the timbre. But a whistle carries farther, especially in dense foliage.

"*Where are you, Coco?*" I imagined the question, visualizing possible answers as I walked. If I only had some help…

There, off to the left, two blocks up, a truck was parked by the curb. Dark green with a familiar logo. "Ronnie?" I called and waved. Nothing

With a last glance over at the forested strip, I bolted toward the truck. Ronnie would be better than nobody, I thought. At the very least, I could send him to fetch Bunbury.

"Hey!" I called again as I got near. "Ronnie, you there?"

"What?" Larry Greeley stuck his head out of the cab, craning back at me. "Hey, Pru. What's up?"

"Emergency." I didn't take the time to catch my breath. "Lost dog. I need you to get help." I gave him Susan Felicidad's address and explained what I wanted, pointing out the street one block away. He'd been doing enough business around here he probably knew the street, but I wasn't taking any chances. Hey, if he did me a solid on this, I'd be happy to recommend him.

"Sure, sure thing." He nodded. I didn't know if he'd ever seen me flustered, but it had gotten his attention. "I'll be right back."

Even before the engine had turned over, I was dashing back to where I'd heard that cry. "Coco!" I called, all the while straining every nerve to catch something—anything—that might come back in response.

"*What? What?*" The truck's rumble—it needed a new muffler—had disturbed a rabbit. "*Who's there?*"

"Lucky bunny." I shook my head. It was a strange day when a rabbit escaped while a dog was grabbed. Then again, the poodle might have been led astray by the scent of that rabbit. We live in a complicated world.

"Coco?" I had crossed over to the forested side of the street by then, trampling through the low brush in my search. "Are you there?"

Nothing. My clumsy passage had scared off most of the smaller animals. The ones who remained were hunkered down, holding their breath—and their thoughts—until I passed. Still, I stayed on guard, stopping to listen every few steps. It wasn't until I heard a car pull up beside me that I stopped and turned back toward the road.

"Ms. Marlowe!" Susan Felicidad stepped out of her Toyota, waving. "There you are!"

I turned toward her, my heart sinking. She was alone. I should have known Larry Greeley would have been unable to convey a simple message.

"Mrs. Felicidad." I met her on the sidewalk. Despite the evidence of all my other senses, I craned to see into her car. "Did you bring Spot?"

"Oh, no." Her words were at odds with the big smile on her face. "I know, you sent that nice young man, but, you see there was no need."

I searched her face, at a loss for words.

"Coco came home," she said, to my obvious puzzlement. "She just came bounding out of the hedges like she'd been hiding in there all along."

Chapter Thirty-four

"She came home?"

The smile on her face confirmed the news I was parroting back. Granted, this was the third time I'd asked, but the answer still made no sense.

"And your neighbor had called for her?"

"Yes, I guess she just didn't hear Merilee. Or, maybe…" The smile faded into a look of bemusement, "maybe she simply found something more interesting than one old lady."

I couldn't answer. This wasn't the behavior of any pet I knew. Something was wrong. "If I may, I'd like to speak to her." I caught myself. "To your neighbor, I mean."

"Of course." The smile was back. "She was very grateful for your prompt response. And that nice young man you sent over—does he work with you often?"

"No." I snapped and caught myself. No sense in alienating a client. "We know each other. Beauville being a small town and all."

She nodded. "So I see. I gather he also does landscaping."

That was a fancy word for it, but Larry had come to my aid, and so I nodded. "Lawns." Simpler was better. "I'm guessing he's explaining his services to your neighbor now?"

"Oh, no." She brushed off the suggestion. "He understood that she was in no condition."

That didn't sound right to me. A vulnerable woman? A chance to make some money? And Larry Greeley was passing it up? But the merry widow misread my silence.

"I'm sure if you want to come by, though, she'd be happy to speak with you. After all, you did go searching."

"Thanks." I wanted to speak to Coco, but the phone buzzing in my pocket reminded me that I had other obligations. "I can't right now. Would you give me her number?"

"Her number?" A musical laugh. "Lord knows. She's the green house two down from mine. Just come by. I'm sure she'll be there."

"Thanks." Relief affects people in different ways. Still, I had to wonder.

"By the way," she said, as I turned back toward my car. "I'm dying to know what brought you out here." She gestured to the spread of trees, but she kept her eyes on me. "I mean, this is blocks from where we live."

"Parameter," I said, with as much authority as I could. I was ready to go further. To come up with some explanation about starting at the woods and working back, but it wasn't to be. Susan Felicidad just smiled that enigmatic smile.

"Of course," she said, as she returned to her own set of wheels.

Tracy Horlick was uncharacteristically silent when I arrived, which I took as the calm before the storm.

"I'm sorry for the delay." I jumped right in. "There was a situation with a missing animal, and that counts as an emergency."

"I hope Orzo is all right." Her eyebrows rose in what I could only interpret as alarm. "Such a handsome dog."

"Urso?" I pieced together her silence and her sudden appreciation for an animal—an animal belonging to a wealthy, apparently single man. "No, Mr. Walz's dog wasn't the one gone missing."

"Oh." Those brows came down in disappointment. But before she could rally, I saw my chance.

"He was very understanding about my morning appointments

being delayed by the emergency." I didn't know how the old witch got her news, but she clearly knew he was a client. "In fact, I'll be seeing him later. And, so…if Growl—Bitsy is ready?"

The crayon of her brows converged, as if pouncing on my mistake. But the luster of the rich man's name—and the appeal, I had no doubt, of future gossip—got the better of her, and soon she was shuffling off in her worn carpet slippers to free the large soul in the small body she called Bitsy.

"*You've been busy!*" We were barely at the end of the block before the bichon turned those black button eyes—and, more crucially, that wet leather nose—toward me.

"A poodle went missing." With other animals, I didn't bother with the names given by humans. Nor was I going to get into the question of what had happened. Growler could pick up the relevant details from my scent, I had no doubt. The fact that there had been some urgency involved he must have already discerned—at this point in our walks, he'd usually still be catching up on the neighborhood canine news.

"*Missing, huh…*" The soft chuff was a dismissal, I thought. It was hard, at times, to tell exactly what Growler thought of me and my world. Tracy Horlick hadn't left him with a great impression of people. Besides, I had some idea from Wallis what most domestic animals would think of the term "missing." They might be in danger, but they always knew where they were. We were the ones who panicked.

With that, the white fluffball had gone back to sniffing a fence post that served as a cross between a meeting place and community newspaper. I watched, trying not to eavesdrop as he catalogued the comings and goings of the various neighborhood animals. Carson and Squeeks had been by again, Carson with his stuffed bunny, taking as good care of it as he did his brindled "sister." Only after Growler had finished his assessment —"*what's with the stuffed animal, man?*"—and left his own liquid update did I voice the question that had been preying on me since earlier that morning.

"Growler, am I losing my hearing?" He stopped and turned to look up at me, and I realized that I was phrasing my query poorly. "Am I getting something wrong?" That was closer. "I mean, I really thought I heard something grab that poodle. I was sure she was in trouble, that something had taken her..."

His dark eyes stared into mine, but I was back on that street. Staring into that remaining strip of forest. What had I heard? I had never met the poodle Susan Felicidad had called Coco. Was it possible that I'd been mistaken and picked up on the final struggles of some other poor creature?

He chuffed again, a soft woof more grunt than bark, and walked on. Animals don't rework the past the way we humans do. While they experience longing and grief and sadness, they understand, better than we do, that time doesn't go backward, for all our wishing. And since the present was all Growler had, I did my best to shut up and let him enjoy it, after that, wandering behind him as he made his way down the development streets toward the river.

The sun was playing through the leaves, by then. Although we were only a little later than usual, the sky was brighter. The air warmer. In the shifting shadows, I saw a robin hop. Somewhere nearby, her mate began his distinctive song. It was all so peaceful. As quiet as a woodland could be, and yet, I found myself stuck to the street, unable to proceed.

Growler, therefore, had to stop too. He was still wearing his lead—after that morning's adventure, I wasn't going to let even the most reasonable dog off leash. Even before he reached the end of its length, though, he would have felt me pause. Caught the hesitation that drew me up at the edge of the pavement—the edge of civilization. Growler, for all his oversized spirit, was still a very small animal, and I couldn't watch over him every moment.

He turned, then, and stared, more in accusation than in a question. In his light, I was doing what every other human was guilty of—seeing him as some kind of toy, a possession to be coddled at times, but not given freedom of choice, or even any kind of real agency.

"It's—" I bit my lip, searching for the words. "There are scary things out there, Growler." I pictured the bear. A wild cat I had once encountered not far from here. The hawk I had seen flying overhead. All of those animals had to eat, as well. All of them hunted for small, sentient prey.

As Growler glared up at me, fury making his compact body tremble, I tried once more to explain my fear. Only, when I tried to put my anxiety into thought, I found myself going back to that more basic question.

"Is my hearing—my perception—off, Growler?" Anxiety wouldn't let me avoid my real concern. "Could I have heard some other animal and not understood correctly?"

A louder chuff, this time. Almost a bark, and Growler turned back toward the woods. "*Predators…*" As I heard his voice in my head, I could feel him looking longingly into the shadows, where the deep leaf mold hid small burrowing creatures. I got an image of that robin, eyes bright as she pounced on an earthworm. "*Predators come in all sizes.*"

Chapter Thirty-five

Those words stayed with me even after I returned the bichon to the harridan who paid me. The idea of different predators—of all the creatures that would make a meal of a small dog—ran through my mind as I drove to Jack Walz's place, once again navigating the cobble and that swath of woods. Had I let my own viewpoint—my own size—cloud my thinking? Even before Growler's disgruntled pronouncement, I'd been considering smaller beasts of prey—the fishers and martens that could easily take down a small dog. But maybe I'd been totally off base about what animal had been calling out in fear.

Maybe Wallis was right, and we humans simply had no clue about the reality of the world outside.

Jack Walz was a walking example of how lopsided our species was. The man who came to the door didn't look like an alpha male by any real measure. Short—barely as tall as I was—and wiry, the strongest thing about him was his nose. That and the deep grooves that accentuated the perpetual scowl on his face.

"Come in, come in." He ushered me into a foyer made frigid with climate control. "Please, have a seat."

I followed him into a living room done in modern male: leather and wood that both gleamed from polish. "Please, I've been hoping we could talk."

I opened my mouth, and realized I had nothing to say. Usually,

I'm the one to suggest a conversation. Most of what I do is actually training people, rather than their animals, and that starts by getting a sense of who they are and how they view the beasts they've taken into their homes. This man had gotten the jump on me, in a manner I hadn't expected.

"Good idea," I said at last. I looked around for the husky even as I settled into a butter-soft sofa.

"I was thinking it would be useful to learn more about your process," said Walz, settling himself into a chocolate leather chair opposite me as if he were preparing for a long talk. "I bet there's a lot I could learn."

That shut me up again. From my brief experience with Walz, I'd pegged him as one of those Wall Street-shark types—men who act like they know it all, even when they don't. I had thought I'd be lucky to get a word in edgewise, especially after he'd dominated our first conversation on the street. But the man sitting opposite me could have been a different person. With his questions and his patience, he didn't seem very much like an alpha male, or even a typical New Yorker, to be honest.

"I thought you could watch me with Urso." He'd kept talking, even as I mused the apparent change, but from his tone—more questions than statements and with an edge that I could only attribute to nerves—he was simply waiting for me to step in. For me to take the lead. Could I have been so off, once again? "Go around the block with us, and point out what signals I'm giving." He was saying. "Or tell me what I should be doing or saying. You know, to make him less likely to run off."

Then again, maybe this behavior wasn't that odd. Maybe there was a reason this man had retired rich. What he was suggesting was exactly what I'd want to do. He either did his research ahead of time, or he was simply smarter than I'd given him credit for.

"I think that's a good idea." I struggled a bit to catch up. Intentionally or not, this client had taken my thunder, and in this situation I wasn't used to ceding dominance. "And, yes, I would like to explain what I do."

"Good, good!" With that he jumped up, as if I'd given him a treat. "I'm sorry! Would you like something to drink? Or should I go get Urso now?"

"Why don't you get Urso." I rose, too, somewhat relieved. "It will be easier to explain if the three of us are together."

He returned moments later with the blue-eyed husky, and we went out to the front lawn. He tried to hand me the leash, then, but I refused.

"No, this is about your relationship." I went on to explain how dogs respond to our body language as well as our voice commands. "What you do travels down the leash to him. Now, let's go through some basic commands."

Twenty minutes later, I was rethinking my entire approach. Urso didn't need me. The husky, who maintained a quiet concentration, waiting for my cues, was already fully trained. From the history I gleaned from Walz, he had arrived that way, purchased from a reputable breeder, who had overseen his education at one of the best training facilities in the city. He heeled and came when called, and despite the inattention of his person—Walz seemed more interested in talking to me and to the occasional neighbor who passed by—he never took advantage. This was not a leash-puller or nipper. If anything, I thought he was too patient. I'd have lost interest in waiting for a signal from a man who spent a solid five minutes discussing the weather with a beleaguered postal worker.

"So, what do you think?" The poor civil servant had finally extricated himself when Walz paused to take a phone call. Humping his mail sack onto his shoulder, the carrier gave me a sympathetic nod. I smiled and did my best to pass it along to the husky, who sat staring up at his person as he spoke on the phone. In all fairness, Walz kept the call short, and in under a minute, he'd turned back to me. "It's good that Urso doesn't try to run or anything, when I'm talking to someone, right?"

I glanced down at the dog. He had eyes only for Walz.

"Yes, it's good." I replied aloud, resisting the urge to engage in a private conversation with the husky. What I'd said about Walz holding the lead was true. What mattered here was the relationship between these two, and any private dialogue I had with the dog could undermine it. "Urso is very well trained, but you need to give him your attention, too."

"Oh, yes." He actually stood up straighter at that. "Yes, sorry. Come on, Urso. Come on. Let's go." The verbal command wasn't necessary. As soon as he began to walk, the husky rose from his haunches and took his place by the man.

"Good." I followed at a distance. Partly to observe, but partly to keep Walz from getting into any more meandering conversations. I had no problem spending time with these two—I was going to bill Walz, after all—but I'd begun to pity the poor husky.

"So you really think that?" Walz stopped on the sidewalk and turned to face me. "You think we've got it down?"

"Really," I replied in my most conciliatory tone.

That's when it hit me. For a supposedly powerful man, Walz was acting like a little dog. That air of entitlement was just so much yapping and jumping around, trying to get my attention. Because of Urso—I liked to think it was the majestic animal, rather than his owner's perpetual scowl—I hadn't expected such behavior. But maybe what Growler had been trying to tell me had some relevance here as well. Outward appearances didn't always matter. Besides, hadn't I had enough experience back in the city, if not in Beauville, with such types? These so-called masters of the universe were as likely driven by their own insecurity as any raging need to conquer. What I'd finally seen was the needy little boy in the man. Or, in his case, the needy little puppy.

Just what made the big man feel so small was a question for later. And after a few more rounds of basic commands—all of which Urso aced, despite his person's distraction—I called the session to an end. The morning's false alarm had put me behind, and I did have other clients.

"Please feel free to call me if you'd like me to come by for a refresher." I handed Walz a quickly scrawled invoice. "Though, honestly, I would be surprised if you need it."

"I will certainly keep you on speed dial." Walz tucked the invoice in his pocket without looking at it. A good sign, I hoped. "The last—what has it been?—ninety minutes have just flown by. An hour and a half, just like that!"

I smiled and kept quiet. Had it really been that long? I checked my watch and kicked myself for not billing for more.

As it was, I spent the rest of the morning apologizing—or trying to.

"You're a heroine!" Celine Lim declared, when I showed up to clip her schnauzer's claws. "Was it a hawk that had that poor woman's dog—or a wolf?"

"Neither, Ms. Lim." I focused on the task. Randolph didn't like his paws being handled, and he certainly didn't appreciate me not giving him my full attention. "Just doing my job."

I had no more role in Coco's return than Randolph here. Then again, a little luster couldn't hurt. And as the day progressed, my reputation grew shinier and shinier. I had no idea how news spread so quickly, but everyone I spoke with seemed to have heard—either that I rescued "poor Coco" or been involved in guiding her back to safety. Somehow, I couldn't see Coco's owner, Merilee, being the source. As I'd gone about my day, I'd garnered an earful about her deafness and her mobility issues. For a Pine Hills resident, the housebound senior was already well known, and I figured Susan Felicidad was more likely the one to have shared the news.

Once again, I found myself wondering about the glossy brunette. Only this time, what I was hearing made sense. She was new to town and seeking to connect. What better way to insert herself into the social fabric of a town than to praise a native? If she could pump the story up with some drama and a happy ending, well, so much the better. While I didn't like the idea of my life becoming social currency, I could understand it. If she boosted my reputation in ways that promoted my business, well, then, maybe we came out even. And if she helped me build up my clientele among the monied new residents of Beauville, well, that would give me some options.

Which reminded me: I needed to get back to Greg. He'd called again while I was with Randolph, and I'd been happy to let that go to voicemail along with two calls from Creighton. Jim sounded businesslike—never a good sign—and both messages simply told me that I should get in touch at my earliest opportunity.

Greg wasn't much better, although he sounded a little more polite—asking me to call back, rather than commanding. "Not about the cage," he'd said, which piqued my curiosity. Still, I could hear the impatience beneath his voice. Impatience, rather than irritation, I thought, though my ears aren't as good for the human male as they are for so many other species. Which could mean that he was wondering where our flirtation was headed. Or it could mean that he had a position to fill, and he needed to know if I was a serious candidate.

"*Big-game hunting, are we?*" Wallis twined around my ankles when I got home. Not out of affection, I could tell, but to catch up on my day through the various scents that had accrued on my boots and jeans.

"I need to do some more research." I answered reflexively, before realizing that to the tabby at my feet the terms were one and the same. "I want to know what I'm getting into before I get into it."

"*Like you don't already know…*" Her mocking rebuttal had the weight of truth. I might not know Greg well, but I knew enough. He'd be straightforward—as a boyfriend as in business. Honest, as far as he was able. And I knew he respected me. In bed? Well, that was another question, and one that I would only find the answer to through direct experience. But maybe that was the problem. Physically, Greg hit the right buttons. After several months of Creighton's lean muscle, I was ready for a man with a bit more meat on him. And predictable would be good, especially as Jim and I veered into dangerous territory. Only… predictable wasn't exciting.

"*Not so domesticated after all…*" Another pass by Wallis, and another purr. I'd opened my laptop by then and begun looking at pay grades for various positions in fish and wildlife.

"Will you cut it out?" I resisted the urge to shove her away, but she either read the thought as it formed or felt the tension in my leg, retreating beneath the table. "I thought you were complaining that I *was* domesticated." I heard the pout in my own voice, as sulky as a teen. "Spending all my time with Creighton."

Wallis didn't respond, and, under the guise of scrubbing her ear, pretended not to hear. In fact, the tuneless humming I got back—part growl, part the kind of murmured purr that functions as an interior dialogue—let me know she considered her point made.

There was little sense in continuing my search after that. Pay grades for state wildlife officers weren't going to sway me one way or another. And so I found myself typing in Jack Walz's info—or John R. Walz, as I soon discovered. Working backward from his Beauville address—he'd bought the house outright—I traced a career in the city that made such purchases possible. Walz wasn't a household name, but from what I could see he had the kind of clients who would prefer discretion. The man I knew only through his dog was a trustee of several major charities and had been a boldface caption at a city gala as recently as last winter.

I focused in on the photo. Yes, it was the same man, his mane of white hair set off against the black tux. But more than that mane—or the bright white of his shirt or even the dazzling fall of blond hair draping the significantly younger woman on his arm—what stood out were his eyes. While his date was caught in profile, laughing or speaking with someone off to her right, Jack Walz was staring straight into the lens with a ferocity that I associated more with a lion than the eager puppy I'd just spent an hour with. That didn't necessarily signify anything: the man in the picture was in his element, surrounded by the trappings of his success. In Beauville, he was an unknown—and I was the person with mastery of the situation. But it did say something about the relativity of dominance, a lesson I would do well to remember.

Out here, all Jack Walz's money just marked him as a newcomer. An outsider, albeit a valuable one to people like me. No, what mattered more here—and here I found my thoughts traveling to Jim Creighton and the way he could size up a situation—was knowledge. Of the land, of the community. Of the people.

Which someone was rapidly accruing. On a whim, I typed in Susan Felicidad's name, curious to see what high-powered life she had left behind. Chair of a board, or at least a big bucks organizer, probably for a major foundation. I was betting on a buyout. She seemed young to have retired out here, and I wondered about her late husband and whether she'd been a trophy wife. Somehow, I doubted it. With her schmoozing skills, she would have been a star as a fundraiser—the kind who gets the rich to donate more than I'd see in five years.

At first, I thought it was a mistake. The wealthy widow was no Larry Greeley, to live below the radar. She must spell her name oddly—Susan with a "z," or something—and so I tried again. When that didn't work, I cut her down to an initial: Felicidad, and then Felizidad, and a few other options that came to mind. Finally, I typed in her Beauville address, expecting at the very least a public deed or tax bill to come up.

It didn't matter. No matter how I spelled her name or what part of it I used, I couldn't find her. The woman I had now met several times was a ghost.

Chapter Thirty-six

I'm not the sort to jump to conclusions. I like my privacy, too, and I certainly understood wanting to hide one's past. That didn't mean I wasn't intrigued—and even somewhat gratified. I'd sensed that something was off about Beauville's new socialite, and the fact that she had given me—given all her neighbors, presumably—a fake name was probably the least of it.

That didn't mean I couldn't find out more. If the address she'd given me wasn't an outright purchase—and I could find no deed on record—that didn't mean she wasn't paying for utilities. No, I'm not supposed to have access to those records. But anyone with half a brain can figure out how to get at least some information.

"Hi, I've got a question about a service call that's scheduled for tomorrow?" I'd gotten through to the phone company's customer service line. "I forgot what time it is."

"Are you calling from the affected line?"

"No." I faked a laugh. Maybe these people were getting better. "That's why I need the service call!"

"Would you give me the last four digits on the account, then, Miss?"

"Hang on." I put the phone down, preparing to return with some random digits when I was, literally, saved by the bell. "Sorry." I grabbed the phone back up. "Someone's at the door. Bye!"

"You don't return calls anymore?" Creighton, and he wasn't happy.

"You wouldn't believe the day I've had." I waited. No kiss, no smile. Either this was a business visit, or this relationship had reached a new low. "Nonstop craziness. Why?"

"Clients?" His voice was cold. "Appointments?"

"Nothing but." I closed my eyes, remembering. "Those new people in Pine Hills are what you'd call high maintenance." I started telling him about the whole situation with Coco when my supposed beau walked past me, heading for my kitchen. I followed and watched as he fetched himself a beer, popped it open, and drained half of it in one pull.

"That bad?" I found myself softening. The man was human, after all.

"I'm just glad you're okay." He used his free hand to wipe his face, and I realized that what I'd interpreted as temper was more likely fatigue or worry. "Yeah. That bad."

I waited, wondering.

"There's been an accident. A stupid…" He paused, his mouth clamping shut as he shook his head. His hand clenched the beer so tightly, I was afraid he'd crush the can, and he swallowed—hard—before speaking again. "Ronnie was mauled by a bear," he said, his voice strangely flat. "I was afraid that maybe you'd—That you'd…"

"I'm okay." I went to him then, wrapping my arms around his waist. "Is he—?" I stopped myself. Clearly, the man wouldn't be okay.

"He'll live, they say." Creighton looked down at me, still stiff with tension. "But when I saw him—I got scared."

"I wouldn't be part of anything that stupid." I stepped back, shaking off a wave of nausea—queasiness and rage. I knew what a bear could do to a human. I didn't need Creighton to describe the deep gouges those claws could make. The way a bear's teeth could pierce muscle and crush bone. Bears are a part of our world out here. Most of us have enough sense not to mess with them. "What happened?"

"He had another one trapped, only I guess there was a problem with the snare." He paused, and I saw his Adam's apple bob as he swallowed. "The main rope was cut nearly clear through. At any rate, it got away—and Ronnie almost didn't. He's lucky he's alive."

The scene I pictured was horrific. I could imagine all too well how panicked the bear must have felt. Trapped and frantic. Ronnie was a big guy, but if he got between a young male like the one he'd caught before and freedom? It wouldn't even be a contest, even if Ronnie had been working with—

"Albert!" I gasped. "Was he—?"

Creighton smiled as he shook off my fear. "Albert's fine, Pru. He's staying with us for a while. It looks like Ronnie was alone, but someone else had been up there. That rope? I don't think Ronnie was cutting it. It had already been compromised—he walked into a trap as surely as that bear had."

"And you thought, I…" The logical follow-up hit me like a punch to the gut. The question about my day. About my appointments. "Jim, you can't think—" I struggled to find the words.

"I had to." That strange, sad half smile. "Someone wanting to free a bear? Someone who always carries a knife? Maybe, if you'd started to cut the bear free, and then Ronnie had come along…"

"No, I'd never." I shook off the idea. "Not like that, by cutting the ropes. I mean, be real. If I found another trapped animal, I'd call Greg, like last time."

He sighed, and I saw his shoulders sag.

"How'd you find him?" My professional curiosity kicked in.

This prompted another quizzical glance, but this time I was rewarded with the hint of a smile. "Do you ever get a feeling about something?" The question was rhetorical, but I gave him a half-hearted shrug anyway. Nothing I wanted to commit myself to. "Well, maybe it was going over Albert's interview. I had a feeling that there was more up at that camp of theirs—something I'd missed or that I needed to see. So I took a drive up there."

It was on the tip of my tongue to ask him about the timing of this hunch—and of the drive. He'd called me twice that day, the first time fairly early on. I didn't think he was necessarily trying to catch me out, but I did wonder.

"Anyway, I was able to get emergency services there in time." He pulled me close again. This time, his body was warm and yielding. "Tackling a bear on his own. When he wakes up, he's going to have some story to tell."

Chapter Thirty-seven

I didn't get around to calling Greg back. But after the inevitable, and rather wonderful, physical reunion—and a better night's sleep than I'd had for a while—I did end up telling Creighton the details of my day's adventure, except, of course, for the part about me hearing the missing dog cry out.

"I guess you're making a splash over in the new part of town." Creighton was scrambling eggs, while I—and Wallis—sat at the kitchen table watching. "Sounds like you're the go-to pet person."

"I guess." I toyed with how to bring up the mystery of Susan Felicidad without exposing my own inept ploys. "Though I'm not sure how it will play out."

"That Walz guy's hired you, right?" He reached for two plates and scooped the eggs out. Beside me, I felt Wallis begin to purr in anticipation. "You like him?"

I took my plate and scraped some of the eggs into Wallis' dish. At first, she drew back in disdain—"*too hot!*"—but then she fell to as if she were starving. "You've looked into him." It was an observation, not a question.

"Part of the job." Creighton knew better than to comment about Wallis, but I did see the corners of his mouth twitch as he forked up his eggs. "Protect and serve."

"You really think a master of the universe type like Walz needs protecting?" I took a bite, curious. The newcomer had seemed so different from what I'd expected once we were alone. "And didn't you hire a deputy to cover Pine Hills?"

"I'm still responsible for Beauville," he said, mouth full.

"And Walz has got more money than God," I filled in the rest. "More than the rest of the town, anyway."

"And everyone knows it." The grin died away, and I thought of Larry Greeley and his crew. At least they were offering a real service—not unlike me.

"I charge them the same as I do anybody else." Call me defensive, but the smile came back.

"I never would have thought otherwise," my beau said as he shoveled up the last of his eggs. Before I could ask if he wanted more—of anything—his phone buzzed, and after one quick peek at it, he stepped into the other room.

"*You worried?*" Wallis loves to tease.

"Are you?" I looked down at her, only to hear a quiet cough. "Just talking to the cat," I said with a smile.

Creighton wasn't amused any longer. "That was my team," he said. "I'm going to need your knife."

"What?" This wasn't the way I saw breakfast ending. "Why?"

"I'll need to take it into the lab." I shook my head, confused. "The trap, Pru. Word has gotten out how angry you were about the bear being trapped, and well, someone was trying to cut those ropes."

"Shit." I closed my eyes, remembering. "Jim, I don't have it. I lost it." I opened them to meet his cold stare. "You can search me. Search the house, if you want."

He paused. He was considering it, and I felt my core grow cold. "Jim?"

"I need to speak to some people." The staties. I was in for it. "Don't do anything stupid." And with that, he was gone.

"*Wasn't that interesting?*" Wallis jumped to the sill to watch as Creighton drove away. "*After all that talk about the hunt?*"

"Shut up, Wallis." I put the dishes in the sink. I wasn't in the mood.

Before I did anything, I had to check on Frank. I hadn't wanted to bring the ferret into the shelter, but leaving him locked in the office alone wasn't kind either. Not that I was overly worried about him. He'd have water from our leaky tap, and I suspected that the beetles and moths that found their inevitable way into our space would offer a healthier diet than whatever Albert probably offered him. Though with that in mind, I made a mental note to clean out Albert's desk—just because bugs were a part of nature, didn't mean he had to actively promote colonization in a workplace I might soon have to take over.

The office had been closed since I'd left it, so I wasn't surprised by the slightly musty smell as I unlocked the front door. In fact, it was somewhat fresher than it had been of late, and I felt a spark of anxiety as I looked around.

"Frank?" I knew his hearing was better than mine, but it only seemed polite to announce myself. "Are you here?"

"*Here!*" The masked head popped up from behind the desk. "*Treats?*"

"Sorry." I kicked myself, as he scurried over and began to nuzzle my pocket. Not only was the poor ferret deprived of company, he was missing his snacks, too.

"*Silly!*" Small claws grabbed at my hand. "*Treats!*"

Frank had never clawed or bitten. We didn't have that kind of relationship, and so I paused, staring down into his eyes. "What?"

"*Treats!*" The tiny nails dug in as his paw tightened on mine. "*Treats. Box!*"

I shook my head. I had no treats. Unless… a glimmer of an idea, as bright as a diamond chip, had begun to take shape in my mind.

"I'm sorry, Frank." I was already turning to leave. Sometimes I could be incredibly stupid. "And thank you."

Chapter Thirty-eight

"I've got something going on." The words rang through my head. Larry Greeley might have started off as a small-time grifter, but if he was trafficking in stolen jewelry—and had somehow involved Albert in his scheme—he'd graduated to something a little bigger. Whether that something included murder, I didn't know. This time, however, I was determined to find out.

On a hunch, I swung through the new development, thinking I'd circle back to Tracy Horlick's house and Growler once I'd made a pass by the new houses and their big, manicured lawns. The old bag would give me grief, but I could deal with her. It was the bichon I felt bad about, making him wait.

Still, I didn't think I'd find anything. Larry Greeley might be a worm, but he wasn't the early kind. This was more me being too riled up to settle into my own work day. Creighton and I are both early risers. For him, I suspected it was part of his work ethic. For me, it was a holdover from the crisis that drove me here. Once you've been drugged and locked up—even when you do it to yourself—you don't sleep that well.

Besides, my visit with Frank had sparked another idea—a slight niggling suspicion that was growing as I rode the curve around the granite outcropping to where the dew still glistening on those perfect lawns. I didn't expect to find Larry here, soliciting work at this hour, honest or not. But he had been here yesterday. On this very street, I remembered as I turned onto the tree-lined block. I'd seen him before my appointment with Jack Walz. Drafted him into action, when the inscrutable Susan Felicidad had told me about her neighbor's missing pet. That he hadn't brought Bunbury as I'd asked hadn't really mattered, as that minor crisis had seemingly resolved itself.

But that resolution raised its own questions, I realized, as I turned up Susan's street. I was driving by rote at this point. By memory, as I worked through the timing. No, it wasn't likely that Larry would have been able to get from here to the clearing, where Ronnie and Albert had their camp. While I didn't know how long Ronnie had been up there, bleeding and wounded, before Creighton found him, I couldn't see even a grifter like Greeley booby-trapping a friend and then racing off to shill his services at lawn care. I mean, he must have been going door to door...

I could almost picture him, bad tooth and all. The morning sun would make his greasy blond hair appear lighter than it did at night, almost like it did when we were in high school. Almost like the man I now saw, hunched over by that hedge.

"What the—?" I hit the brake so hard it startled me out of my reverie. Yes, I'd come cruising through the development, searching for Larry. But I hadn't really expected to find him. Not now. Not this early, and especially not since I started to realize the impossibility of him being behind the bloody crimes out on the state land.

While it was impossible to make a vintage GTO with a custom paint job disappear, I swung into reverse and retreated slowly down the road, grateful that I'd resisted the muscle car stereotype of mistaking volume for power as I eased back up the block.

There was no reason for him not to be here, I told myself as I brought my car to a halt by the curb. Especially if I was wrong about what I suspected, it made sense for Larry to be out and about first thing in the morning. This would be the time to get yard work done, wouldn't it?

Only, if Larry were engaged in honest labor, why wasn't I hearing a lawn mower? Was he leaning into that hedge with shears or a rake?

There was nothing for it. I parked and got out. I didn't know exactly what I wanted to ask Larry, as I pocketed my keys and began to walk up to where he was standing, leaning into that hedge. All I knew was that I had questions.

Chapter Thirty-nine

It all proved less difficult than I'd feared. As is usually the case with animals, if you act as if you know what you're doing, they'll respond to that confidence—and your ignorance may go unnoticed. Of course, an unweaned pug would probably be faster on the uptake than Larry Greeley.

I'd been smart to be quiet, though. By approaching more or less silently—though I'm sure Wallis would disagree—I got to hear a bit of a conversation that confirmed my suspicion that not everything with the hulking lawn boy was on the up and up.

I hadn't meant to eavesdrop. Not really. I mean, I'd been walking quite openly up the street to where he stood, to all intents and purposes, leaning into the tall, thick boxwood. It wasn't until I'd gotten within hearing distance that I'd noticed him nodding his head. And when I'd heard him respond—"uh huh," he'd said. "Yes, ma'am"—I'd frozen.

Yes, *ma'am*? Whatever I'd expected, it hadn't been that. But taking my cue from millennia of hunters before me, I'd stood as still as a rock. Not until he began murmuring again, his sloppy drawl a little tighter, a little more anxious than usual, did I move slowly over to the nearest tree—a copper beech that Growler would have loved to mark as his own.

What I heard was clearly the tail end of an argument. Larry was protesting, still. "Honest, I didn't," he got out before he was interrupted. "That wasn't my idea at all." I didn't need any more than that. I'd known he was crooked, and it sounded like someone else had caught him out, too. What I hadn't expected was what happened next.

"Good morning!" A perky voice as loud as a goldfinch made me start, as—from the other side of that hedge—Susan Felicidad stepped away from the greenery, decked out in another crisp poplin shirt. She was facing my way, of course. But I had the distinct impression that her bird-bright dark eyes would have spotted me anyway, and the smile she spread across her face was in direct opposition to the blanched and guilty stare on Larry's as he whirled around and saw me standing, not ten feet away.

"Good morning, Susan." I strolled up to her as if I hadn't been hiding. "What brings you out so early?" It was an inane question. This was her neighborhood, after all. But I wanted to start this conversation by putting her on the defensive. The right questions would come after.

"Why not be out on such a day?" The ease with which her grin broadened made me wonder what she knew. She was a deep one, all right. "Right, Larry?"

"Right." The would-be landscaper rubbed his mouth as he answered, as if he could hide behind his hand. Susan's eyes darted over to him, and I wondered if she saw this too. At any rate, she spoke again quickly, as if to cover.

"I've been chatting with this nice young man," she said, raising an arm as if to embrace him—or perhaps to shield him from me. "He's been so kind and helpful, and he knows the area so well."

"I'm sure he does." I was growling, and Larry's eyes widened in response. Whatever these two had been discussing, I didn't think they were talking about the neighborhood. He was clearly the more scared of the two, and so I turned to question him. "So, you're doing lawn care this morning?"

Granted, the heavy emphasis I put on "lawn care" might have signaled my disbelief.

"Yeah, I—I am." I'd never heard him stutter before. "My—my tools are in the truck."

He pointed, as if toward salvation, and so I let him pass, determined to follow and find out more. "Good to see you again." I nodded at the neat newcomer, who still stood there, smiling like a Cheshire cat.

"Always," she replied.

Larry caved pretty easily after that, at least to his own considerable sins. As he pretended to fuss with a mower in the truck bed, I laid out what I suspected. Granted, I may have made it sound more definitive that it was. And, perhaps, I implied that proof existed of what I had merely postulated from the clues. I was careful about not pushing too far.

But the longer I spoke, the more sure I was that my suspicions were correct. Wallis would say I'm lousy at body language. As a smaller predator, she's got a strong sense of which way an animal—prey or foe—is going to jump. As a woman, I've learned to read men pretty well, too, for much the same reasons. And, yeah, all those animal behavior classes hadn't hurt either.

At one point, I got concerned. As I spelled out my conjecture, he turned from the mower—a vintage model roughly the same age as my car and not as well cared for—and reached for a rake. I stepped closer to him then, not so much to intimidate him as to limit his ability to swing it. But there was no fight left in him by then. He really did appear ready to pull the rusty old thing out of the truck bed and carry it door to door. Only I had other ideas for how he could make amends.

"You could even earn an honest living, Larry," I told him. "And if you behave, I won't turn you in."

"You won't tell anyone?" Even his voice had collapsed to something small.

"Not a soul." I wasn't completely committed to that. It made a good bargaining chip, though. And at this point, I cared more about expediency than honesty.

"I want to know everything." I fixed him with my best dead-eyed stare.

"I don't know the details." He kept harping on that point, even after I got him to put down the rake and look at me. "I just know it was a gig, you know?"

"A gig." I didn't even try to keep the ice out of my voice. "Spill, Larry."

He stared up at the sky then, as if the white puffy clouds making their way across the blue could help him skate too. But he was no robin, flitting tree to tree. And I was in my ultimate hawk mode, pinning him with my best raptor glare.

"I don't know." He shrugged, when I finally got him back to earth. "I wish I did, okay? Paul and I, we fought about it ..."

Maybe he heard me catch my breath. Maybe it was the implication of his own words that stopped him, but he turned, staring at me, his eyes wide and—could it be?—watering. "Not like that," he pleaded, willing me to believe. "I wouldn't—only, he had his own thing going on, right?"

"His own thing?" I didn't like this, only there was something in Larry's voice. A pleading and a sadness that felt honest, if not adult. I believed that he felt left out. I didn't know if that was enough to kill for. "His own pot of gold, and he was cutting you out."

"It wasn't..." Larry wasn't big, in terms of muscle. But he was tall and I could believe him capable of violence. Only the man before me seemed suddenly shrunken, as if our confrontation had taken all the air out of him. "Look." His voice sadder and in some way more human than I'd ever heard before. "If I'd done—that. If I'd done for Paul and taken over his gig, why would I be here, anyway?"

One hand waved toward the truck, with its rusty mower and lawn tools. The other, toward the manicured hedge. I didn't like it, but I couldn't argue. The man had a point. He'd also raised another question for me.

"So, what were you and Susan Felicidad talking about?" I nodded toward that wall of green. "I heard most of it, but I want the details."

"Susan?" He blinked.

"Come on," I prompted. "Glossy brunette. Older. Called you a good boy or something like that."

"Oh." He looked down at the curb, and an alarm sounded in my head. I'd thought there was a good chance he was scamming the older woman. I'd even wondered if he was making moves on her, though the pretty newcomer would have to be fairly lonely to consider Larry Greeley. "No." He answered to my unspoken question. "We weren't talking about anything."

"I heard you, Larry." I kept my voice level, even as I desperately thought back to what I had overheard. Damn it, I knew that woman was hinky in some way. "I think she figured out your scam, same as I did, and she wanted something."

That was a mistake, akin to leaving my flank exposed in a dog fight. Never offer more than you have to. But even as Larry clammed up, I saw his eyes twitch back and forth, for all the world like he was seeking an escape route.

"Larry?" I pressed on.

"She wanted to know about the neighborhood." It was weak. He had to know that. "The plants and such."

"The plants?" I didn't hide my skepticism. If nothing else, Susan Felicidad knew her flora.

"And, you know, who my other clients were. Like, for recommendations?" He raised wide grey eyes at me, but there was nothing of innocence in them. I narrowed my own and watched his Adam's apple jump as he swallowed.

"Come on, I promise," he said. "I'll ask around, and I'll call you. Just—you don't have to tell her, do you? You don't have to tell anyone."

"Not if you hold up your end." It was time to beat a tactical retreat. "I expect to hear from you. Soon."

He was nodding and agreeing as if I'd suggested we go for ice cream. I didn't trust him for a minute. But he had given me some information. More, probably, than he was aware. Larry Greeley had agreed to ask around about who was paying to trap a bear—a scheme that had gotten one man killed and another mauled. He was going to do this because he was afraid of me. But what he'd let me know with that last bit of evasion and those slippery glances back toward the hedge and beyond was that I wasn't the only person he was afraid of.

I had information that could upend Larry Greeley's livelihood. Susan Felicidad, however, had him afraid for his life.

Chapter Forty

It was a little hard to care about Tracy Horlick after that, but I did my best. If the house-coated harridan couldn't get a rise out of me, she'd take it out on her dog. And Growler didn't deserve to pay for my preoccupation. So I did my best to simper and apologize when I pulled up, late, to the old lady's house.

"I hope this isn't getting to be a habit." She reared back, so she could look down at me from her lofty perch on the top of the stoop. "Because that would be unacceptable."

"I understand." I dipped my head, the human equivalent of a submissive posture. I'd roll over if I had to, though the idea of those smoke-stained teeth on my throat made my own jaw clench up. "And I'm sorry."

She snorted, sending twin plumes of smoke into the morning air, and made me wait a few moments more. I didn't mind, really. I had a lot to think about—like how I could best use the leverage I had over Larry if he started to get squirrelly. And what Susan Felicidad could be up to.

I had pretty much decided, when I heard a grunt. Not Growler, not yet, but his person had turned back into the house. And so I stored away my thoughts on interrogating one of my newer, more affluent clients to take charge of one of my most loyal.

"*Finally.*" I couldn't tell if the bichon was more annoyed with his person or with me. It didn't matter. I knew I was responsible.

"I'm sorry, Growler." I kept my voice low, aware that his person was watching us from the stoop.

"*Not you.*" He chuffed, as he paused to sniff a curbside tree and then water it. "*You do what you've got to.*"

I thanked him silently, hoping my appreciation translated down the leash. After that, I tried to stay silent. Bad enough I made him wait. Put the woman who held his life in her hands in a bad mood. The least I could do was shut up and let the fluffy white dog enjoy his social outing.

"*Leo, watch out.*" He'd moved onto the next tree now, and from the way his tail was vibrating I knew it had caught his interest. "*You keep eating like that, you'll get gout.*"

I stifled a laugh. Clearly, I was distracted, and my unconscious translation of the little dog's concern for his friend had taken on language that he would never have intended. My smile faded, though, as I turned to the white dog.

"*Great.*" A low growl rose in his throat. "*You can't listen, and you find me funny.*"

"Sorry, Growler." The dog had a point.

"*Samuel...*" Mollified, he returned to his rounds. "*So sorry to hear that. And with a hound, too.*"

To give my charge his privacy, I let my mind slip back to my own preoccupation. Had Larry been involved with what happened—the bear, and the murder of Paul Lanouette? It wasn't impossible that he'd pursue more than one scam at a time. But the man I'd known for half his lifetime was not what I'd call industrious. No, I let that one go. As much as he'd like more money, laziness would probably win out—making the case that he'd laid out, rather eloquently, back at his truck.

That didn't mean I trusted him. The deal I'd made with Larry was that he'd call me as soon as he heard anything. He had to know that I wasn't going to sit waiting for my phone to ring, however. Just as he had to know that I didn't believe him about his conversation with the widow. What I wasn't sure of was how

I should proceed. A follow-up call and visit to Susan Felicidad were surely in order, under the guise of good customer service. But she'd already deflected my questions about Larry, and she'd probably seen me talking to him, after she took off. If she was as involved as I was beginning to think, she'd be on her guard. Without any leverage on her, she'd be a tough nut to crack.

"*You can get more out of that weasel, you know.*" The comment caught me off guard. I stopped myself before I fired back with a question. Again, I had to remind myself that animals don't use metaphor. The world they live in is colorful enough. I'd been distracted, and the unconscious translation of thought and impulse into language was, in my case, imperfect at best.

"Oh?" I held myself to a simple interrogative syllable. The better to leave the question open.

"*Yes.*" The bichon at my feet grunted, to accentuate his response. "*I can smell him on you, you know. I can smell where he's been. And walker lady, that little weasel knows more than he's letting on. He's scared, and he's got reason. From what my nose says, he saw it all.*"

Chapter Forty-one

Wallis was no help. By the time I got home, I was regretting my deal with Larry. I was ready to track down the sleazy landscaper and turn his life inside out. But cats are nothing if not consummate strategists, and as she circled my ankles, she pointed out the flaws in this plan of action, as simply as she would teach a kitten to hunt.

"*Hmmm...*" Her purr served to underline her own confidence in her words. "*Let's see, right now you control him, right?*"

"More or less." I was grumbling, even as I shredded the half a chicken we'd both share for dinner. "As much as he's controllable."

"*And if you pull him apart like you're doing that bird, this helps you.... how?*"

"It would feel good." I snuck a sliver of the juicy thigh.

"*You're hungry...*"

Again, that translation problem. "I want answers. I'm overdue for the truth."

"*Well, then, hmmm...*" I felt her hunker down by my foot. "*We should figure out how best to get that, yes?*" And with that, she leaped to the counter top and, quick as a wink, grabbed a chunk of the dark meat for herself.

"I was going to … nevermind." I pushed the plate toward her and reached instead for my laptop. I had no better luck finding anything on Susan Felicidad than I had the day before. I was standing there, tapping on the keyboard, when I felt the tickle of whiskers against my wrist.

"*Trying to lure something out?*" Wallis bent over the keyboard, staring at the screen.

"Right." I caught myself before the snark could go too far. Wallis might have been jesting. Then again, she can't read, and at times I think she's a bit sensitive about this. "I was looking for something."

Too late. She turned her back to me and sat heavily, leaning on the keys and making it impossible for me to type. "*Doesn't have the sense of a kitten.*" She began to wash, and her rebuke was accompanied by the taste of fur.

"What?" I tried to modulate my tone. I'd offended her unintentionally, but that didn't matter. Forget what I said about other beasts, cats can hold grudges. At least, Wallis can.

"*You think this is about … that box?*" Her rhythmic licking lent a rhythm to her words. She also was much better at hearing my thoughts than I'd like.

"It isn't?" Sometimes honesty is the best policy.

"*Silly person.*" Lick, lick. "*Petting a machine when there's a witness you could interrogate instead.*"

She was right, of course. And if Creighton had come by, I'd have worked on him to give me access to Albert. The portly animal control officer hadn't been willing to tell me anything about the bear, but if I could get him talking about what he'd seen, maybe I'd be able to piece together what had happened. After all, I had access to information that Creighton never would—from sources that he'd never credit, either. Both Growler and Wallis had been pushing me in that direction. And although animals might not understand the challenges of questioning a witness, something in the scents that I was carrying had prompted them both to speak to me of witnesses and revelations.

Creighton didn't come by, however. And while I liked to think that my tossing and turning had more to do with a dead body and a bear at risk than my own personal romantic dilemma, I'd be lying if I didn't give that at least some of the blame. The man and I were growing closer—but there were parts of my life that I could never reveal to him. To anyone, really. Even if Creighton didn't try to have me committed, I doubted he'd ever truly understand. He'd be sympathetic, at best. Condescending, at some point, as he humored what he'd have to consider a delusion. To me, that might even prove worse. It would certainly kill any passion between us. Which left me wondering, would I ever be able to really share my life with someone—someone other than Wallis, that is?

Such thoughts darted through my brain whenever I began to drift off. When I did sleep, I found myself caged, like that bear, and just as scared and alone.

I would have sworn I wasn't asleep when my phone rang. The muttered curse as Wallis jumped to the floor put the lie to that, but I certainly didn't feel very rested as I grabbed up my cell. A number I didn't recognize, and I prepared to let loose.

"Pru? It's Larry." I swallowed my protest. "You said to call."

"What's happening?" I poked around for paper and pen. A pale light was only beginning to leak through the trees. If Larry was awake at this hour and sober, too, then he had news. "What did you find out?"

"Nothing much." I was about to slam the phone back down. Good thing he couldn't read me like Wallis did. "But I was at Hap's last night."

Of course. The dark booths in the back served as a clearing-house for all kinds of shady deals. "Yeah?"

"There's some kind of deal going down at the camp." He spoke softly, as if afraid of being overheard. "They're looking for muscle."

"Muscle?" A lot of things went down in the woods. I didn't particularly care about drugs or untaxed cigarettes.

"I heard something about cages." Greg was right. Whatever had happened to Ronnie, someone still wanted a bear.

"You still at Happy's?" Officially, bars in the state had to close by two. All that meant was that Happy would turn out the light over the door. "I'll pick you up."

"Me? No!" His voice squeaked. "You said call—I did."

"Larry..." I was growling.

"Look, if you just show up, they won't know I told you. But I was there."

"They who, Larry?"

"That's just it." The fear in his voice was palpable. "No one's saying. Only that they'll pay and pay good—but, well, someone said Paul was a lesson."

"*That's what you're taking?*" Wallis was staring as I filled my travel mug. "*Coffee?*"

I knew she didn't like my brew—or any brew, for that matter. Though she'd been known to lap at cream. "*I haven't been sleeping that great.*"

"*I noticed.*" She sniffed and pulled her head back in disgust. "*But really? For some...animal?*"

"For the bear?" I poked about in the fridge. I still wasn't hungry, but I've been involved in animal care long enough to know that we all function best when we've eaten. "Or did you mean Albert?"

"*Whatever.*" She crossed the counter to stare over my shoulder. "*Neither one is ...*"

"Family?" I grabbed a roll—and pulled out a can of salmon for Wallis.

"*In danger.*" She corrected me, as I forked the fish into a dish. She was right, of course. One bear had been freed and relocated, another had happened into that clearing and been trapped—but had escaped. The odds of a third young male being caught in the same area were slim. Even if she meant Albert, the same held true. The town official was still in custody. Effectively caged, and thus safe.

For now. But unlike Wallis I had a sense of the progress of time. At some point, Albert would be released—and if he knew something… if he had seen something, even if he wasn't fully aware of what he might have witnessed, he might become a target. Much, I realized with growing horror, as Ronnie must have been.

I had tried to explain to Creighton, but I'd gotten distracted by talk about Greg, about who was responsible for what: I wouldn't have freed the bear by cutting through the ropes. Nobody with any sense would, not when it had a functioning release mechanism. No, the trap had been compromised intentionally, and then Ronnie had been sent to deal with it.

"*No loss.*" Wallis lapped daintily at the salmon. I couldn't bring myself to respond to this, not now when I had to get moving. Besides, there are some arguments that I knew I would never win.

As I drove out to the state road, I found myself asking my own version of Wallis' question. What was I hoping to accomplish, besides putting myself in a possibly dangerous situation?

Some of it was obvious. My species was preying on others. And while I was no stranger to the natural order of things, I did my best to even the score every now and then—though not in a manner that would put another person at risk. Granted, this kind of work was technically Greg Mishka's responsibility. But not only was he overextended, he lacked my resources. What was I going to say? The animals of Beauville had clued me in that I could blackmail an old and disreputable colleague? No, I didn't think that would cut it.

That didn't mean I wasn't going to use every resource in my capacity. As I slowed and let my GTO drift onto the shoulder, I rolled down the windows, listening. The sounds of the waking forest, unfazed as yet by my intrusion. There was only so much I could do to hide my car. A short bumpy ride behind some bushes was the best I could think of. But if the flora didn't help much, the fauna didn't seem to care. Granted, I'd affronted a chipmunk, rolling over an acorn he'd had his eye on. But they have such short attention spans, it wasn't like he was going to report me to Greg.

He wouldn't have to. I was fully intending to call him, I reminded myself as I got out of the car and crept, as quietly as that chipmunk, over toward the camp. The moment I saw or heard anything that could be called actionable. Besides, with everything else going on, I wouldn't mind having a feather in my cap—the kind even that one noisy jay flying by would be proud of.

"*No fur, no hide to speak of!*" Wallis had huffed, as I'd headed toward the door. "*Where are your claws? Your fangs?*"

"My kind do enough damage without." I wasn't going to waste time arguing. Wallis was on about something, but for all I knew, it was simply envy. She sees herself as the hunter in the family.

"*Alpha predator indeed.*" The thought had followed me out to the car. "*Teeth can't even pierce the skin.*"

I didn't need her to point out my limitations. As I settled in to wait, I realized how awkward and obvious I was.

"*Who's there? Who?*" Mourning dove. Reacting to me, most likely, but I hunkered down lower, to make myself appear less threatening if not less noticeable.

"*Who?*" After a while, the bird fell silent. Not long after that, the whole forest grew quiet. I could hear my own breath as my pulse began to race. I'd been here long enough that the woods should have begun to get used to me. Something else was out there.

"*Intruder! Intruder!*" Blue jays are tough. If this one was blasting a warning, he had a reason. "*Watch! Watch!*"

That's when it hit me. I was unarmed. I never had gone back to Happy's to ask about my knife. Never replaced it either. I closed my eyes in disbelief, wondering at my own stupidity. That's what Wallis had been saying to me—trying to say. While I'd been arguing about human responsibility, she was pointing out my complete vulnerability. Now I was in the middle of the woods. If I was lucky, the only thing approaching was a bear.

If I wasn't.... I looked around. A branch about as long as

my arm and as thick was within reach. As quietly as I could, I grabbed hold of it and pulled it toward me, once more crouching behind the scant brush. Somewhere close, a branch cracked. I held my breath. The slight sigh of leaves compressing came next, a sound so soft that were it not for that earlier crack I would have missed it.

And then nothing. Whoever—whatever—was out there was waiting, too. Listening as I was, and perhaps sniffing the air for signs of company. Around us, the forest held its breath. Wallis was wrong on one point—we were alpha predators. This silence? It meant something big. Something big—or something human.

That's when it hit me. I had to pee.

Now, I'm not squeamish. Like that bear, I'll go in the woods. But I was certainly not going to make myself more vulnerable to whatever or whoever was out there. Cursing the coffee, I chomped down on my lower lip, willing the urge to pass.

I was rewarded by the quiet rasp of branches not far away. Doing my best to push my discomfort aside, I tried to open my awareness—my thoughts as well as my ears. Like I've said, I'm no good with wild animals, but still, if it were a bear, I should be getting something. A sense of hunger or wariness, or even ursine fatigue.

"*What? What?*" I caught my breath. But, no, a vole had surfaced and the silence had caught her by surprise. She had been in the process of cleaning her soiled nest; that third baby was a terror. She scrabbled in the leaf mold, and I was aware once more of my own growing urgency.

"*Come on, Pru. Deal!*" The force of my internal command stopped the vole in mid claw, and with one quick flip, she dived back into her tunnel. The movement, subtle as it was, had an effect. I felt, rather than heard, a gasp. Yes, whatever was out there was listening too.

In other circumstances, I would stick it out. This was a contest I could win. If only I hadn't finished that coffee. Besides, by now, my position crouching in the low brush was taking its toll. My leg was cramping. Wallis, who never found herself in an uncomfortable position, would have a field day.

As carefully as I could, I shifted, bringing my cramped leg forward to relieve the pressure. Only I had stiffened more than I'd known; parts of my calf were numb—and my foot dragged over the crumbling plant life that carpeted the forest floor, rustling the dead leaves just like that vole had.

Only whatever was out there heard, and knew the difference. Something about the stillness, as if the morning itself held its breath. And that's when I decided. Maybe I could out wait whatever was out there. Maybe my bladder and my patience would hold. But if I've learned anything from the animals around me, it's that there are different styles of hunting. Different ways to cope.

What if I drew out whatever it was that waited? What if I made him—it—reveal itself? All I had was the branch, but it might be enough. From what I'd been able to piece together, Paul Lanouette had been beaten, not shot. I adjusted my grasp on the bough, dragging it over the fallen leaves.

It was enough. Even as I pulled it toward me, I heard the crash of something—someone—breaking cover. From my hiding place, I couldn't see, but I could hear, and as the sounds came closer I rose and shouldered the bough. I've never been one for sports, but as the bushes in front of me parted I swung for the fences with a yell. Thwack! Before my shout had died away, the branch made contact, and a figure fell forward. A figure with glossy brown hair, an outstretched arm clad in floral poplin. Susan Felicidad.

I dropped the branch in relief—and then I heard it. More footsteps, crashing through the brush. In a panic, I stumbled backward, desperately trying to balance. To pull the bough back for another blow. Only to see the shrubbery part and reveal— *Greg?*

I dropped the branch, panting. "Greg, oh, man…"

"Pru." I'd never heard so much bitterness in one syllable—and my mother had been a master. "I didn't think..."

"Wait, no!" He didn't understand. I saw that. "I got a tip. Animals—smuggling—and this woman is in on it."

On the ground between us, Susan Felicidad groaned and tried to sit up. Greg knelt, and to my surprise, he cradled her upper body, as if he would help her stand. "This woman?" He shook his head as he lifted her gently to her feet. "You better hope she's all right, Pru."

"Okay, maybe it wasn't justified. But she's a criminal. Animal cruelty, at the very least."

"Animal cruelty?" Another slow shake. "Pru, you're crazy. This is Susan Phelps. Special Agent Phelps of the U.S. Fish and Wildlife Service."

Chapter Forty-two

Greg had his hands full, literally, helping the groggy agent back toward their truck, which he'd hid farther up the road. He didn't like that I'd excused myself, but I'd promised to come find them—and did, a few minutes later—desperate to make sense of what had just occurred.

"So you got a tip?" Greg had helped the federal agent buckle herself in by the time I found them. From the glare she gave me, she was going to be fine, if a bit banged up. Now he stood, hands on hips, doing his best version of the same.

"You know I've got contacts." I let him think I was only talking about the human kind. "And someone told me something was going down." His eyes narrowed. "Okay, it was Larry Greeley." I had no reason to protect the sleazebag. Especially not now. "Only, there wasn't anything solid. I was going to call you as soon as there was."

I pulled out my phone, which had Greg's number ready to go. It could have been a stunt, quickly put together while I was off behind the trees. Only Greg seemed to believe it. At any rate, he nodded as if what I was saying made sense.

"That's what we heard too," he said, and it hit me, much like that log.

"I saw them talking." I put two and two together. "Susan Fel— Phelps and Larry. I thought there was something odd going on."

"Susan had leverage on Greeley," Greg acknowledged. "We thought his information would be good."

I nodded. "I did too. I wonder what went wrong?" We stood in silence for a moment.

"Greg?" Susan didn't sound great. "If you want to stay…"

"No." He called to her. "This was either a mistake or a setup."

I thought of my own failed attempt. "Someone wanted to draw us out. Or—" Another idea popped into my head. "Draw us away from something—or someone."

Someone like a witness? But who—

"I guess we should be grateful that Albert is still in custody." Was I becoming fond of that fat, stupid man?

"He's not." Greg's voice grew cold. "I spoke to Jim Creighton before coming out here this morning. Someone talked Albert into calling a lawyer, and Jim had to release him."

My car was faster than Greg's truck. Besides, he needed to take care of Susan. I had some vague notion of what my liability would be if she were more seriously injured than she appeared, but that took a backseat to my fears for the bearded ferret keeper I knew so well.

"Call me." Greg shouted, as I raced back to my car. It was a command, not a request.

"I will," I yelled back. I only hoped I wasn't too late.

Driving is a skill like any other, and I know how to drive fast. I should have felt guilty about the family in the RV that I nearly scared off the road—the father's blanched white face stuck in my rearview for a moment like a screech owl—but I didn't. Lawyered up. All my best intentions had put Albert at risk. If anything happened to him, Frank would never forgive me.

I made it to Albert's apartment in record time. Greg probably hadn't even gotten Susan halfway to the hospital yet. I raced up the stairs to his second-floor entry to find the door ajar, the lights out.

"Albert!" I called as I kicked the unlocked door wide. My

voice fell flat. The apartment was empty, every sense told me, so I stepped inside. To an untrained eye, it looked like his place had been tossed. Clothes were everywhere, spilling out of opened drawers. A stench of old garbage—and worse—emanated from burst bags in the filthy kitchenette.

Only my knowledge of the man who lived here kept me from panicking. This might seem like a disaster zone, but for Albert, this was its normal state. Still, I didn't breathe easily until I'd walked through the cluttered studio. No body, no discernible blood. If Albert had returned home and been taken out forcibly, I could see no signs of it. But maybe it was that thought—or maybe my general nosiness—that had me running a hand over the clutter, gingerly pushing aside the fast-food wrappers to see what else the portly man kept around. Unopened mail. A flier about a boat for sale. Another offering to "buy your junk."

I thought about keeping that one. I really could clean out my mother's place. But as I lifted it, a familiar gleam caught my eye.

"Son of a…" It was my knife. My missing knife, on Albert's dresser. The knife I'd thought I might die without less than an hour earlier. Here, as if it were simply more of the apartment's detritus, or, rather, one of the shiny, pretty things Albert liked to collect. Without thinking, I picked it up—and immediately froze.

Its appearance here was wrong, and I struggled to figure out why as my mind raced back to when I must have dropped it. To when I thought that my own lack of self-control—okay, my drinking—was to blame. I went back over that night, what I remembered, anyway. Albert hadn't been at Happy's that night. He'd still been in custody. I thought back to if I might have lost it earlier—maybe when I gave Albert a lift back into town. If that was the case, maybe he'd have returned it, if he'd been free. Unless I had lost it at Happy's, like I'd thought, and one of his friends had dropped it off here.

Since I'd already picked it up, I examined the blade, hoping it could give me the answers. Someone had used it; that was clear. Fibers were wedged in the bolster, where the blade was attached to the hilt, and I reached for them gingerly. Not animal hair, I realized with relief—though there was something of the wild in the twisted threads. No blood either, for which I was grateful.

I turned it over in my hand. Creighton's people had searched this apartment only days before. I didn't know what they were looking for, but I was grateful that my knife hadn't been taken in. And since it hadn't….Well, as my recent experience had proved, I had more need of it than Albert. After wiping down the blade on my jeans leg—I didn't trust anything in that apartment to be clean—I replaced it in my boot, feeling its presence against my ankle like the touch of an old friend.

I shoved that flier—"buy your junk," indeed—into my pocket as well. Whether Albert had intended to return my knife or whether he had stolen it with the intent of pawning it, didn't matter. I was the judge and jury in this case, and I saw intent. He had also forfeited any right to privacy, in my mind, and I began to rifle through Albert's drawers. Two shot glasses very like the ones Happy settled on the bar. The Town of Beauville stamp we're supposed to use on official documents. Damn, the man was more magpie than muskrat.

What I didn't see—to my relief—was anything that would tie him in with Paul's death, or with that initial trapped bear, for that matter. His lame alibi of having gone along for the ride might just be the truth. Albert might be a petty thief, but I'd like to think he was innocent of anything to do with that bear—or his friend's death. Innocent of anything other than terrible judgment.

That didn't mean he was safe. Somebody had sabotaged a trap and sent Ronnie to check on it. Which meant somebody was covering his tracks. Or—it was possible—looking for something. Something that might reveal who was behind this violence. Someone knew something...

"*That little weasel knows more than he's letting on.*" The words rang like an echo in my head.

Growler had said that, picking up on the scents I carried. And while I'd been thinking of Larry, I'd made the same mistake I was always warning myself against. Growler wasn't using a metaphor. He didn't mean Larry. He meant Frank, whom I had also spoken with that morning—and whose musky aroma would certainly be more distinctive and probably more revealing than that of one scared and clueless man.

"*He doesn't know. He can't know.*" The words came back to me, with new meaning. I had thought that the ferret was talking about Albert's general cluelessness. His inability to see his sleek pet as anything more. But the ferret was alert and aware, as any smaller animal must be. He'd been awake when Albert had been passed out. And although he had been trapped in the car that morning, he did have the run of Albert's home—and Albert's office.

If, say, Albert had picked up something—something that might implicate him—Frank would understand that it was dangerous and try to keep his person away. Even if it was something shiny. Something that Albert might, like his pet, consider a treat. Something a ferret would do his best to hide, tucked away in a box.

Chapter Forty-three

I drove like a fury back to the office. Yes, I was angry about my knife. But mainly I was pissed off—at Albert, at myself. At Creighton, for following the rules. At the stupid, useless greed that had already caused so much pain.

My tires announced me before I was parked, and my engine was ticking as I pulled open the front door. For a moment, though, I wavered. I could go left and see Creighton. Put this whole thing to rest—and clear my name, while I was at it. Or I could go right, into the office, and interrogate the witness myself. Because if Albert was gone—taken or on the lam—only one creature would be able to give me anything like a lead.

There was no question, really, although I did look back over my shoulder—my entrance had to have been audible in Creighton's office—as I unlocked the Animal Control office.

The bellow that greeted me made me jump back a foot. The sound—a very unferret-like roar—emanated from a flailing bulk, like a landed walrus. Feet, I made the connection, and belly, as, behind the desk, Albert regained his balance along with his consciousness and righted himself.

"Pru!" He sat up, blinking. "I thought I—uh..."

"You did." I held up my keys. Yeah, I was relieved to see him unharmed. That didn't mean I was going to go easy on him. "I'm covering for you. Remember?"

"Yeah, right." He stroked his mop of hair, as if to groom. "I didn't get much sleep last night."

I nodded. That didn't surprise me. Then again, Albert had the ability to sack out anywhere. But I didn't have time for the niceties. Neither, I figured, did he. "Did you see Frank?"

"What?" More blinking, and this time I didn't wait. Walking around his desk, I reached and opened the bottom drawer, sighing with relief when a familiar triangular head popped out.

"Hey, Frank." I kept my voice level. He'd be able to read my mood easily enough, and I didn't need Albert butting in. I had too many questions to clear up before someone came over from the cop shop.

"*He's free! He's here!*" The little beast appeared understandably excited, and Albert giggled like a little girl as his pet ran out to nuzzle his bristling beard. There was something underlying the ferret's agitation, however.

"I'm glad Creighton let you out." I was speaking as much to the flustered ferret as the man. Neither was paying me full attention, though, and I didn't have much time. "I think I've figured it all out."

"Huh?" Albert turned toward me, mouth open in confusion. "I didn't see Jim."

"*No! No!*" The ferret jumped down to the desktop and ran to the edge. Nose twitching in the air, he was doing his best to reach me. To explain that his person wasn't simply freed from the cage next door. He was—

"Maybe you didn't realize you'd picked up evidence," I continued, interrupting the ferret's emotional outpouring. "Maybe you didn't even know what this meant."

I opened my palm then, revealing the diamond-studded cuflink I'd found in the ferret's tackle box cache.

"What?" Albert sat up, blinking. "I never—I mean, yeah, I found that."

"*No! No, you didn't!*" Frank leaped to the floor and ran up to me, sniffing the air eagerly. "*I did! Mine! It's mine!*"

"If I could find it, others could have, too." I stared down at the button black eyes. Panic, pain, and a deep sense of sadness came to me, and while I wished I could soothe the little creature's distress, I knew the only way out of this was through full disclosure. "And he—or his henchmen—wouldn't take the time to ask questions."

"Wha?" Albert's obvious confusion stopped me. I had questions of my own—but then I realized what the problem was.

"Henchmen," I explained, biting down on the word. "You know, toughs. Someone like Jack Walz doesn't do his own dirty work." Even as I said it, the missing parts started to fall into place. I should have known as soon as I'd seen the sparkling little circle that it was a cufflink and that it had to belong to one man—the only man in this town who would wear his money on his sleeve: Jack Walz. Now I realized why he'd needed me to be at his place yesterday, and why he kept me so long at our appointment.

I was his alibi while Ronnie was being mauled by a bear.

All of the variables flooded my brain. The fibers in my knife—the compromised snare—a call to the state police, to make sure my law-abiding beau didn't let me slide. Was I going to be framed, or was this somehow going to fall on Albert, once he'd been released?

What I couldn't figure in was Greg's observation—that whoever had been behind all this had significant local knowledge. Walz wasn't working alone. But with Paul Lanouette dead and Ronnie in the hospital, I was running out of ideas. Larry Greeley—well, I knew now what he was up to. Mack—that job in Pittsfield? No, as much as my ex had let me down, I didn't see him as the type to get involved in something this violent. He'd have a long way to go before I ever trusted him again, but the man I'd seen at Happy's was trying to get himself straight.

I didn't have time. *We* didn't have time. "Albert?" I used my best command voice. "Who else was out there, that day?"

"I—" He began to stutter, but it was too late. Just then,

the door pushed open and I looked up to see Chuck Carroll, Creighton's deputy, burst in, his face set in anger.

"This came from the scene of Paul Lanouette's murder." I held out the cufflink. I couldn't defend my driving, and from Chuck's thundercloud expression it was obvious I couldn't wait for Creighton, either. "It belongs to Jack Walz."

"Really?" He stepped toward me and reached for the small, gaudy thing. I scrambled to come up with an explanation—one that didn't involve a ferret stealing from his person and then hiding evidence to keep him safe—as I waited for Chuck to ask me where I'd found it. Who had had it, and what it might mean. After all, his territory was the new part of town. Instead, he slipped the little golden disk into his pocket and looked up at me, his face breaking into a smile. A smile I'd seen before. At Happy's, talking to Ronnie.

"You." I felt like I'd been punched in the gut.

"What?" Albert turned from the deputy to me and back again.

"The knife." I swallowed. "My knife. You planted it in Albert's apartment during the search."

The fat man's head swiveled, his mouth open wide.

The deputy's grin widened. "Interesting you found that." A smile as cold as a shark's. "I bet we'll find evidence on it—traces of rope and leather—linking it the trap that gave way. Poor Ronnie."

Albert's eyes were saucers.

"Chuck's the connection." I said as much for myself as to enlighten him. "The man on the ground who's been organizing everything." Suddenly, even Albert's inarticulate protests made sense. His refusal to talk while in custody. His fear. "He released you today, too. Didn't he?"

"Yes, I did." Chuck cut in. "We're hoping he'll lead us to his boss. To whoever was holding out—holding this." He patted his pocket. "Of course, we can't be responsible for what happens then."

He stepped closer and I felt time slow. Backing up, I reached behind me, almost as if I had stumbled. Balancing myself by reaching backward, as if for the desk.

"Son of a—"

I had a knife, *my* knife back again. But he had pulled a gun. And while I was sure that Creighton would question its use, I couldn't be certain I'd be around to explain. I dropped the knife that I had slipped into my hand.

"That's enough," said the deputy. His smile was unnerving, even though I now knew what it meant. He pulled his cuffs from his belt and stepped toward me. "I think we need to go for a ride to discuss things. All three of us."

I swallowed hard. I had an idea of what would follow.

"Maybe we'll take your car," he said. "Everyone knows how you like to drive." And I knew for sure.

I was thinking fast. I knew I couldn't get in a car with this man—not any car, but especially not mine. With my reputation, it would be too easy to stage an accident. I didn't know what they had used on the bear, but I had a bad feeling that some strong sedatives were involved—and this man wouldn't hesitate to use them on me. But just as he reached to fix the cuff around my wrist, he stumbled and then kicked out.

"What? No!" Bouncing back on one leg, he glanced down and kicked. And as Frank flew off—teeth still bared for the bite—I saw my moment. I leaped, carrying Chuck to the ground.

We landed hard. He'd been off balance and my weight had his body pinned. But not his arms. Too late, I saw the hypodermic. Felt the jab through my sleeve. And even as I drew breath to scream—to yell for Creighton, for Albert, for anyone—the world shrank to a pinprick. As it whirled, I saw Frank, a giant foot, and flying furniture, and then all was gone.

Chapter Forty-four

I swear it was Albert's breath that brought me back. I opened my eyes to see him staring down at me, and, yes, I shrieked.

"It's okay, Pru!" A dirty hand replaced the face as he pulled back and then pointed. "I hit him with the chair."

"You what?" I sat up. My head was swimming. A needle still hung from my arm, its plunger only partway depressed. I pulled it out with a curse and struggled to my feet. Sure enough, the deputy was laid out flat on the floor, Albert's upended desk chair by his head.

"I was so mad." Albert's face was red as he stared down at the prone man. "He kicked Frank! I mean, an animal! He kicked a poor defenseless animal."

Nevermind what he did to me—what he was going to do. I closed my eyes and thought of the bear. Albert was a work in progress, but maybe we could make an honest animal control officer of him yet.

"Whoa, Pru!" I felt a hand on my arm and pulled back, nearly tumbling over. Clearly whatever I'd been injected with was going to be with me for a while.

"Sorry." I shook my head. A mistake, but I managed to make it over to the desk. "Wait." I blinked. "Where's Frank?"

"*Here!*" The ferret popped up. He'd been sniffing his tormenter, who was now groaning and beginning to stir. "*Not dead.*"

"No, he isn't." I smiled, then saw how confused Albert was. "Sorry." I raised my hand to my forehead. I felt like I'd been the one decked. "I guess I'm a little loopy. But, Albert, what happened—what really happened that day?"

He shook his head so slowly I had to wonder if he'd been drugged too.

"I wish I knew," he said. "I wasn't even in on the job, you know? I was just tagging along with Paul and Ronnie. It was hot, and we were drinking. Paul was getting cranky, and then Chuck showed up and he and Paul got into it. Paul was going on about how he was doing all the hard work, moving the bear, and I guess I fell asleep—"

He stopped short, aware of what he'd just let slip.

"So you knew about the bear." My head was beginning to clear. It was also starting to throb. What had Chuck given me?

Albert shrugged. "It wasn't like they were going to hurt it. It was going to a collector, or something." I had no words. "Paul wasn't getting any work. I mean, I've got this." He opened his hands, taking in the room. Animal Control in Beauville, and I knew then I couldn't take this from Albert. It was all he had. This and—

A squeal made us both turn. Chuck was standing, a scowl on his face. In one fist, he held Frank, extended away from his body. I didn't know how he'd managed to grab the ferret, but I could feel the wordless panic—the rage, the fear—as the agile beast flipped and strained, desperate to bite his tormentor. In his other hand, Chuck held his gun.

"No." I fought the temptation to close my eyes again. Maybe if I hadn't been dopey, I would have thought to secure the weapon. Maybe if Albert weren't Albert, he'd have picked it up. And Frank? Well, the ferret had already done what he could, once before.

"Drop it, Chuck." The voice as calm as coffee made us all turn. Jim Creighton stood at the door, his own service weapon in his hand. "You know this is over."

"Jim—" His deputy made a strangled sound.

"Drop the gun," said Creighton once more. "Drop it, and kick it toward me. And then you can put the ferret down, too."

Chapter Forty-five

"What kept you?" I was irritable. Hospitals affect me that way, and I'd been lying in the bed being poked and prodded for over an hour by then. "You were almost too late."

"I bet you'd have figured something out," said my beau. The warmth had returned to his voice, and he leaned back in his chair like someone who's done a hard day's work. "But since you asked, I was answering a complaint call—about you."

"My driving?" It wouldn't be the first time.

"More like animal cruelty." Creighton laughed at my obvious annoyance, and explained. "Jack Walz wasn't too clear on the details, and I had the distinct impression that he simply wanted to hold me there, listening to him complain as long as possible."

"As long as was necessary." My lids were growing heavy. I really wanted to get home, not that I thought I could drive right now. "While Chuck cleaned up the mess."

"Something like."

I opened my eyes. "Chuck killed Paul, didn't he?"

A nod. "Walz is behind it, though. He may not have ordered Chuck to kill Paul. But he did tell him to rough him up. Best I can tell, Chuck either waited till Ronnie had left or sent him home. Albert had already passed out by then. Paul had been threatening to blackmail Walz, and Walz thought he had his missing cufflink. That somehow Paul was going to use that to place him at the camp.

"Maybe he was." My honey looked bemused. "I can't see any-one wearing diamond cufflinks out in the woods, no matter how rich. But whether Walz was that careless or Paul stole it earlier and brought it out there to frame him doesn't matter. Paul didn't have it. Albert had picked it up by then—claims he 'found' it, then lost it again." Silence, as he waited, curious. I wasn't going to give up Frank, though. Not when the ferret had been doing his best to hide the evidence and protect his person.

"At any rate," Creighton began again, "I gather things got out of hand. Paul probably wouldn't have given it up anyway. He was a big guy, and neither of those two were the kind to back away from a fight. Chuck either got around behind him and hit him with something or Paul fell on a rock on his own—the coroner wasn't clear. At any rate, Chuck panicked. Locked Paul's body in the shed lest Albert woke up, and hightailed it back to town. To his shift."

He paused, the bitterness showing in the lines around his mouth. He swallowed it and continued. "Walz must have sent him back. Told him to clean it up. Find that cufflink and get rid of anyone who could talk. He'd been lucky in that they'd snared another bear."

Not luck, the spring behavior of young males. The thought jumped into my fuzzy head. Now wasn't the time for a lecture on animal behavior though. Creighton, for once, was still talking.

"Chuck had your knife. I gather he'd picked it up a few nights ago, thinking it might be useful." Those blue eyes were piercing. "Maybe he would have used it on Ronnie, if there'd been nothing in the trap. Claim you and Ronnie had a fight or something, but when he saw that another bear had been snared, he got creative. Cut the ropes almost through, and called Ronnie to go check on it, then left the knife where one of us would find it. I knew—well, I suspected something like that. That's why I wanted to hold Albert. I should've picked up Ronnie, too, only I couldn't find him in time."

"Spring." My eyes were growing heavy, but I caught the quizzical tilt of Creighton's head. "Young males, looking for territory." I could have been talking about the bears. "Walz confess?"

A terse shake. "Not yet. Said he had met Chuck on his rounds and hired him for protection, so it isn't his fault things got out of hand."

He fell silent. We both know that wouldn't hold up in court. But the tickle of an idea wouldn't let me rest. "Walz was wrong," I said. "The cufflink—I don't know when Albert found it, but I don't think he got it from Paul. He—well, he has a tendency to pick things up." Now that push came to shove, I felt protective of the man.

"Nobody should be killed over a cufflink." I didn't think I had to worry about Albert. Not right now. "By the way, what did you have on Larry? I gather he was helping you."

I smiled, and let myself sink back into the pillows. "I'm not telling," I said—or thought I did. Sleep was coming on strong. "Just...no more pets are going to go missing over in the new part of town."

In truth, I wasn't sure what Larry could even have been charged with. His scam wasn't kidnapping, per se. It wasn't even dog—or catnapping. For one thing, he never asked for ransom, being content with the tens and twenties that the residents of Pine Hills gave out in gratitude. But what he'd been doing—luring vulnerable pets with treats and then grabbing them—had put animals at risk, even if he didn't realize it. Not to mention the grief he caused, even temporarily, among those pets' people. And then offering his services as pet care? No, I wasn't going to give him to Creighton, not when the only legal penalties would hinge on the value of living creatures as property. The man had been a menace...a menace I had dealt with, in my own way.

"Excuse me?" The voice was very far away.

"No more rewards for 'that nice young man.'" I formed the words, I swear I did. But then I heard a soft chuckle. I felt the warmth of lips on my forehead, and the conversation ended.

Like everyone else in town, I followed the trial. Beauville isn't that big a place, and we'd lost one of our own. Two, if you count Chuck—though he'd long ago forfeited any local loyalties when he threw in his lot with Walz. I had sensed early on, that night at Happy's, that he'd given up his old friends. I'd made the mistake of thinking he'd given them to join Creighton's team.

Chuck took the bulk of the blame, of course. I guess I shouldn't have been surprised. Walz and Chuck couldn't turn on each other fast enough, once they were arraigned, and Walz surrendered his contacts—a Colombian syndicate that supplied so-called "exotic pets" for the bored rich—which won him some credit with the feds. Plus, he brought in a big-deal lawyer, some city slicker who actually argued that his client should get off. He didn't, of course. Once the verdicts were in, I turned my attention to other things, but I heard they were both going to do serious time.

The rest of the fallout was unsurprising. Albert kept his position, getting off with simply a warning once he agreed to testify about the little he could remember. Ronnie did, too, though I thought that was more because the condo association couldn't be bothered finding someone else to plunge the toilets now that high season was upon us.

As for me, I turned down Greg's offer. As attractive as the idea of the opening—or the man himself—might be, I couldn't see committing to a full-time gig. Especially now that my client roster was healthy again, thanks to the good word from Tillie and Helen, Ernest Luge, and, yes, even Susan "Felicidad."

Our mysterious newcomer wasn't going to be staying. She had already brought Bunbury back to his real owner—a nursing home where the smart, social creature served as a therapy cat. I should have known he was a working feline from the start. Then again, Wallis always says I'm blind when it comes to what I should pick up.

Some things I do get. Billy Wagner, for example. The boy and his loyal puppy came to County's first companion animal training session—accompanied by his mother. I saw his father a few times over the next few months as spring turned to high summer and then into a gentle New England fall. And while I didn't have great hopes for his marriage, I like to think Billy's father was getting help with his anger. At any rate, as the leaves began to turn, both the boy and his dog were filling out, the haunted look leaving the young child's eyes.

Wallis, of course, thought the whole thing was ridiculous. "Runts," she grunted, when I came home from a September session with the smell of the bonded pair on my hands. *"If they can't fend for themselves…"*

"Not runts, Wallis." Some things need to be said. "Children."

"Huh." Having voiced her complaint, she fell silent. In the cool of the evening, she rubbed against my ankles, and I found myself wondering what kittens were in her past and who had showed her kindness or cruelty before I came along.

"The past is past." The words rose up to me as a rejoinder. Cats, like all animals, live in an eternal present. They don't regret anything, nor do they fear what they cannot yet sense on the horizon. It's as good a way to live as any, I thought, as I put the bills away, paid for once, and walked into the kitchen.

Wallis joined me there, jumping up to the window as her tail lashed the air. We stood there, enjoying the moment. The fading light made the birches glow even more than usual. The nights would be getting cold soon, and so many things would change. For now, though, the scene was beautiful. Golden and calm, and broken only by a set of familiar headlights coming up the drive.

To see more Poisoned Pen Press titles:

Visit our website:
poisonedpenpress.com
Request a digital catalog:
info@poisonedpenpress.com